'57, CHICAGO

'57, CHICAGO

a novel

STEVE MONROE

talk
miramax
books

HYPERION

NEW YORK

Library of Congress Cataloging-in-Publication Data
Monroe, Steve, 1961–
    '57, Chicago : a novel / Steve Monroe.—1st. ed.
      p. cm.
    ISBN 0-7868-6730-2
       1. Criminals—Fiction. 2. Chicago (Ill.)—Fiction. I. Title: 1957
    Chicago. II. Title.
  PS3563.O533 A615 2000
  813'.6—dc21   00-048886

10 9 8 7 6 5 4 3 2 1

For my mother
Your love, talent and encouragement
stacked the deck

"A man with a financial surplus can control circumstances . . . but a man without a surplus is controlled by them."

Quotation credited to Harvey Firestone, found on a scrap of paper in the coat pocket of slain banker Leon Marcus. The slaying made headlines on April Fools' Day, 1957.

'57, CHICAGO

March 21, 1957

"My old man leered at those dice like a child molester ogling a lollipop. Everything that happened over the next few minutes changed my life forever, and what do I remember the most? His eyes. The way he looked at those dice like he saw a future. That's what I always remember, Gene. The guys that play through us see a future, and you know what? They ain't got one, and neither did my father."

"So this is inside a church?" asked Gene.

"Yeah. This old church is being renovated, and my old man and some other guys are using the sanctuary to hold their weekly crap game. So I'm hiding up in a tree, peeking in through a hole in a stained-glass window. Anyway, there I am looking through Christ's outstretched arms, when my father hits a hard six. He doubles his bet and the fat guy to his left covers him. These guys are coated in sawdust. The place is a mess, and there they are, throwing dice against the altar; all of the pews stacked in the back, carpet rolled up. So everybody's coupled up on bets except for one guy. He wipes down the shooter's area like an umpire cleaning home plate. Now my father starts rolling, trying to hit the hard six. He and the fat guy are jawing back and forth, and my father just can't hit the point, but he ain't crapping out either. Finally, he looks up like he's praying, shouts, 'Lord, let's teach brother Brand a lesson,' and flings the dice against the altar. They carom off of the bottom step, dance back toward my father, and finally come to a stop inches from his face, cause he's laying down now, coaching them—a pair of threes, six, the hard way."

"No shit? Hey, it's your play."

"No shit," said Al as he leaned forward and threw a five of spades on the discard pile that lay between the two stalls. "The last roll of his life and he hits his point. Six. The hard way. Anyway, the fat guy starts bitching and moaning about his wife and kids and how he needs the money, and my father says 'Fuck you, I got a kid too,' and pretty soon they're going at it. My father kicks the living shit out of this bum and heads for the door when I see the gun. The fat guy pulls a pistol from his . . . , oh shit I need that."

Al picked up a queen of hearts from the discard pile, threw down the two of diamonds and pushed his pants a little farther down around his ankles. "So he pulls a gun from his jacket and yells at my father to turn around. My dad just laughs, and heads for the door. By now, all of the other yahoos have all scrambled out the back door and I'm beating on the window, yelling at my dad to turn around."

Gene interrupted. "I can't see your discard, Al. You've got to throw your card right in the middle or I can't see it."

Al pushed the card over with his foot. "The first shot tore off a piece of his scalp and I dropped straight to the ground. Screwed up my knee bad enough that I've still got a bum wheel. So, I run toward the front door just as the fat guy starts to open it, and I pick up a two by four with a bunch of nails sticking out the end. He steps out and I swing like Mickey Mantle and catch him right in the forehead. He's so surprised that he was probably buried before he realized he was dead. Meantime, I run in and grab my old man. He's gone, no last words, nothing, so I run back out and grab the money from the fat guy and run home to tell my mom. Gin."

"Shit," said Gene as he looked down at Al's gin hand. "I was waiting on that seven."

Al peeled off paper and shifted his weight. "Let's get over to the bar. I think the book on these NCtwoA games is getting out of balance."

"Hey," said Gene as Al exited the stall and headed for the sink. "Was all that true?"

"You asked me why I became a bookie," said Al, laughing as he zipped up his pants. "I thought you'd like a story."

Gene blew a tommy gun that made his stall rattle.

Al washed his hands, smoothed his hair and stepped out of the bathroom muttering. "Thirty-six dollars. All over thirty-six dollars."

"Robert J. Lipranski. Bobby Lipranski. The Lip. I like that! Well, Mr. Lipranski, I learned at a very young age that a smile can part doors, legs and men from their money, and I do like your smile," said Lincoln Johnson, jowls shaking. "But I'm not quite sure why you are sitting here in front of me, smiling and asking me for money."

The Lip leaned forward, used his thumbs to pop his knuckles. Despite fine tailoring, his suit coat clung to his biceps and the shoulders were stretched to their limit.

"I'll tell you, Mr. Johnson," he said, gazing at Lincoln Johnson and his associate, Reg Lewis. "I came to you because I believe that an association is mutually beneficial for both you and Junior Hamilton. Junior is going to be the next heavyweight champion of the world. He's strong and quick, and, being a Chicago native, and a son of Bronzeville, it's only fitting that you achieve a valid relationship with him. You are the Mayor of Bronzeville. Everyone knows that you run this area. Therefore, when Junior needs a bit of help, it's obvious that he should look to the most important man in his world."

"That was a splendid load of crap," said Johnson, leaning back from behind his desk. "I enjoy a good blow job now and then, but certainly not from a man who is asking me for thirty thousand dollars. So, since I have a young woman from the neighborhood waiting in the lobby and I want to get to the heart of the matter quickly, and you obviously don't, I'm going to ask my good friend Mr. Lewis here to give me his take on the matter."

Reg Lewis strode forward and sat on the corner of Johnson's desk. He, like Johnson, was dressed in a conservative three-piece business suit, with the jacket hung neatly behind the door to the office. He tugged at his vest as Johnson began to clean his glasses with a handkerchief, feigning disinterest.

"Lip," said Lewis, "my man behind the log tells me that, by contract, you aren't allowed to handle the money for the fight. It's being held in an escrow account at the Southmoor Bank and Trust and a third party divvies it up after the fight. You owe both camps money, and you've got bills to pay at the Tam O'Shanter and the Palmer House. You can't go to Sam Giancana because he hates your guts and your only real friend is a bookie, and he can't loan it to you because it makes him look very, very partial. My guess," he concluded, glancing back at Johnson, "is he figures if you loan him the money, you'll push our people to the gate to insure your investment."

The Lip hadn't moved during the monologue. The man wasn't too far off, except for the shit about Momo, and he figured that it was better to acknowledge the heat and hope for a fan.

"You've got me pretty well pegged, Mr. Lewis," he said. "My prison time didn't make me an ideal candidate to hold the money, so it's sitting in the bank. We've run up more debt than expected, but nothing that the gate won't cover, and I do believe that this is a great deal for both Mr. Johnson and Junior. Also, I hope that you'll push the Negroes to the gate to help a brother, not because it's some kind of collateral for my loan."

Johnson put on his glasses and nodded. "I agree that an association with Junior Hamilton will be advantageous, because I have been told that your assessment is astute. He will be the next heavyweight champion of the world. Shit, even I can see that he's an amazing fighter. But as we consider the terms for any loan, please don't take me for a fool. I may be a fat, old, colored man, but I'm still a good judge of character. Reg."

Reg Lewis threw the dagger. "Your prison record has nothing to do with the fact that you're not handling that money. You're a liar, a cheat, and a drunk, and nobody would trust you with their money. You did time for manslaughter because you beat another drunk to death when he didn't pay off a ten-dollar debt, and you have the audacity to beg a stranger for thirty thousand dollars."

Johnson piped up before the Lip could reply. "But I don't mind that, Mr. Lipranski. I'm a businessman at heart, and I do what's right for my people. I'll loan you the money on two conditions. One, I take fifteen percent of the gross on the gate and television rights and, two, Junior fights an exhibition during the Bud Billiken parade. Nothing serious, just a few jabs with another local and smiles for the crowd."

The Lip did the arithmetic. The coons were raping him; 15 percent equaled around $60K, and the last Bud Billiken had a crowd of 30,000 in the park and 500,000 on the streets. Selling pop, food, booze, whatever, they'd make a fortune with only a little something to the sparrow cops to protect the pot.

One shot. "I didn't come here to get insulted or to sell a piece of my fight. I've got other avenues, but, I thought just once you would like to help one of your own. Junior Hamilton lived most of his life in a kitchenette with his mother and sister. They had a hot plate, a bed and an icebox. The first time I met his mother, she offered me their last piece of bread. I made that woman one promise, that I would help her son become the heavyweight champion of the world so that he could provide hope and inspiration for others in their community. Mr. Johnson, I'm damn near a pariah among my own people because of my position with colored people, so I don't have to listen to your friend insult me. I need thirty grand for two weeks, and I'll find someone who'll help because they believe in us."

The Lip stood up. "Good day, sir," he said.

Johnson smiled broadly and began to laugh. "I wish that I had a stethoscope on your heart right now. I'll bet that if I let you walk out that door, you'd be prancing back in here in less than a minute. And I must say, you earned your nickname with that last soliloquy, but I'm not so sure that you deserve your reputation with my people. I've heard conflicting stories."

Johnson let it hang in the air before concluding. "Now sit down and work out the details with Mr. Lewis. I've got to take that young lady back into one of the other offices to offer some counsel."

They settled at fifteen percent, with the Lip getting ten percent from the Billiken parade. He smirked at Lewis as they left, hearing the moans coming from a back office.

The Lip stepped out onto Michigan Avenue, hailed a cab. A colored man scooted out of a doorway, begged for money.

The Lip kicked him. "Beat it, nigger."

He stepped into a cab, thinking that he had better find out where Junior's mother lived.

She came to him like she always did, piercing the darkness. The film room was full. Wee Willie ran the projector, talking incessantly about Jack Johnson while the fighters watched him toy with Jess

Willard on the screen. Jack Albano, the former football player turned sparring partner, tried to maneuver his ass on the metal chair, prayed for it to stop itching. Howie the Hat, over 6'5" tall and 265 pounds, straddled a stool, chewing sunflower seeds, spitting the shells into one of his old felt hats. Three other fighters, legs stretched out in front, arms folded across their chests, feigned interest, and Spider Gomez, the lightweight who couldn't speak a lick of English, sat at rapt attention. But Junior, he saw her.

Her visits were always a shock, but never unexpected. She could come to him in the film room, during a jog, in the midst of a conversation, or, God forbid, during a fight. And of course, she came to him when he slept.

He hugged himself tight. Her dark face and eyes tried to penetrate his grip and he shut his eyes as tightly as he could, but it was Wee Willie's deep voice that drove her back into the shadows.

"Hammer, look at Johnson move. He's playing with him. That footwork. The jabs. Damn it, if this don't show 'em he threw it nothing will. His old lady waits for the rest of the money until the twenty-sixth round and then Jack, he goes down."

"You know," said Howie the Hat as he spit out a mouthful of sunflower seeds and turned to Junior, "you do look a lot like him."

Junior nodded and looked up at Wee Willie.

"I don't think he go down on his own," he stammered.

"Watch!" yelled Willie.

The screen: Johnson, tiring but leading the fight, suddenly goes down, and while he's counted out, appears to shield his eyes from the Cuban sun.

"Get up, you mothafucker," yelled Willie.

"Get up," yelled a couple of the other fighters.

"Get the fuck up," yelled Howie the Hat.

Johnson stays down. Silence. A sob. Everyone turned to see Junior, hugging himself, shaking, eyes shut tight. His lips fluttered as he sucked for air.

Spider Gomez said it first. "Un grand fuckiiiiing problema."

•   •   •

Stevie was watching the door and nodded as Al and Gene bounded up the steps. Once inside the building, they climbed the inside staircase until they found Unit B on the third floor.

Seven men looked up as they entered, but returned to their telephones without missing a beat. Pete Barnes shuffled in front of the folding tables, removing the slips of paper that each man had piled up, replacing them with blank sheets.

"We're getting all sorts of action on Kansas," said Pete.

Al nodded. "The house limit's thirty K for both games. Bump 'em a half point every fifteen grand. How's the action in the N.C.–Michigan State game?"

"Everybody's on North Carolina right now, but we'll bump it to three pretty soon."

Al turned to Gene as Pete sat down. Pete's girth seemed to bump with the spread, and he was sweating profusely, despite the cool temperature of the room.

"I thought you figured all of the Michigan Staters would play early?" said Al.

Gene nodded as he glanced down at Pete's tote sheet.

"I figured they'd take anything. They think that this is their dream season and that Jumping Johnny Green's gonna take 'em all the way."

"All right, Pete, I wanna take North Carolina up a half point to three," said Al, "and I want you to keep an eye on Kansas. They started at eight, but I don't want 'em to go past nine and a half. I'll start laying off tomorrow afternoon, but I don't want to have to dump too much. If you start to get too out of balance, call me. I'll either be at home or at my uncle's."

Pete stood and turned to the other tables that were lined up, classroom style, across from his table. The seat of his pants was damp and he pitted out near his belt line. He strode over near the windows and plucked off a large salami that hung in front of the blinds. He hacked off a piece with a pocket knife and popped it into his mouth. "Okay, fellas, move Carolina to three." He was about to repeat it when Tommy Spector began gesturing rapidly for him to shut up.

"You're in," said Tommy as he hung up the phone. He finished writing and looked up at Pete. "That was Poochie. He put two large on Michigan State at two and a hook."

The room burst into laughter and Al put his hand on Pete's shoulder. "In that case, move 'em to three and a half. Shut down in an hour and I'll be back here tomorrow afternoon. Gene's gonna open up and we'll shut down at game time. Any action on the NIT?"

"Not much. Can you believe that CBS is showing the NIT final on Saturday and not the NCAA?"

"I know, it's ridiculous. Things are changing. Hey, we're listening to the Michigan State game at my uncle's. Why don't you come by?"

"Thanks," said Pete, wiping his brow.

Al and Gene left the building, Gene slipping Stevie a ten spot at the door. They jumped into Al's big Buick and Al told the driver, Sandy, to head to his uncle's tavern.

"Al, I think you oughta take a position in both games," said Gene as he turned to face him.

Both men sat in the back and Al sighed as he looked out the window. He could see shades of his reflection in the glass, his dark hair thinning on top, crow's-feet next to his eyes, deep circles beneath them. He was only a few years older than Gene, but he looked his age—near fifty, while Gene, despite his thick glasses, barely looked thirty.

"I never take a position," said Al, running a thumb and forefinger over his brow. "I do just fine taking the juice."

"You could make a bundle in this game. Shit, you could probably make a ton on Kansas. Chamberlain can outscore Frisco by himself. They ain't got Russell or K. C. Jones anymore, and a lot of people are betting they'll repeat. But Al, I tell you, North Carolina's the play. They're undefeated and they play in a hell of a better conference. Michigan State ain't got shit."

"Geno, we've been through this. I don't gamble. I pay everybody. I pay the boys. I pay the winners. I pay Sandy here for driving and I pay you. And I gotta tell you. I'm getting tired of you ragging on me to take a position."

"Come on Al, it's just a suggestion. I seen too many easy games and I just wish you'd listen to me now and then."

"I listen. I listen when you tell me that everybody's gonna play

Michigan State at two and a half and what happens? Everybody's playing North Carolina. I'm a layoff bookie, Gene. I'm a businessman in a service industry. I'm a fucking bank. I don't have five-dollar players calling me. I've got bookies calling me with ten grand to lay off. Shit, here it is the day before the games, and Poochie's laying off two grand."

Gene took off his glasses and rubbed his nose. "That's a great example, Al. Fucking Poochie never wins. You've got two grand of his to play with. Throw it on North Carolina."

"And then I'd be Poochie. You're busting my balls here, Gene. I pay you a good salary and I trust you, but I do not want to hear another word about this. I don't take a position. I clear four, four and a half percent and that's fine with me. You want to become Poochie, you go work for somebody else."

"No, no, no," said Gene, putting on his glasses. "I'm happy working for you. I just think that you could make a little more."

"Yeah, I could make more all right. I could make more for Momo and the boys. There's the racket, Gene. They take fifty percent of my cut and all they do is pay off the cops and 'protect' us. And what do I do? I pay the sheet writers. I pay the lookouts. I pay Old Bones to rent our offices. I pay Tom and Jerry to take care of the phones and I pay you. You want to make more money, next time Angelo comes by, you tell him that you want to replace Momo. Then say your prayers."

Gene smiled.

Al looked back out the window, unconsciously rubbing his bad knee.

Sandy looked back in the rearview mirror. "Hey Al, you wanna go see *Twelve Angry Men* at the State Lake? I love that Henry Fonda."

Al shook his head.

Gene continued to look at him, smiling.

The bar reeked mahogany and crimson. Small tables were scattered throughout the room; a candle served each as a centerpiece. A colored man sat playing the piano in a corner, and a waitress scampered between the tables and bar, where a solitary bartender poured drinks and rang the register.

The Lip sat with three men, smoking cigars, finishing another late round of drinks. His suit coat hung on the back of his chair but his tie wasn't loosened. He motioned for the waitress, knocked a bit of ash into the ashtray and blew a stream of smoke into the air.

"This fight'll outclear Robinson–Fullmer, easy. They're middles and no matter how good, people want to see the big fellows."

"Sure they do," said Dally Richardson, his glasses slipping down his nose, fraying tie loosened, shirt sleeves a full inch from tasteful. "But your guys are up-and-comers. Nobody really knows them yet."

"Yeah," said Mike Lantz. Lantz was Richardson's competition from the other daily newspaper. "And it's gonna be tough with the Robinson–Fullmer fight scheduled for May first. That's only four weeks after your fight. People only have so much money."

The Lip ran numbers through his head. 15,000 was his break-even with paying the coons and everyone else, but it wouldn't help him with that other matter. He needed at least 16,500 paid tickets and another $200,000 for the radio and television rights. A sellout was a dream at this point.

"There are plenty of fight dollars out there. I need you guys to help me drum up business. If people get an eyeful of these fighters they'll pay."

Herb Bradley, the fight publicist, finished off his drink. "Last year, the Patterson–Moore fight drew sixteen thousand two hundred forty-eight people to the Chicago Stadium. The fight was blacked out for a hundred fifty miles surrounding Chicago and WMAQ ran the radio broadcast, and you know what? It wasn't enough. You guys ran three-inch headlines when Patterson won, covering everything from the size of the purse to Patterson's wife popping their kid right before the fight. This town's a fight town and we've got to fill that stadium to make sure that Chicago keeps drawing the big fights."

"Isn't it going to be blacked out again?" asked Dally Richardson.

"Yeah, but that helps all of us," said the Lip. "If it was on local television, fewer people would go to the fight and fewer people would have to read about it the next day."

"People will always read the newspaper," said Mike Lantz as the waitress stepped to their table. "It's part of their daily routine, like shaving, shitting, and brushing their teeth."

"Looking at your teeth, I'd guess that you don't read the paper or shit either," chortled Richardson.

"Kiss my ass," replied Lantz.

"Drop your shoulders," said Richardson.

The waitress arrived, bent over to pick up their empty glasses and asked if anyone else wanted a drink. The Lip ordered for all of them.

"Four Moscow Mules."

The Lip's early buzz was fading. The beer and vodka would help.

"Say, Mr. Lipranski," asked Richardson, "why don't you tell us about the prison yard. Isn't that how you got involved with Junior Hamilton?"

The Lip glanced at Herb Bradley. Bradley cleared his throat and set the ground rules. "This is definitely off the record then?"

Both men nodded.

"There's no secret," the Lip assured them. "It's just that the focus of any publicity should be the fight. The winner's assured a shot at Patterson and the heavyweight championship of the world, and that should be enough to draw interest."

The drinks arrived and the Lip swallowed half of his in one gulp. He pulled a fresh cigar from his pocket, clipped one end, and lit the other, drawing on it and twirling it to get an even light. He had only told this version a couple of times, and he puffed on the cigar while he pieced it together.

"It was the last month of my last year at Statesville. I'd spent most of my time reading and working out, but I'd become friends with a colored man named Henry Hamilton. Now, you've got to understand that prison attitudes aren't much different from those on the outside, but prisoners are much more bold in their interpretations. In this case, neither the white nor the colored population appreciated the fact that we had become friends. But word had filtered in that I couldn't be touched, and when Henry and I hung out, that applied to him. Mostly we talked about books, because, believe it or not, he was a reader, but we also talked about his nephew, Junior. Junior's mother was Henry's sister, and he loved that boy like a son. Junior's father had left home years before, and Junior was slinging hammers for the railroad. That's where he got his nickname. He was a gandy dancer. Anyway, I had determined that I was going to get into the fight game. I knew a few of the faces and I also knew that the I.B.C. was bound for trouble. It was obvious that they were monopolizing the championship fights and that the opportunity was ripe for someone else to start promoting. He'd have to pay Norris and Wirtz to use the Stadium, but they'd have to start listening to other promoters, or face government charges."

Richardson interrupted. "I heard that they're going to trial in May."

"Right. Anyway, Henry convinced me his nephew had real potential as a fighter, and I promised to look him up when I got out. So, one day we're in the yard and I notice that the warden's walking through with a group of people. It turns out that they're part of a magazine crew. He's showing off some new angle of rehabilitation or something, and every guard in the place is zeroed in on him and his group. Well, I wasn't the only one that noticed, because as Henry and I walked toward the back of the yard, three guys rushed us. They were carrying shivs, and one of them had an iron bar, and the next thing I know, he's swinging it at me while the other two guys start chasing Henry. I duck his swing and he falls forward, so I trip him. He rolls over as he hits the ground and I send my right elbow into his throat. That paralyzes him, so I grab the iron bar and whack him across the skull. He's done, so I turn around to help Henry. This all happens so fast that nobody sees what's going on until I bash that bar across the next goon's head. Just then, the guards look up, and it must've looked like Henry and I are going to kill this other guy, because the guards start sending shots at us. I hit the ground, but the other guy sinks his shiv into Henry before he falls to the ground. Now, I can see that Henry's hurt bad, so I crawl over to him as the guards start rushing us.

"When I get there, he's nearly gone, but he looks up at me and says, 'Take care of my boy,' and then he goes. By now, I'm bawling because I really loved this guy, and I'm not afraid of anything, so I pick up his body and hold it over my head, showing everybody what they've done. I start walking around in a circle, holding Henry's body up in the air. That's when the photographer snaps that picture that ended up on the cover of *Life*."

"Shit," muttered Richardson and Lantz.

"The real bitch of it is that the warden called me in to give my story and didn't believe a word that I said. He threw me in solitary until that picture came out and there was a public outcry. Some more reporters showed up and talked to a few of the guards who told them that I was the only white guy that ever sat and ate with the Negroes and that Henry and I were buddies. Then the warden didn't really have a choice. He dropped the charges and threw me back into population for my last couple of weeks. And when I got out, the first thing that I did was look up Junior Hamilton and his mother. We've been like a family ever since."

"Well, it's worked out all right for you," said Richardson, a bemused look on his face. "I understand that Arthur Wirtz and James Norris will both be forced to stop promoting fights at any spot in which they have a financial interest, such as the Stadium."

"Pure luck," said the Lip.

The waitress came back.

"One more round?"

"Sure," answered the Lip.

"Not me," said Richardson. "I've got an early morning."

"Me too," said Lantz, pulling on his suit coat.

Herb Bradley made his pitch.

"Fellows, if there's anything at all that you need, please feel free to call me at any time. We need a bit of help now, and we won't forget it when we're promoting a championship bout."

Dally Richardson dangled it. "Any cheap tickets left?" he asked, as he pulled his fedora onto his head.

"I'm glad that you asked," replied the Lip, standing. "We've got four great seats for both of you, in case you have family or friends that want to see the fight."

He gave each man tickets, shook their hands and watched them walk out into the lobby, headed for their cars. Neither of them had questioned the story or asked him about the other men. His theory hung true: always mix fiction with a strong dose of fact.

Herb pulled his coat over his lap and finished his drink.

"They'll be fine," he said. "The booze and tickets helps, but their readers eat up fight stories. We still need something else. We've sold about seventy-five hundred tickets so far, so we're lagging a little behind."

"Just what I was thinking," said the Lip, softly. "That's a nice little behind."

The waitress strode up to their table. "Mr. Lipranski, could you spend a minute with Ramon at the bar?" He nodded and told Herb to head home.

The Latino slid him a fresh beer as he sat down at the bar. "Thanks."

"Not a problem, sir," said Ramon as he handed the Lip an envelope. "This was sent over for you earlier this evening. I didn't think that you would want me to trouble you in front of your guests."

The Lip looked inside. A check made payable to Robert Lipranski. A bit short.

"Mr. Lewis also asked me to tell you that he took the liberty of paying your hotel bill out of the proceeds. He said that Mr. Johnson has an interest and that he appreciates your consideration."

Ramon started wiping down glasses.

The Lip chugged his beer and set his glass on the bar. He also pulled a twenty-dollar bill out of his pocket and set it next to the empty glass.

"That won't be necessary, sir," said Ramon, filling the glass.

"That isn't for the tab," replied the Lip. "I like my business to remain that way. Anything that I want to share with Mr. Lewis or Mr. Johnson will be shared in person."

Ramon pocketed the bill and nodded.

The Lip went back to his table and polished off the beer.

The waitress returned. Black hair, dark eyes, nice rack.

"Anything else?"

"A shot of bourbon and a schooner."

"Taking our drinking seriously tonight, are we?"

"Taking everything seriously tonight."

She went to the bar and brought back a shot and a beer. "We're closing. This is it."

"Care to join me?" he asked.

Her eyes sparkled. "I don't drink with the customers."

"If you're closed, then I'm not a customer."

"If we were in the middle of Marshall Field's you wouldn't be a customer."

"Attitude, I like that. Does Miss Attitude have a name?"

"None that will do you any good."

"Try me. A few drinks and I get a lot better looking."

"After a quart of tequila, Olive Oyl thinks that Bluto's good-looking."

"I love your taste in the arts. So you think that I look like Bluto?"

"Same build, less hair, not quite as smart."

"You heard it too young."

"What?"

"That you're beautiful."

"You heard it too old."

"What?"

"That you're ugly."

"Only a quart of tequila. I can afford that."

"You couldn't afford your bar tab. Somebody bailed you out with an envelope of cash."

"I'm a few weeks from rich."

"They all say that."

"You're a few years from law school."

"We all say that."

"You bring the tequila and some beer. Fucking room service is raping me."

"Better you than me."

His head swam. The shot clarified everything for just a moment. Her name tag read GILDA.

"This ain't funny, Mr. Hansen," said Wee Willie. "This boy is breaking down. He ain't just tired."

"Aah, he'll be fine," replied Hansen. "We all go a little bonkers when we don't get any sleep. Hell, I got married after working a double shift!"

Wee Willie shook his head. He kept his voice quiet, so it wouldn't echo in the corridor. Even their breathing echoed.

"I'm not joking around here. Junior's got a problem. He's always been jumpy, but lately he's gotten worse. Bawling in the film room is only the start of it."

"Well, what do you want us to do?" asked Hansen.

"Postpone the fight until he gets some help."

"Not going to happen."

"Mr. Hansen, me and Junior need the money as bad as anybody, but he isn't prepared to get into that ring. Albano and the Hat are both knocking him around the ring."

Don Hansen ran a hand through his thick white hair. He stared down at his loafers, pretended to be lost in thought, but they both knew that, despite the honorary title of manager, he had no control over Junior Hamilton or the fight. He was just the Lip's mouthpiece.

"Let him lay off for a couple of days and then we'll talk. But I can tell you this. This fight is going to come off. This is the big shot for you and Junior and if he blows it, he'll end up pounding spikes for the railroad again."

"Then at least close the workouts to the press. They get him all nervous."

Hansen laughed. "Are you a junk hog? We're struggling to sell tickets and you want to keep the press away. Jesus, I'll bet that you'd tell the Good Humor man to stop ringing his bell. The press stays. Junior stays. All he needs is some zzz's and he'll be ready to go."

"That ain't all," said Wee Willie. "We need some money. Lipranski promised that he'd pay us last week and we still ain't seen no money."

"I'll say something," said Hansen. "But I wouldn't hold your breath. He's paying a fortune for all of the training and the food. Hell, these sparring partners don't come cheap, either. You'll get paid right after the fight."

"Better," grumbled Wee Willie.

Junior heard their conversation trail off down the hallway as he rolled over onto his stomach. Mama always said that you can keep nightmares away by sleeping on your stomach.

Mama. She'd slaved for him for nearly all of his twenty-two years and he wouldn't let her down now. His father had left when he was barely four years old, and his sister had turned into a jabber, but Mama was always there. She worked for Mr. Daniels, cooking and cleaning and she was a fine Christian woman and she always led her Junior right. So she could never know. That didn't even need to be said. He'd die before he told her.

Thinking about Mama made him homesick. He fell back to his standby. His mind wandered and suddenly he was back working for the railroad, hammer in his hand, pounding spikes.

He had loved working for the railroad. As Johnny, the old Indian foreman, always said, it offered constant visible progress. The back-hoe would work in the morning, tearing out the old track. Then Junior and his crew would plant their tongs into the railroad ties and carry them over and line them up before the rail would be set over them. Finally, they would drive spikes into the ties, their tips anchoring the rail to the tie.

His crew loved him, of that he was sure. They respected his work habits, and were awed by his physical ability, but loved him for his gentle nature and honesty. Old Johnny would always have a smile for him; Paco, some of his home-made burritos; and Alvin, a crude joke. The pay was good, and for that he could thank Mr. Daniels, who had gotten him the job. He would have stayed there forever if he hadn't loved driving lag screws.

One hot summer afternoon, his crew had been assigned to put in a new road crossing. The backhoe had performed its job in the morning and they had filled the crossing during the early part of the afternoon. The only thing that had remained was to secure it with lag screws. The lag screws were nearly a foot long, and most of the men hated to pound them, because it required using a heavy sledgehammer, rather than the long, thin spike hammer. Being screws, they were harder to insert than spikes, but that was why Junior loved banging on them. He challenged himself to see how few swings he could use to pound in a screw, and he loved how he felt when the crossing was secure. His energy was drained, his back and shoulders fatigued, but his muscles were flooded with blood and he was filled with the thrill of accomplishment.

That afternoon, he and Johnny had remained at the crossing, while the others had moved on down the line to lay more track. He'd been pounding in the last lag screw when he'd seen Johnny arguing with a man in the street. The man had pulled his car over to the side of the road and was screaming. He'd told Johnny that the reason traffic was so screwed up, and that he was being forced to make a detour, was because the track was being laid by one "shiftless nigger." They exchanged words, and then the man, who was a foot taller and fifty pounds heavier than Johnny, suddenly backhanded the old foreman, sending him to the ground. Junior hadn't thought, only reacted. He dropped his sledge and leaped over the track. The man had faced him and squared up, but Junior had slung both hands like hammers in wide overhead arcs. The man had managed to nearly slip the first two, catching them on his shoulders, but the third one had crushed the top of his skull. Only Johnny scampering to his feet and tackling Junior had stopped him from killing the man.

Despite Johnny's testimony and the reluctance of the man to file charges, the railroad held its own hearing two days later and he was fired. Once again, Mama went to Mr. Daniels, and the publisher, upon hearing the story, made his own inquiries, and then sent Junior to see Wee Willie.

His first few days in the gym showed his inexperience, but also offered proof of his physical skills. He was strong and quick and had surprising balance, no doubt, surmised Wee Willie, because of his time bent over the tracks, swinging hammers. Junior fell in love with the discipline that the sport required: the long runs, hours spent in front of the speed, heavy and double-end bags, the art of shadowboxing, grueling exercises, endless rope jumping and sparring. But above all, he loved the other boxers. His friends and peers. His crew.

Junior rolled over onto his back, unable to sleep. Secrets, he knew, kept a man awake at night, so he confessed again in his prayers. Once more, he told God what had happened and begged his forgiveness.

He rolled back onto his stomach, his breathing slowed and his eyelids grew heavy. His last waking thought was of Jack Johnson, lying in the Cuban sun, shading his eyes. Why was he smiling?

Friday, March 22

Al sat down at the patio table, spread open his newspaper, took a swig of orange juice and began to read. His high-rise apartment overlooked Lake Michigan, and despite the fact that it was only a small one-bedroom unit, was his only indulgence. Janet had helped him decorate it, choosing white leather, ivory trim, tasteful paintings and money green in the bedroom.

The morning was warm by Chicago standards, where March could offer snow, and he sat out on the deck, wearing only his white terry-cloth robe and a pair of slippers. It was the time of year when he began to crave warm weather.

He'd slept like shit again the night before, waking to sopping sheets and the morning shivers. The morning papers were piled on the chair next to him, including his stepfather's Chicago daily. It was his morning ritual to read each, digest the news and sports along with his bacon and eggs and black coffee.

Gene had been way off with his assessment of the North Carolina–Michigan State game. He had North Carolina favored by three and a half, and the action on Michigan State was minimal. He'd have to lay off, unless popping it up another point brought on some Michigan State action. That's what would probably happen, and he was glad, since the bookies down in Charlotte couldn't handle all of his action, and his peers on each coast were probably running into the same problem. The Kansas game was definitely a layoff, since nobody was going with San Francisco. He'd call Goldie Rubenstein early afternoon to warn him of the bet. It was a professional courtesy for Goldie to accept his bet and he owed the advance notice.

Gene. Something was up with him. He'd known Gene all of his life and all of a sudden he'd started hounding him to take a position. Ninety-nine percent of all bookies took a position, and ninety-nine percent lost when they did. It was a cardinal sin, one that layoff bookies like him and Goldie avoided. Lay low and lay off. That was the credo. Avoid publicity, the limelight, the IRS, and Momo. That was it. Avoid attention.

Tom and Jerry, the exterminators. It was time to change apartments and he'd need the phones hooked up. Crazy bastards, but the best.

Uncle Pat. Call him and tell him to set up a couple of tables in the back room. They'd listen to the game there tonight.

He lit a cigar and leaned back into the chair. Clouds pooled, the temperature started to drop, and the breeze froze his nuts. His back and knee hurt and his eyes burned. Stress was killing him. His body testified. It was time to get out.

The Lip smoked an aspirin-laced cigarette. His head was pounding and he could feel the sugar gush through his system. He stepped across the carpet into the bathroom and brushed his teeth. Damn, that was a little bit better. He ran the water for a shower, stripped off his underwear and stepped under the hot stream.

Bills paid, a slight pad. Only 7,500 tickets sold. 9,000 short with two weeks to go. There had to be a way.

Fights at the Marigold Garden tonight. A quick pitch over the PA. Check out the ring girls.

Now, Lincoln Johnson was in for 15 percent. Twenty percent for Junior, 25 for Gordon, 30 percent for the Stadium and expenses. Shit, he'd only get 10 percent and that wouldn't cut it; he was in for more than that. Attendance of 15,000 averaging $14.77 per ticket and $150,000 for radio and television equaled $371,550. Pumping the attendance to 16,500 and the RTV rights to $200,000 added another $70,000 or so, or $7,000 to him. Forty-four grand. Still not quite enough, but closer. Maybe he could screw with the expenses, but that would take some doing. Only a sellout and guarantee of a rematch would convince radio and TV to add $50,000. A sellout. 19,000. He'd be covered, but how could he get there? Sell love or sell hate. Take your pick.

He closed his eyes and let his head slump forward; water blasted the back of his neck. His skin started to tingle as the water got hotter, and when he shampooed the short, dark hair on the sides of his head and let the water rinse it off, the headache started to ease.

He stepped out and began drying himself with a towel. A trip over to the Tam O'Shanter to watch Junior train and then a late lunch at Fritzels with Abe Rosen, Tomcat's manager. The fights this evening and maybe pop into the Chez Paree or check Carol Channing at the Empire Room. Fuck Carol Channing. No tits.

He stepped back into the bedroom. The lights were still off and she was sleeping. He walked over to the bed, pulled back the sheets and stared at her naked body as she mumbled awake.

"Ugh, give me back the covers."

She tugged at the sheets, lying on her side. She pulled them up over her shoulder, but he reached forward and jerked them back. She yelled into the pillow as she rolled onto her stomach; her breasts popped out underneath.

He slipped in behind her, spread her legs and pulled her toward him. She buried her head in the pillow, put her hands on the cheeks of her ass and spread them. Puckering.

She yelped as he entered her.

Screw Junior's workout.

Gilda. He felt like he was making it with a frigging movie star.

The bell rang and Junior stopped to catch his breath. The room was basement gray, and smelled of musty sweat. A ring had been set up in the far corner, and five canvas-covered heavy bags, varying in size, hung in the back. Mats were laid out near the entrance and two double-end bags and several speed bags lined the perimeter. It was a fighters' training camp, and fighters stood at each bag, slung each medicine ball, performed exercises on the mats, shadowboxed near the ring and sparred within it.

Kid Spinelli stepped by Junior, wearing a plastic coat and pants.

"How many more you got to go?" asked Junior.

"Eleven friggin' pounds," said Spinelli. "My Angie's just too good of a cook. Between fights I balloon up to a hundred and eighty and then got to drop back to one sixty. It's torture."

He picked a rope out of a pile and began to skip rope. "They got me eating a half a hard-boiled egg and a half a can of soup for break-fast and the other half for lunch. For dinner I get a slice of beef liver and all the celery I want. Pure torture. Not even any sauce for the damn celery."

The bell rang again, signaling the end of the one-minute rest period, and Junior turned his attention back to the double-end bag. The bag was anchored to the floor and ceiling with thick rubber bands, and with each blow, it would rebound crazily. Amateurs could play quite the fool, attempting to land consecutive solid blows, but the seasoned professional could rattle off a series of punches, pum-meling the bag like it was somehow attached to their gloves.

Junior kept his eyes trained on the bag, stung it with jabs and crosses. His gray T-shirt and sweat pants were drenched, and the muscles in his biceps knotted like grapefruit. Sweat dripped down his brow and flew airborne with his rhythmic snorts. Sometimes he felt like he was making music; banging the bags like drums, expelling air like brushing the cymbals, dancing.

He had slept well the night before, no doubt having released a lot of tension during the film. He had awoken refreshed; his morning jog went well, and he finished nearly twenty minutes before the others. Wee Willie witnessed his sprint to the finish and seemed relieved.

The bell rang again, signaling the end to the three-minute round of exercise, and he stepped over to the heavy bag. Wee Willie and his assistant, Aaron Green, stood by the bag.

"Aaron's gonna hold for you, Hammer," said Wee Willie. "I want you to remember to stick and move. Tomcat's about your size, but you got a big edge with your reach. Keep 'im off with your jabs, pop-ping him with your right cross and setting up your left hook. And don't forget to combo your hook."

Wee Willie leaned into the bag and simulated a left hook near the middle. "When you come into the ribs with a hook, he's gonna drop his right elbow. That'll give you the chance to follow up upstairs."

He touched the middle of the bag with an open hand and sud-denly hooked the bag at eye level, open handed, loudly popping the canvas. "Now show me."

The bell rang and Junior opened up with a series of left jabs, followed by a right cross and a strong left hook.

"Now, stick and move," yelled Aaron Green.

Aaron was Wee Willie's nephew. He looked up to his uncle and wanted to follow in his footsteps. However, he didn't have the nature to become a fighter, even though Wee Willie had been a top bantamweight. Therefore, he had made his mark as Wee Willie's assistant trainer, and, although he was barely thirteen, he had become Junior's closest friend among the crew.

"Come on, Junior, grunt when you hit this thing," screamed Aaron over the gym noise, turning to seek his uncle's approval. "Scare that old bag. Let him know you're coming."

Aaron wrapped his legs around the bag and grabbed hold of the chains that anchored it into the ceiling. Junior continued to pound the bag; Aaron rode it like a carnival ride, laughing and giggling as it jerked with each punch.

"Get on off of that," yelled Wee Willie.

Aaron jumped down, turned to Junior and gave him a mischievous grin. Junior smiled warmly, then started to pepper the bag again.

Junior completed two more rounds on the heavy bag, endured three rounds of situps and three rounds catching the medicine ball in his midsection, and finished his workout with a series of pushups. He was exhausted as Aaron strode up beside him and unwrapped his handwraps.

"Let's go get some lunch and then rest for a while. Uncle Willie's got someone coming in to spar you this afternoon."

"I ain't sparrin' Jack or Hat today?"

"Nope. Uncle Willie's worried 'bout you after the last few days. He's gonna see how you do this afternoon and if you don't do good, he's gonna try to cancel the fight."

"He cain't do that," said Junior, his brow furrowing in concern. "I gotta get this fight so I can move up."

"Why you think I'm tellin' you this?" asked Aaron, throwing the wet wraps in a bag with the sixteen-ounce training gloves.

"I was just tired."

"You better not be this afternoon. He's letting the newspaper men in to watch."

Junior's stomach went acidic. *She* paid a quick visit. "Who's he bringing in?"

"Crandy Williams."

"He ain't nobody's sparring partner."

"That's what I'm tryin to tell ya. You'd better be ready for a war."

The hell with Wee Willie, trying to ruin his fight.

He needed the fight. They needed the fight. *Mama* needed the fight. He might have to kill Crandy Williams.

They had turned the space heaters off, but the apartment was still warm. The phones were ringing, the clerks were taking bets, Gene was tabulating the totals and Al sat in the bathroom, sweating out his breakfast.

He walked out moments later and strode behind the tables, looking at each clerk's sheet.

Too many sticks and slashes for Kansas. Nothing for San Francisco. North Carolina getting a lot of action, not much yet on Michigan State.

Gene looked up at Al, tucked a pencil behind his ear and sighed. "We've got sixty-five thousand on North Carolina, so we're pushing them to four," said Gene. "That should start the Michigan State money in. Nobody's playing Frisco. We've got Kansas action at fifty large, so they're going up to eight and a half, but I don't think you'll get much on Frisco, no matter how high the line goes."

Al pulled a folding chair up to the table and sat down next to Gene. He wore a pair of light wool slacks, a white cotton dress shirt and a hand-painted tie. Dressed for business. He pulled out his reading glasses and slipped them on as he began to tally the figures. He didn't look up as he addressed Gene and Pete Barnes, who leaned on the table in front of him. "Press 'em up a half of a point. I'm gonna call Goldie and try to lay off some of the Kansas and N.C. action. Gene, you try Jimmy in Detroit, and Pete, you check with Miami. I don't want a lot of exposure on Kansas."

All three men picked up phones. The exterminators had wired nine phones into the rooms. Only one line was registered to the address and nobody used it, except to place a couple of calls to local, unaffiliated numbers. The remaining lines were patched in from the main telephones line and were untraceable. Miles and miles of telephone lines crossed the city and it was impossible for the authorities to confirm that every line went to a registered household. Like the bug men told him when they spliced off his first lines, "Look like the phone company, act like the phone company, everybody thinks you're the phone company."

Gene lit a cigarette and blew the smoke straight up in the air, leaned back in his chair.

Cradling the phone, Pete Barnes tucked the back of his lucky red and black Hawaiian shirt into his pants. He tagged it lucky because he had been wearing it the day that his wife had fallen off of their cruise ship, disappearing into the ocean. Sink or swim, he had thought, kind of like bookmaking.

Al got Goldie Rubenstein on the line. They dispensed with small talk. "I got too much action on Kansas, G. Where you got 'em?"

"I ain't. I've got 'em at eight and a half, but I can't sell San Francisco, so I'm not taking any Kansas."

Al's stomach knotted. "I'm exposed. Anybody taking Kansas?"

"Probably not," rasped Goldie, "but you can try Miami."

Gene threw an arm around Al. "Hold on one second, G," said Al.

Al turned to Gene. Gene pleaded: "Al, Jimmy ain't taking any Kansas, but he's still got Carolina at three and a hook. Throw your exposure on Carolina."

Al shot back, disgusted. He turned back to his phone, dismissed Gene. "What about North Carolina, G? I should balance out soon, but I may try and drop something a little later."

"We're showing Carolina minus four and a half now, probably going up to five within the half hour."

"That's where I'm heading too," said Al. "Thanks anyway."

"Lay low, A."

"Lay off, G."

Al hung up the phone and looked at Pete Barnes.

"Sorry, Al, Miami's not taking any Kansas. This fucking Chamberlain's got everybody."

"All right," said Al. "Bump Carolina to four and a half, and push Kansas up to nine."

Pete nodded and walked the tables, writing down the new spreads.

Al turned to Gene. "Don't start in on me today, Gene. If I'm exposed on Kansas, that's one thing, but I will not voluntarily risk my money."

Gene put out his cigarette, grinding the butt into the ashtray. The smoke tickled his long, hooked nose, and he sniffled as he kept his eyes trained on the tab sheet. "If you never risk anything, you'll never make a killing."

"I'm only worried about making a living."

"Angelo's thinking that maybe you aren't producing enough."

Knots again. When? "When did you talk to Angelo?"

"I saw him last night at the Trocadero. My brother and I went to see some titties and have a few beers."

"And he just happened to be there."

Gene sat up. "That's right, he just happened to be there. Don't make a big deal out of it. He just said that since Joe Batters put Momo in charge, he's looking to make an impression. He figures that, since you're the man, maybe you can make a little more money."

"I make them plenty of money, and if I start betting, I'll lose plenty of money. Angelo wants to make an impression, see what kind of impression he makes if I start losing. They love me when I'm making money, but that stops, see how fast they come down on me."

Pete Barnes came back. "Action's starting to come in on Michigan State. I think we'll be okay."

"At what point?" asked Al.

"Four and a half."

"So the most of the North Carolina money is giving three and a half or less, and the bulk of the Michigan State money gets four and a hook?"

"Yeah," said Pete.

Gene lit another cigarette.

"I'm exposed at four," said Al.

"Huge," said Pete Barnes.

"You can still get Carolina giving three and a half from Detroit," offered Gene.

"I'd rather take my chances on the point," replied Al, taking off his reading glasses. "The odds of the game finishing on four are rat-shit small."

Pete shuffled nervously. "Tommy just took twenty thousand on Michigan State from Gamey Donato."

Al looked at him quizzically. "Gamey ain't playing twenty grand."

Gene interrupted. "He's gotta be bearding somebody."

"Search me," said Pete. "He's good for the money, so I can't blame Tommy for taking it, but Gene's right, he's gotta be bearding for somebody."

"I don't like it," said Al. "On settle-up day, ask him who he played for. If somebody's playing through me I want to know who it is, not their damn beard."

Pete nodded. They booked for another hour, then unplugged the phones, folded up the tables and chairs and emptied the place, save one phone for Tommy Spector to take any late Kansas–San Francisco bets.

The totals: Fifty grand on North Carolina giving two and a half, fifteen at three, fifteen at three and a half, fifteen at four. Michigan State bettors playing $80,000 at four and a half.

Virtually no risk. Unless it ends on four, it's around an $8,000 win. It hits four, shit, don't even think about it. Four equals a loss of $160,000.

Everyone on Kansas to the tune of fifty-three thousand, giving between eight and nine; Frisco only took in $25,000. Exposure at $28,000, minus juice—$25,500.

Al slipped into his jacket. It was still too damn cold. He stooped into his car, slid over to make room for Gene and Pete, tapped Sandy on the shoulder.

"Hit Pat's."

Sandy started the car and pulled away from the curb.

The rearview mirror: the other men trickling out of the apartment building.

Gene and Pete began talking about the game.

Al looked out the window as night fell, a cold breeze whipping trash across the street.

Exposure. Over twenty-five grand. Cumulative, a good chance of dropping $17,500. Shitty business.

Cold air shot through the car as Gene tossed a cigarette out the window.

Time to leave it all behind. Maybe Florida.

The Lip stood in the locker room, rapping his knuckles against the wall. Spider Gomez and Wee Willie walked through the door, talking. Spider took one look at the Lip and turned around.

Wee Willie stopped about four feet short.

"Just what the fuck are you doing?" asked the Lip.

Wee Willie stared at him, silently.

"I said, what the fuck are you doing!?"

The Lip, back to the lockers, slammed his open hands against them.

"Don't just stare at me. Explain to me why you risk everything and don't even consult me."

"I couldn't find you."

"You couldn't find me, so you go ahead and call in Crandy Williams. And you call the press. The press! What the hell are you trying to do? Can you answer that one simple question for me. Please. What the hell are you trying to do?"

Wee Willie stood his ground. "I tried to talk to Mr. Hansen the other night but he wasn't listening. This boy's got some problems, so we're gonna find out right now whether or not he can fight."

The Lip moved close. "He can fight. He will fight. I've got a lot of money on the line here, and you're not going to jeopardize it."

The Lip surveyed the floor, ran a hand over his scalp. His suit felt three sizes too small. "Here's what we're going to do. You tell Crandy to take it easy. Let Junior catch him a couple of times and we'll pay him off and send him on his way."

"I can't do that," answered Wee Willie.

"What?"

"I can't do that. If Junior can't take Crandy Williams, he could get hurt against Tomcat. That boy ain't right! If he's screwed up and he gets into the ring, he could get killed."

"So you call one of the top heavyweights in the country to spar with him?"

Wee Willie spit passion. "That's right!" he yelled, eyes bugging. "Today he's gonna have on headgear, but in a couple of weeks it's for real. I'm not sending the boy out there if he isn't all together."

"Well then," said the Lip, crowding, "I guess I'll have a little chat with Mr. Williams myself."

Wee Willie dropped subtlety. "No you won't."

"Why won't I?"

"Because if I don't think that Crandy's giving it his all, I may have to talk with Junior about that prison yard."

The Lip stared at him.

He stared back. He fucking knew.

"If you've got something to say, say it."

"No need to, unless Crandy Williams looks like he's loafing."

Stalemate.

"If Junior screws up, you're dead."

"If Junior screws up, he may be dead."

The Lip ducked out of the locker room, adrenaline gushing like he was climbing into the ring. He brushed past Spider Gomez, who held his gloves tight, crotch level. When the Lip cleared the doorway, Spider sprinted inside, looking for a stall like a scared rabbit hunting for a hole in the ground.

The Lip walked up to Crandy Williams, sans the Wee one.

"Good, but not too good."

The fighter nodded as he pulled on his headgear. Jack Albano brought over a pair of gloves and held them open for him as he slipped his hands inside.

Aaron Green talked excitedly to Junior, who already wore his headgear and gloves.

Wee Willie strode up behind them, put his hands on Junior's shoulders and leaned forward, speaking only inches from Junior's ear. "Don't you get all riled on me now, Hammer. This is just a little test for you and I know you're gonna come through with flying colors."

Junior shrugged Wee Willie's hands free. "He ain't nobody's sparring partner."

"Now, look at it as an act of kindness on your part. Crandy's done lost his license for fighting, so you're giving him a job."

Junior snorted. Wee Willie ignored it and bore in. "Now, I want you to work your hooks. Crandy's about Tomcat's size and his style's the same. So, I want you to concentrate on hooking the body and comboing up top."

Aaron stepped on the bottom rope and pulled the top one high. Wee Willie slipped through, followed by Junior.

Junior began shadowboxing around the ring, whipping jabs, pulling his elbows up to block shots, hooking, bobbing, weaving.

Crandy Williams climbed into the ring. He was taller than Junior expected and that just made him look bigger. Junior figured that he could've substituted for a backhoe, ripping railroad ties out of the ground with his bare hands. His skin was coal black. Red, broad scars riddled his arms. He was shirtless, so the long, thick scar that wrapped from the back of one shoulder around to his stomach was also visible. His legs were long and strong, and he pumped them like pistons, shook his head, loosened up his neck.

Junior moved over to his corner.

"Now don't you worry," said Aaron as he inserted a mouthpiece. "He probably ain't near as mean as he looks."

Junior's look said, "Thanks a lot."

Wee Willie clapped his hands and the two fighters came together. They touched gloves and then Crandy Williams fired a couple of half-hearted jabs at Junior. Junior easily slipped them and sent a quick hook to the body.

"Follow that!" yelled Wee Willie, leaning in from a corner.

Junior threw another lazy hook and Crandy Williams caught it with his elbow and popped back with a quick jab. The jab glanced off of Junior's headgear and Crandy followed it with a hard right, but Junior leaned away from it.

"Damn it, Crandy, we ain't paying you for a half-assed effort!" screamed Wee Willie.

Junior began firing jabs, circling around his opponent like he was wrapping him.

Crandy stepped hard left, cut off the ring and bore in on Junior, hooking to the body with both hands: mallets pounding drums.

Junior skipped back, faded left and then threw an overhand right lead, surprising Crandy, snapping his head back.

Junior backed off, let Crandy recover.

"No, Junior, no. You're a headhunter! A killer. You don't let him go!"

The bell sounded and both fighters went to their corners.

Wee Willie pointed at Crandy Williams. "You give my boy better than that. I demand it! We want your best!"

The Lip shot Wee Willie a hard glance. Don Hansen came up behind him and dropped an arm over his shoulder. He nodded forward, looking at Dally Richardson, Mike Lantz, and Herb Bradley. The nod asked, "What are they doing here?"

"Where have you been, you asshole?"

"Getting my hair cut," said Hansen, smiling. He ran his hands through his thick, white hair. "My looks are the only thing that gets me up in the morning." He laughed; his alcohol-reddened face glowed.

"Well, for your information," said the Lip, turning to face him, "your fighter is in there with the former number-one contender. A cut, a head butt, a broken hand and our fight is off."

"Then why the hell is he sparring with him?"

The Lip glared at Wee Willie. "Because that little maggot of a trainer of his is worried about him. He said that if Junior can't perform against Crandy Williams, he's going to pull out of the fight."

Hansen bolted upright. "What?"

The Lip dismissed it with a swat at the air. "Don't worry about that. He's going to fight. Just pray he doesn't get hurt."

"Did you approve this?" asked Hansen, taking off his sportcoat and hanging it behind the folding chair.

"No, I've been a little distracted."

"I hope your distraction was pink," said Hansen, chuckling.

The Lip ignored him as the fighters climbed back into the ring.

"Now, let's see some action," yelled Wee Willie.

"Stick and move, Hammer," shouted Aaron Green, leaning over his uncle.

Wee Willie shoved him back onto his stool. His look dictated "shut up."

Crandy Williams came in hard, firing hooks to the body. Wee Willie's taunts fed him anger.

Junior backpedaled, jabbed his distance safe.

Crandy rushed, heaved an overhand right like tossing a grenade. Junior slipped it and popped his face with a left hook. He faked a follow-up right hand and sent a left hook to the body. Crandy blew air like a drowning victim spewing water.

"Good combo," shouted Aaron.

"Rock him," yelled Wee Willie.

Crandy threw his arms around Junior. He caught the Lip with the corner of his eye. He screamed a mental "fuck you!" and shot his head upward, hoping to catch Junior's chin with a head butt. All rules were off.

Junior pushed him away, digested the head butt.

Nothing's stopping the fight.

Junior circled left, shot jabs. Crandy rushed again and Junior slipped right, measured the distance with a jab and followed with an overhand right. The punch buckled Crandy's knees and Junior leaped forward, threw a left hook combination to the head.

Crandy fell Buddhist, worshiping with his face digging canvas.

Scenes: Aaron Green jumped in the air; Wee Willie took a wet sponge to Junior while Mousey Morris helped Crandy to a stool; the Lip addressed the press. "Not even the former number-one contender is an adequate sparring partner for Junior. Shoot, if Rocky Marciano would come out of retirement, we would consider, and I do mean consider, hiring him as a sparring partner."

Wee Willie unlaced Junior's gloves and unwound his handwraps. He looked up into the fighter's eyes, popping intensity. "You found it again today. You haven't had any focus or confidence lately and you needed to find it. Now, you've got to hold on to it."

Junior shuddered in relief. His thoughts were nearly duplicate. Hold on. Just hold on.

• • •

"Jesus Christ, it's freezing," bellowed Gene as he entered the back room. "This city, two months of summer, no spring, no fall, ten months of winter."

Three tables had been pulled together in the middle of the room, where Al played gin with his Uncle Pat, while Pete Barnes was pitted against Pat's friend Duffy. The rest of the room, which Pat rented out for parties or opened up during big evenings, was empty. The chairs all sat, upside down, on top of the tables, and the lights behind the long oak bar were dark, despite the neon glow from a beer sign.

The radio, piped in from the front bar, competed with the noise from the bar crowd; glasses clinking, laughter, cheers and jeers.

"It's tied at the half," said Al, looking up from behind his hand of cards, acknowledging Gene. "Where you been?"

"The Troc," said Gene as he peeled off his jacket, threw it over a chair and walked to the back bar. "Open, Pat?"

"Pour your own," said Pat. "Bar's open until I whip your friend here."

Al peered over his reading glasses.

"Which means it never closes," confirmed Pat, returning his attention to his hand. "Now how the hell could you need that three of hearts? You didn't pick up the damn two."

Gene flipped over a stool at the bar and sat on it, leaning against the bar. He faced Pat and Duffy, while Al and Pete Barnes had their backs to him. He pulled his upper lip taut and pretended to peer over Al's shoulder, then grinned mirthfully at Pat.

"I don't need any of your help," cackled Pat. "Except to get me another beer. A draft of Canadian Ace, if you please."

"Anybody else?" asked Gene. He stepped behind the bar and filled a glass with beer. Pete and Duffy both nodded and Al held up an empty whiskey glass. The usual, bourbon and water.

"I saw Poochie on the way in," said Gene, setting the drinks at the tables. "He told me Michigan State is a lock. I even told him that he bet too early and missed out on a couple of points, and you know what? He told me that it didn't matter, Michigan State is going to win outright and he didn't want to jinx the feeling by waiting."

"A pad isn't a lock for Poochie," chortled Pat. "He's just like his father, they shit through money like last night's corn. No common sense for the games. His father played my Chicago wheel more than anyone and I swear he's the only one that never won. He'd come in here and play 26 all night and never win. Never seen anything like 'em. Like father, like son. Am I right, Duffy?"

"Like father, like son," agreed Duffy.

Pete Barnes wolfed down a handful of peanuts and splayed his cards. "Gin."

"Shit," said Duffy, dropping his hand. "I was waiting on that four."

Duffy stood up, pulled his pants up underneath his large belly, tucked in his shirt. Navy tattoos ran up and down his arms.

"Take my place, Gene," he said as he waddled by Sandy, who was watching the door. "I'm gonna hit the can."

Gene sat down across from Pete.

"Hollywood, three across," said Pete, shuffling the cards.

"Fifty cents a hand, buck a game?" asked Gene, taking off his glasses, placing them inside his shirt pocket.

"Sure."

Pete dealt the cards. Gene picked them up and turned to Al. "There's this new broad at the Troc that's absolutely amazing," he said. "Me and my brother must've given her twenty bucks."

"You've been spending a lot of time there," replied Al, dropping a card on the discard pile. "Is this broad the attraction?"

"God as my witness, you've never seen anything like it."

"Just another cash cow," said Al. "Gin. That's one fifty-five, game. That's two games."

"Criminy," said Pat, slapping his cards on the table. "You've got no right to treat your uncle this way. What've I ever done to deserve such treatment?"

They all smiled as Pat hopped to his feet, his bowling shirt hanging loose over his slacks, his thin, wiry frame in constant motion. He grabbed a cloth off the bar and wiped off a table, then replaced the cloth. "That's been bothering me all night."

"Jesus, Pat, you're as bad as Al," said Gene, concentrating on his hand. "You guys need to relax a little. Come on over to the titty bars with me."

There was a knock at the door and Sandy, stationed on a bar stool, let Duffy back into the room.

"It's crowded out there," said Duffy, pulling up a seat at an adjacent table.

"Say, Duff," said Pat, chuckling. "Gene here thinks that titty bars are the place to relax. Would you agree with that assessment?"

Duffy shook his head in disgust. "Give me a whorehouse any day."

"You can't really blame them," spat Pat. "When the Lester sisters moved on, whoring just wasn't what it used to be."

Sandy took the bait. "Who were they?" he asked, turning his huge frame on the stool, popping his knuckles with his thumbs.

Pat got a glint in his eyes and a warm smile crossed his face. "They were the two loveliest matrons ever to run a house of ill repute. They were businesswomen, shining lights and pillars of the recreational community."

"They were a couple of baggy madams," said Al, shuffling the deck. "My uncle gets weepy over them because they catered to the same men."

"I acknowledge that my sentiment is a bit business-oriented," replied Pat, as he strode behind the bar and began pouring drafts. "But the sisters were the Las Vegas of prostitution. They bought a couple of houses up on Dearborn and turned them into these wonderful dens of iniquity. Am I right, Duff?"

"Right, wonderful. Wonderful."

"Mina and Ada called themselves the Everleigh sisters, and the Everleigh Club was the most exotic, fantastic club of its kind. I myself preferred the Oriental Room."

"I liked the King's Room," said Duffy, as he grabbed another handful of peanuts, discarded the shells into an ashtray.

"The Oriental Room contained authentic oriental furniture, deep, thick rugs, and rice-paper walls surrounding the beds. Asian women in native garb would serve you."

"I'll bet," said Al, resigned to wait out the end of the story before resuming the card game.

"No you won't," laughed Pat, "and I admire you for it. But that was, without a doubt, the best head of my life."

"The King's Room beat it hands down," said Duffy. "A king's harem. And it was all classy-like."

"Real classy," said Al. "Just what you want from a whorehouse."

"He's right, my self-righteous nephew," cackled Pat. "Women would enter, very softly, wearing wonderful evening wear. They would ask your permission—your permission—to dance, and you would end up dancing back to a room. That's how I've always pictured myself leaving this world, dancing off with one of the Lester sisters' girls."

"What did they charge you?" asked Gene.

"Fifty bucks an hour," replied Duffy.

"Or," added Pat, "two hundred for the night. I had an account there. They'd press your clothes, bathe you, dress you, treat you like royalty."

"You had an account there?" asked Al. "I can't imagine Aunt Rose being too happy about that if she ever found out."

"Well, you know, certain things are better left unsaid. However, a problem did arise. I would always settle my account with a check, and it would come back endorsed by the Kingdom Come Novelty Company, a name that I still hold dear. Anyway, your aunt began to notice that I was spending an exorbitant amount of money there, so, I told her that I was buying stock in the company. At that time, one of my numbers games used certain numbers from the stock market, and since your aunt played them religiously, she was quite familiar with reading the New York Stock Exchange report."

Pat sighed, continued. "So, one day she looked up Kingdom Come Novelty Company and when she couldn't find it, she looked it up in the phone book. Of course, she still couldn't find it. Rose was a resourceful woman, so she started asking around and finally, someone, I've always sworn it was Duffy, who had a crush on her, told her the address of the company."

"I never said nothing," said Duffy, indignant.

"Of course you didn't. Anyway, Rose marched up there and somehow got in the front door. She was putting on quite a show when Ada finally came down to see what was causing the commotion. Ada explained that their dear father owned a company of such name and that this wasn't the first time that there had been such a problem. I was just about off the hook when Mina came lumbering down the stairs, and when she heard the tail end of the conversation, she said, 'and besides, Pat ain't never been here.' Well, when Rose heard my name, she ran out of there and was waiting for me with a rolling pin when I got home."

The men roared. A strong knock at the door caused Sandy to glance out the peephole, then open it slightly and step outside. He entered moments later and walked over to Al, placed a hand on his shoulder and whispered in his ear.

Al nodded. "Give me a couple of minutes," he said, standing up.

"Take your time," said Pat. "I'll practice up on Duffy here until you come back."

Duffy pulled up a chair and sat down while Pat shuffled the cards. "I never had no crush on Rose," he said.

Pat laughed. "Duffy, my boy, sometimes the one with the crush is the last to know."

Al peered around the bar, searching for Poochie. It was a great crowd, clustered around the bar, listening to the game. Not a bad cash cow, either.

He looked over the top of the crowd and saw Poochie, waving to him from a corner table. He sat alone, but there were three additional empty glasses, and since Pat was a stickler for having his people clean off the tables right away, Al knew that Poochie had asked his companions to give them a few moments alone.

Poochie wiped a stool down as Al approached. He then pulled it out and sat back down, gesturing for Al to sit across from him. He folded his arms across the table, tugged at his tie, and brushed at his graying hair with the palm of his hand.

Poochie always looked distressed, like a worn-out basset hound, hence the nickname. Additionally, he talked in a soft, hoarse voice, as if every conversation hearkened impending doom.

"Al," he wheezed. "How bad is it?"

Al shook his head, accepting a drink from a B-girl, who recognized him, acknowledged Poochie's nod and walked off.

"You know I don't talk business in public, Pooch, and you act like if you keep asking me, the figure's gonna change."

"I'm sorry," replied Poochie. "I've just got a lot on my mind, with all of my cigars back-ordered. I really don't remember."

"You're down fourteen thousand five hundred dollars, with a two-thousand-dollar bet on Michigan State getting two and a half points."

"Jesus, Al, I keep forgetting that it's getting that high. Excuse me for asking, but can you give me until I get rid of this next inventory of cigars? They should be here within the week, and they're almost all sold already."

Al shook his head again. "I should not be doing this, but I'll give you the time. But you'd better pay soon. I don't want word getting out that I'm some kinda pushover. You lose, you pay."

"I swear on my mother's grave, I pay within a couple of weeks."

"Your mother ain't dead, you putz. You think I forget your family."

Al laughed and Poochie took a swig from his beer, relief written on his face like "Schlitz."

Poochie chuckled for a moment, looked off to the B-girl, holding his empty beer bottle high, and dug in. "I'm pretty confident tonight Al, and I shoulda told you, but you know my luck."

"Yeah," said Al, getting up. "I'm not worried about getting your tips."

"Can I bet the fight?" asked Poochie, grabbing Al's arm, eyes pleading.

"Sure, Pooch. You win tonight, maybe you're on your way to settling."

Poochie rose up in his seat. "Yeah, yeah. Kind of like golf. Once I hit a good shot, I really start to roll."

Al clapped him on the shoulder and started for the back room.

Kind of like golf. Play like shit all day, hit a good shot and you can't wait to get back the next day. Credo for guys like Poochie: hit and hope, bet and beg.

Al heard Poochie whoop as the door to the back room shut behind him. There was no mistaking his yell; a train whistle with a hole in it, "Whooo, whoooo!"

"What's the score?" asked Al.

"Michigan State's up by five," said Gene, grinning.

Pat flipped cards to Duffy, asking, "You fellows exposed on Michigan State?"

"No," said Al, sitting down. Pete Barnes was in the john, so Gene sat down across from him. "Gene's just smiling because he wanted me to take North Carolina. If North Carolina covers, he'll act pissed, but if the Spartans cover, he'll be grinning, thanking God that I didn't play 'em."

Gene shuffled the cards. His pupils looked like they had been burned into his eyes by the light magnified through his thick glasses. He flipped the cards back and forth between his hands. "Hollywood, three across, buck a game, fifty cents a hand."

Al frowned. "I don't bet."

"Come on, Al, just one set."

"A saloonkeep shouldn't drink. A bookie shouldn't bet. That's it."

Pat gave him a quick glare.

Gene sighed, shook his head, dealt the cards; eleven to Al, ten for himself.

The radio sputtered. The bartender must've turned it up.

And Green's free shots tie the game at fifty-eight. Undefeated North Carolina, in search of their thirty-first victory of the year, is getting a mighty test from the Spartans of Michigan State.

"North Carolina will hold for the last shot," said Gene, surveying his cards.

"We're looking okay." replied Al, shifting in his chair. His knee began to hurt. The bourbon didn't help.

Pete Barnes returned, pulled up a chair at the end of their table. "You guys mind if I camp here for a minute?"

Both men shook their heads, and Pete sat down, the chair creaking under his weight.

No good. Michigan State rebounds. The Spartans have a chance to knock off the country's top-ranked team!

The men all set their cards face down on the table. Pete Barnes sweated. Gene sat forward in his chair like a jockey riding a fast mount. Pat and Duffy stared at the speaker, willing a picture.

Al stared at the bar, rats eating at his stomach.

The front bar was silent. Glasses tinkled, a collective breath was drawn.

It's going to Quiggle. His shot is up and . . . in!

A roar erupted in the front room. Gene leaped to his feet. Duffy and Pat sat back, laughing. Al blew air, listening to Poochie's open hand slap the door.

"Whooo, whoooo!"

Hold everything. They're saying that it doesn't count. The shot came after time expired. Holy manoley, we're going to overtime.

The slap of Poochie's hand turned into a dull thud. He was banging his head on the door.

"Son of a bitch," said Gene, as he paced the room. "That's why I hate this game. The last few minutes are the only exciting part, and now they screw it up."

"Who needs one?" asked Pat from behind the bar.

They all responded affirmatively, Al holding an extra finger against his glass.

"Keep going like that and you'll never make the next game," said Pat as he handed Al his drink.

"I don't know if I want to make the next game," replied Al.

Sandy shuffled over to the tables and set a box of cigars in the middle. "From Poochie," he said. "He said that he forgot to give them to you earlier."

Al doled out cigars, matches and a cutter.

"How bad?" asked Pat.

Gene interrupted. "We're exposed heavy on Kansas. Everybody was taking them."

Pat looked concerned. "That's not right," he said. "The West Coast should be all over San Fran. People bet with their heart, not their minds."

"No business," said Al, lighting up. "Let's play cards."

Overtime: Al held his cards; ace, two, three, four of hearts; three kings, six and seven of clubs. Five of hearts, king of spades, five or eight of clubs; winning cards.

Gene threw the five of clubs.

"Gin," said Al, displaying his hand.

Jumpin' Johnny at the free throw line for the Spartans. If he hits this one, it's just about over for North Carolina. For a three-point lead, it's . . . . no good . . . . . . Four seconds left, Brennan shoots from just beyond the free throw line, for another tie, he hits! Call your kids, we're going for number two.

"I can't believe that with all of these Jew kids, McGuire can't bury Michigan State," said Gene, tossing his cards on the table. "He imports them all from New York, they haven't lost a game all year. They should slaughter these bastards. Shit."

"Rosenbluth's probably got twenty-five points already," said Duffy. "But he ain't hitting but one out of every four."

"How the hell would you know?" cracked Pat. "You've been swilling beer and telling stories, not listening to the game."

"I heard it when I was in the can."

Second overtime: Gene got a great draw. Four hands in, Al knew that Gene held queens, fours and a hearts run.

"How high does it go?" asked Al, tossing the king of hearts.

Gene ignored it and went to the discard pile.

Al couldn't go down early. Ten point gin, but he needed twenty points to go out on the game and match.

"Gin," muttered Gene, dropping his cards.

He must've drawn the fourth queen.

So, Green and Rosenbluth trade buckets and, yep folks, we're heading for a third overtime.

Gene took the deal, dropped Al eleven cards, kept ten. Both men rearranged their hands as Pat stepped back behind the bar, filling drink orders. Pete Barnes asked for more peanuts.

Pick up a card. Discard. Grab his discard. Toss him one, feel him out. A run. How high?

And North Carolina has opened this third overtime with six straight points to take a seventy-two to sixty-six lead.

Pat took out a broom and began sweeping behind the bar. Duffy and Pete Barnes casually tossed their cards.

Twenty points for the win. Al held three aces, the two, three and four of diamonds, and the ten, jack and queen of spaces. Winning cards: the ace of hearts, five of diamonds, nine or king of spades.

"Why couldn't we get rid of any Kansas, Gene?" asked Al softly.

Gene, perplexed, "Huh?"

"Or more importantly, why didn't K.C. call us? These games are being played to sellouts in Kansas City. We'd be the first one they'd call with a layoff."

Gene dropped a card. It flipped over on the way to the table. "Search me, Al. Shit. I'll call in the morning."

Al stared as Gene turned in his chair.

"Al," yelled Pete Barnes, leaping up. "This could be it."

"What?" asked Al.

"Jesus," said Pete, standing behind his chair, hands on its back. "Haven't you heard this? Anderegg's at the line for Michigan State. They're down by six."

"Time?"

"Not much."

Duffy peered at Pete's exposed hand, noting cards.

Gene threw his cards, face down, on the table.

Pat stopped sweeping, stared at Al.

The rats invaded Al's stomach.

And the first one is up and good. We've got a five-point game.

No. Nine-to-one odds, a bare friggin' minimum. Can't happen.

Here goes the second one . . .

please, please, please, please, please

and it's good too. So, it's a four-point North Carolina lead . . .

The back of the chair that Pete Barnes was leaning on broke, sent him spilling to the floor.

as they run the clock out and move on to play tomorrow night for the NCAA championship and an undefeated season.

Poochie's wail could be heard from the front room.

"Holy shit, I'm sorry, Pat, Al," said Pete, scrambling to his feet. "I'm so . . . I'm sorry."

"You're fine," said Pat, as Duffy brushed off the front of Pete's shirt. "Don't you worry about a thing. But maybe we'd better call it a night."

They all nodded.

"Al," said Gene, reaching across the table, gently touching his arm.

Duffy sighed, "What? Somebody die? It's only a fucking chair."

Pat stared at Al. His eyes were bloodred; the lids looked raw. Suddenly, Al showed every day of his fifty years, and Pat's hand trembled as he grabbed the bottle of bourbon and stepped around the bar. He leaned over his nephew, rested a hand on his shoulder, filled his glass. "Your exposure?"

Al didn't move.

Gene nodded.

"Middled?" whispered Pat.

No response. Response enough.

Duffy gasped, eyes resting on Pat. Pat motioned him away and he and Pete Barnes left the room, Sandy following them.

Gene got up to leave.

"Al, I . . ."

"Gene," said Al, sitting still.

"Yes, Al."

"Tell Poochie his bar tab's covered."

Gene slipped out, left Pat and Al sitting at the table. Pat started to fill Al's glass, when Al reached out.

"You want the bottle?" asked Pat.

"Gin," said Al, flipping over Gene's errant discard. "King of spades."

"How bad?" asked Pat, as he sat down across from Al, poured himself two fingers of bourbon.

"The worst."

"Mattress or the safe deposit box?"

"Safe deposit box."

"Mother of God."

Pat tried to speak again, but couldn't, so he went out to the front bar and bussed tables. After an hour or so, he slipped into the back room, brought another bottle of bourbon and a bucket of ice.

Middled. Winners on both sides of the line. Win giving up to three and a half. Win getting four and a half. Only $15,000 of push money. Winners to the tune of $160,000.

Hours later, Kansas wins 80–56. Another $25,500 in losses.

A single day of losses at $185,500. Near ruin.

Pat slipped back in early A.M. The crowd had gone home. The bar was pitch dark, save CANADIAN ACE.

Pat granted one last request. He replaced the bourbon and whisky glasses and brought out a tall glass, straw, cardboard coaster and a bottle of rum.

Al tinkered for a moment, leaned back and enjoyed his creation.

The tall glass was filled to the brim with rum. Atop, a make-believe umbrella made from the straw and coaster.

Al passed out dreaming sunny, limping on the beach.

The Lip swallowed another bennie as he reached the top of the stairs. Crowd noise told him that it was packed to the gills—500 easy. The maître d' ignored his condition as he entered the room. "Welcome to the Chez Paree. Tonight, for five ninety-five you get a complete seven-course meal, after-dinner liqueur, dancing and the show. Ann Sothern is our headliner tonight and her next show is at two fifteen A.M."

He handed the maître d' a ten spot and moved toward the bar. Don Hansen, wearing a camel's-hair jacket, leaned against it, a drink in his hand, eyes wandering over the crowd. White tableclothed tables, no booths, a stage and dance floor, mood music piped to a crowd anxious for the headliner. A smell lingering: fresh baked bread, sizzling steaks, cheap perfume and overpriced booze. "Why so late?" asked Hansen.

"I stopped at Club Alabam for a few pops," replied the Lip, holding up two fingers, signifying two more bourbon and waters. "Abe Rosen met me there."

"He's no more a fight manager than I am," said Hansen.

The Lip nodded, chugged his drink and ordered another. "He's a mouthpiece for a group of wealthy Jews that own Tomcat, but he isn't too bad. He's got Tomcat making appearances and hyping the fight. I can appreciate that."

"Some great cooze here tonight. There's a couple at a table over there," said Hansen, pointing toward a table near the dance floor.

"Joliet Josies," said the Lip, smirking.

"Sixteen to sixty," replied Hansen, tightening his tie. "I'll go break the ice. You come over in a few."

Hansen strode away, slipped between people, made his way toward the table. The Lip watched him lean over the table, dropping lines, and smiled as he pulled out a chair and sat down.

"Hello, Lip," said a voice behind him. Angelo Carpacci: charcoal pinstriped double-breasted suit, white shirt and pocket hankie, gold cufflinks, more rings than a phone bank. Black hair and shoes shining.

Their eyes met, no handshakes offered. "Angelo."

"How're ticket sales?" asked Angelo, waving back at his table. Thugs and quiff. Typical night on the town for an up-and-coming mobster.

"Fine. Not to worry."

"Not to worry? You still owe me seventy large and you say, 'Not to worry.' Lip, if I were you, I'd be worried."

"What good does worrying do? I'm working my ass off to sell tickets. Shit, I just had Crandy Williams come in to spar Junior to drum up more press. You'll see articles tomorrow."

Angelo took a toothpick off of the bar and begin to work it between his front teeth. "That sounds like desperation. How'd he do?"

"Junior beat the piss out of him."

Angelo flicked the toothpick onto the floor. "I'll tell you what. I'll have Mike Fritzel introduce you tonight and talk about the fight, 'cause by my calculations, you need to sell a whole lot of tickets to pay me back."

"By my calculations, you'd better keep your face shut. You don't want Momo or the Big Tuna to know that we were business partners."

"Watch the way you talk to me, Lip," said Angelo, cool. "I don't want our business to become public and you don't want our business to include Vic."

"I'm just reminding you. Our business is just that, you and me."

Angelo drew back, laughing. "And Henry Hamilton. So, don't get hostile on me. Some things went sour. We both know you'll pay me. Hey, come on over and join us for a couple of drinks. We're celebrating."

The Lip looked over at the table. Vic D'Antonio waved a drink, wild eyes lolling. "What are you celebrating?"

"Tony Torrio got married last night. You remember him. That's him and his wife sitting with Sal."

The Lip glanced at the couple. An Italian dame, laughing, happy, drunk. She still didn't know what she'd gotten into. "She's a doll. Tell him congratulations."

"She's more than a doll, she's a great lay," said Angelo, gauging the Lip's reaction. "I had her last night."

The Lip stifled a grimace. "You sure know how to gain allegiance, don't you?"

"Hey, if it was good enough for Big Jim Colosimo, it's good enough for me. Besides, Tony was glad that I liked her. Made him feel kinda special."

Angelo looked at the Lip, giggled. His brow furrowed as he finished his drink. "Hey Lip, you don't look so good, are you feeling okay?"

Don Hansen waved from the table; girls looked at him quizzically. Sal howled. The music blared and the bennies kicked in. He started to sweat. "I'm out of here."

He turned and headed toward the door, banged through the crowd like a pinball. Angelo yelled after him, laughing. "Lip, you're gonna miss Ann Sothern."

The Lip shoved his way to the door and lurched down the steps as he heard Mike Fritzel announce his name over the microphone, but he didn't stop. He hit the street wondering if there was an actual moment in his life when God decided to hate him.

Saturday, March 23

The air scorched Junior's nostrils as he rounded the final turn. His lungs burned and his arms ached, but his legs flew in rhythm. "Two oh seven," yelled Aaron Green. "Two oh eight, two oh nine and . . . two minutes and ten seconds. Nice run, Hammer."

A total of ten 880-yard dashes with one minute of rest in between; running wearing his mouthpiece, sucking for air like a diver with a faulty hose.

"Okay, big man, one minute of rest and we start running stadium steps."

"We?" asked Junior between gulps of air. He stood with his hands at his sides, facing the sun, his gray sweatpants and shirt dark with sweat.

"We'll both be running," cried Aaron. "You'll be running the steps. I'll be running the stopwatch."

Junior sauntered across the track and stood poised at the bottom of the first row of the high school stadium's steps. The stadium was empty, save Junior, Aaron, Wee Willie and Kid Spinelli, who was running in his plastic suit.

"Go," yelled Aaron.

Junior leaped forward, pumping his arms, taking the steps two at a time. He could feel the strain in the backs of his thighs and calves as he pushed off each step, pulling his legs high, keeping his eyes trained on the concrete. He turned right as he reached the top, cascading down the next row a step at a time. Wee Willie had told him that the Russians always trained by running downhill, and he knew why. He could feel the incredible strain on his legs as he hit each step, touching it briefly, legs flying like spike hammers.

"C'mon, Hammer!" screamed Aaron, jogging down the track to greet him at the bottom of the steps and send him off to the next set. "Three times around and we can go back for breakfast. Frances is making biscuits and sausage gravy and hash browns and cold orange juice!"

"Fuck you!" gasped Kid Spinelli as he ran behind Aaron, rolling up the sleeves on his plastic suit.

Junior ran on in the distance, the sun slowly rising to burn off the slight mist. When he reached the far end zone, behind the goalposts, trudging up the steps, all that could be seen was his huge frame, a dark figure in the rising sun. His breath rose above him like smoke signals, and the cold air made his eyes water. It was 5:00 A.M.

The booze wore off early A.M. and Al woke with a start. His room; Uncle Pat on the couch. Head throbbing; thirstier than hell; nauseous; reality spitting in his face. He was still dressed, so he shed his clothes and stepped into the bathroom. He grabbed his toothbrush, covered it in toothpaste and scrubbed the inside of his mouth. After a couple of minutes, he still tasted booze and cigars.

Problems: $185,500 to distribute, figuring out what in the hell happened.

Solutions: muscle from Momo, call K.C. and Goldie, maybe check with Bookie Shaffer.

Results: safe deposit box closer to empty than full; change the office, phone lines, lay off some phony bets.

Al shaved, showered and dressed and saw that Pat was up as he stepped into the kitchen. He filled a huge glass half full of orange juice, then topped it off with cold tap water and chugged the entire thing. He repeated the process after swallowing a couple of aspirin.

"Good luck getting rid of that hangover," said Pat, sitting up, rubbing his eyes. "You need a big breakfast, a couple of cold beers and another three or four hours in the sack."

"No more rack time," said Al, as he pinched his nose between his eyes, willed the headache gone. "The NCAA championship game's tonight and so's the NIT. I've gotta make damn sure that I stay balanced tonight or I'm in big trouble."

"Are you going to be able to settle up on Tuesday?" asked Pat as Al opened the front door and retrieved the morning papers.

"Of course," said Al.

"As long as you can settle up, you're okay. Hell, I'll never forget August twelfth, nineteen thirty-seven. I had to pay a big ticket on a Chicago wheel, and I was running a horse parlor at the time. Every damn bettor must've won that day, and the next day I realized that if I came up a loser again I'd have to go to Frank Nitti for a loan. You know what that meant—I'd be a virtual prisoner! But the odds caught up and nearly every bettor lost that day. In fact, thirty-seven turned out to be one of my better years."

"I'm not sure that it was the odds that caught up with me," said Al, glossing over a preseason article on the Cubs. "We didn't have any late layoff action at all. Just the rich guys."

"Not even from Kansas City?" asked Pat, incredulous.

"Nope, and Goldie wasn't taking any Kansas action, either."

"But even those degenerates on the West Coast are homers. They would have been betting on their San Francisco brethren."

"That's what I thought," said Al, "but Goldie wouldn't fuck me. I think this Chamberlain's caught everybody's imagination. But the K.C. office isn't big enough to take all of that Kansas action. They should've dropped a bundle with us. Gene's gonna call them this morning to see what happened."

"Be careful. When the climate changes, there's generally a reason."

"I'm watching, Uncle. I'm watching."

The phone rang as Pat slipped into his jacket and tweed driving cap. Al stopped him as he reached the door.

"I'll go down with you. The doorman says that I've got a visitor."

They took the brief elevator trip down and strode through the lobby. Pat took a quick right outside the building when they saw the long, dark Lincoln parked out front. Vic D leaned against the car, wild hair blowing in the wind. As Al moved toward the car, Vic hopped back into the driver's seat and Angelo Carpacci slipped out. His hair was freshly combed, but his suit was rumpled and the pants were lined from riding down near his ankles.

"Al," said Angelo, thrusting out a hand. "Why does your Uncle run off like that? I've always liked that old character."

Al shook his hand briefly. "He's running late. What's up?"

"No small talk for you, eh," said Angelo, smiling. "I heard about last night and wanted to see if you'd need anything, like maybe a loan."

"No loan," said Al. "It was bad, but not that bad."

"Not that bad? I hear it was a fucking tragedy. Are you sure you can cover it?"

Al ignored the question. "Where you hearing all this?"

"It's like a bank run, Al. A bookie gets middled and people panic."

"Well, I'm fine. Maybe the odds just caught up to me. It happens to everybody."

"You just don't want to make a habit of it. Can you cover all of your action tonight?"

"I'll be fine," said Al, peeved.

Angelo threw up his arms in defense. "Hey, I'm just looking out for you. I figure that since Momo took over, you might be a little worried, but I want to make sure you know that you're our guy. Do you need anything, say a little cover when you settle up?"

Al looked at the Lincoln, which was shaking. Vic sat in the front seat, eyes locked straight out the windshield. "Looks like you've got a little problem with your shocks," he said.

Angelo laughed. "That's just Momo in the back with one of his Polack broads. Damn, he loves those Polacks."

Al pulled out a cigarette, offered one to Angelo, who declined it. Al drew on the cigarette, said: "I may take you up on the muscle. Let me think it through. Is there anything else that I should know about?"

"Why?" asked Angelo.

"Because I didn't get a layoff from Kansas City and I couldn't lay off on the West Coast."

"I don't know anything about that gambling shit, Al, so you're wasting your breath on me, but there's nothing going on. Tony's still the Man, but Momo and I have moved up. Momo's running everything now and I'm gonna start looking after more of his interests. That's why I'm here at eight fucking A.M.—to let you know that it's business as usual."

Al looked back at the car. Sam Giancana sat up in the back seat, tightened his necktie, lit a Camel. "You're on your way home," said Al, nodding in greeting to Momo.

"It was a late night," acknowledged Angelo, "but we didn't have to stop. We just wanted to let you know that we're here."

Al patted him on the shoulder and opened his car door. "I appreciate it. I'll let you know about the muscle."

Angelo slipped into the car and Sam stuck his head out the window, sunglasses already perched. "Al," he said. "Give us one for the road."

Al played the game. "Zeppo Marx."

"Is he funny?" asked Giancana.

"His bets are," said Al, dropping his cigarette on the sidewalk and stamping it out.

Giancana laughed. "Head over to Duro Brothers and get fitted for a suit. Anytime I have a bad day I just go buy a good suit. You know, when things are shit, that's when you need to look like you're on top of the world."

The car rolled away, and Al could see Angelo looking at him through the back windshield. His hangover kicked in hard and the subtlety wasn't lost on him: "We just wanted to let you know we're here."

The doorman opened the door as he walked back toward the lobby. "How are you this morning, Mr. Kelly?"

Al glanced up as he stepped inside. "I'm on top of the world."

The Lip drove through Rogers Park, trying to find Gilda's house. He passed it up, but threw Don Hansen's Rambler into reverse, shot back up the street and parked in the driveway. A two-story brick home with a welcome mat out front, drapes wide open, and a brass knocker on the door that said Mommy and Daddy Gilda lived here and everyone was invited in anytime. He stepped out of the car and walked up to the door, ignoring the knocker, beating the back of his fist on the door. Gilda yelled, "Come in."

He opened the door and stepped inside. The beige carpet was spotless and made him want to take off his shoes. The front room was large and well furnished: a long, cream-colored couch with matching walnut end tables, a coffee table with a picture of the happy family, a baby grand piano and a television set the size of a small refrigerator. He could see into the dining room and hear Gilda in the kitchen.

"Sit down and turn on the television, if you like," she yelled. "I'm making our lunch. I'll be out in just a minute."

"No problem," yelled the Lip, tossing his sportcoat on the arm of the couch, sinking into a corner. He leaned over and picked up the picture to get a better look. Daddy was tall and lean with dark, thin hair, deep-set, compassionate eyes and the unkempt look that said "scholar." Mommy, however, warranted a closer look. She held Daddy's hand, and that was the only indication that she would acquaint herself with such a man. She too was tall, but the similarities stopped there. She had long, dark hair, an olive complexion and big, captivating eyes. The old photograph couldn't do her justice. She was beautiful.

"They were a great couple," said Gilda, emerging from the kitchen. Flour dusted her face and her apron was spotted with batter. "My father was a professor at the Northwestern and my mother had been a dancer."

"What happened?"

"My mother died of cancer four years ago and Daddy killed himself a year later to the day. He used a Luger that a friend had brought home from the war. They found him in his car in the school's parking lot. He loved her so much that he couldn't live without her." She blinked quickly, quelled the emotion.

"I'm sorry," said the Lip.

"So am I. Do you have a family?"

"Orphan. Two foster homes governed by assholes and on my own at twelve. I was big enough that everybody figured I must be at least sixteen and they never really asked where I went at night."

"Did you go to school?"

"Not after I checked out of foster home number two."

"You come across as educated."

"A friend and I delivered papers, so we read a lot."

"Where did you go at night?"

"For a while, I slept anywhere that I could. Then, I stayed with a friend and his mother for a couple of years. Finally, when I was sixteen, I got an apartment."

"How could you afford an apartment at sixteen?"

"I got a job."

"Doing . . . ?"

"Doing things."

"Okay, mystery man. Are you supposed to be intriguing or afraid?"

"I'm afraid I'll have to be intriguing."

"Very funny. What did you do?"

The Lip sighed as Gilda looked down at him. "When I was a kid, a buddy and I were selling newspapers at the entrance ramp to the highway. Then we'd go to the Cubs games and scalp tickets. One day, we tried to sell tickets to a group of men. The men started to complain about the price and my buddy Al told them that they weren't paying a premium for the tickets—they were paying for the newspaper where he was hiding them. He told them that it was a sold-out edition and that they were actually paying for the paper. A cop saw the group and came over to bust us for scalping the tickets, but one of the men pulled him aside and talked to him. That man was Preston Daniels. He took us into the game, bought us all kinds of food and sodas and hired us to work for him at the paper."

"The publisher of the daily," said Gilda. "I suppose he liked your friend's newspaper angle."

"And his mother. They married a year later."

"That's pretty wild," said Gilda, "but you still didn't tell me what you did."

"We both started out working the trucks and selling papers, but we'd also run errands for the press-room guys. We'd drop off their betting slips, pick up their food, whatever. When the summer ended and school started back up, Al went back to class, taking bets from the other kids. He'd let them bet a nickel that a certain baseball player wouldn't get five hits in a game, and if the player did, he'd pay off a quarter. He collected a lot of nickels. Me, I stayed at the paper, listened to the older guys and learned how to make a buck."

"It doesn't take a lot of nickels to make a buck."

The Lip laughed. "It takes twenty, baby. That was always the difference between me and Al; he'd take the slow, sure route—no chances. Me, I'd go after it all at once."

"What ever happened to him?"

"He's a layoff bookie here in town. He takes bets from other bookies and big-time gamblers."

"I thought you said that he took the slow, sure route. Gambling doesn't sound slow and sure."

"Gambling ain't; making book is. He moves the odds around, keeps even money on both sides of the bet and lays off any exposure. Bettors pay an extra percentage for their losses, and that's the only way Al makes his money. Some bookies take a position, not Al. No way."

"Do you ever see him?"

"I like him too much to see him."

"What's that supposed to mean?"

"It doesn't look good for a bookie to be seen with a fight pro-moter. Especially me. It reeks of a fix. I'll see him again, but it'll be down the road."

Gilda stared at him. "You care for him, don't you? You never talk about anybody like this."

"Before I met Al, nobody had ever done anything for me. He took me home with him, helped me learn the rackets, got me a job at the paper."

"And what did you do for him?"

The Lip got quiet, looked at the picture on the coffee table. "I guess I added some color to his life."

Gilda backed out of the room. "I'd better check the oven."

She returned a moment later. "The casserole's done, but we'd better let it cool down."

The Lip looked at her from the couch. Flour still dusting her cheeks, pouty lips curled, the apron not hiding any curves. "Nothing's cooling down."

She stepped forward and sat on his lap, facing him. "You're big on innuendo."

"I'm big on you."

"You're just plain big. You could substitute for a backstop."

"You got your looks from your mother."

"And my brains from my father."

"What was she doing with him?"

"What am I doing with you?"

"So you're saying good taste runs in the family?"

"She overlooked his flaws, he overlooked hers. What are your flaws?"

"I'm dishonest, greedy, desperate, and dangerous."

"Minor flaws. Why are you desperate?"

"Because if I don't sell one hell of a lot of tickets to the fight, I'll probably end up in the Chicago River."

"Why are you dangerous?"

"Because if I end up in the Chicago River, I'm not going alone."

Gilda pulled up her apron—nothing underneath. "Then you'd better get some exercise. Think you can carry me upstairs?"

"If I stop, it's not because I'm out of breath."

He picked her up and carried her up the stairs, stopped in the room where she grew up. A white, flowered down comforter, stuffed animals still working the corners, a canopy over the bed offering sanctuary. She told him about her parents' deaths, living alone, growing up Jewish. She asked if he cared and he said no, that he didn't mind kikes anymore than niggers, wops, bohunks or dumb Polacks like himself. She punched his chest.

He told her about living with Al and his mom; hell breaking loose when she started fooling around with Preston Daniels. Al moved in with his uncle, learned to work a book. He started bearding for newspaper men, took some of their action on his own, laid money on the street. Approached by Tony Accardo one day, edict: keep sharking money to the Polacks, but pay the street tax or die. He paid the street tax, offered muscle, beat some bookies for Tony, started his own numbers game. He began to enjoy the beatings. For a while things were great, then they went south fast. A friend of his, Davey Gronowski, flat out refused to pay him back a ten-dollar debt. The money was nothing but the refusal was everything. One night, too many bennies, way too many drinks. He followed Davey out of the bar and started swinging; halfway through he saw his first foster dad and went blind. Next thing he knew the cops were sapping him quiet. An eight-year sentence for manslaughter, paroled after making the cover of *Life*. He left out the business with Angelo and Henry Hamilton, embellished his heroics during the prison fight.

They spent the afternoon in bed, ate cold casserole late that evening, then headed back for more smacking and moaning. Booze-free for the day, energy spent. He rolled onto his back, pulled her head across his chest, cupped a firm breast. He could feel her heartbeat and breathing slow down and she fell asleep on top of him. The Lip looked up into the canopy and wondered how long he could go without hurting her.

Al sat in the office, shades closed, space heater off, betting slips covering the table. He'd rechecked the figures three times—no mistakes. There had to be a reason why he couldn't lay off, and there was definitely more to the Kansas City business. He heard a rustling at the door and Gene stepped inside, dressed, as he was, in full suit and tie—all business.

No pleasantries exchanged. "I talked to K.C. this morning. He said that so many Missouri fans hate Kansas that he was able to even out his book."

Al tucked his reading glasses back into his shirt pocket. "Do you believe him?"

"It washes. When Notre Dame plays we have a shitpot full of people here who bet against them just because they hate 'em."

"I don't know. They always lay off with us and I just can't believe that they ended up exactly even. K.C. doesn't like any action, if you know what I mean."

"Yeah, he always lays off," said Gene, pulling up a chair. "But what are you going to do, you know? If the guy doesn't lay off, he doesn't lay off, there's no crime in that."

"But it doesn't fit," said Al. "This is a people business even more than it's a numbers business and it just doesn't fit with him," he said, sighing. "I guess what's done is done, but I can't take another hit like that."

"Are you okay?"

"Yeah, but any more and I'm working for somebody else. That's a lot of money."

Al leaned forward, elbows on the table, rubbing his temples. "I'm gonna let you run the show tonight, Gene. Just remember to move the line a half of a point when the action hits a hundred fifty percent of the house limit. I think that people are in love with this guy Chamberlain, so I'm gonna start Kansas out minus one and a half. The house limit'll be thirty thousand, so if the difference reaches forty-five thousand, then move it a half of a point in that direction. But for God's sake, no, shit, for my sake, don't leave a middle. I've had enough of that for a lifetime."

"So what do you want me to do if North Carolina action hits ninety thousand? Do we make it a pick 'em?"

"No, that ain't gonna happen anyway, but if it does, move

Carolina to minus one. And no matter what, I want you to lay off twenty thousand with Goldie."

Gene tucked his head and looked at Al, his thick glasses slipping down his nose. "Why do you want to do that?"

"I'm just sniffing out the playing field. If there's something in the air, I need to know about it."

Al stood up, retrieved his hat from the desk and pulled on a light topcoat. "I'll call you early evening. I'm gonna relax tonight and try to forget that yesterday even happened."

"I hear you," said Gene. "What time do you want to open up for the fights on Monday?"

"Three o'clock or so. We're changing offices on Monday, so I need you to call Old Bones and tell him to rent us another apartment north of the river. When you get the number, call the exterminators and tell them to open up six phone lines as soon as they can."

"How come you're moving so soon?" asked Gene.

"I've just got a feeling," replied Al, shuffling toward the door. "Something's going on and I don't want to let my guard down."

A knock at the door woke Al from his nap mid-evening. He slipped his trousers back on and tried to straighten out his tie and smooth the wrinkles in his shirt—he'd failed to take them off before sleeping. He stumbled to the door and opened it; Janet stood in the hallway, holding a bag full of groceries.

"The doorman just let me in," she said, sliding past Al. Her dishwater-blond hair was cut short and her bangs curled on her forehead. She wore a cream-colored angora sweater and black skirt and Al admired the way her calves balled as she scurried past him to the kitchen.

"You sounded pretty out of it, so I thought that I'd cook for us tonight," she said, setting the bag on the counter and starting to empty it. "Chicken, fresh green beans, potatoes. Do you have any flour?"

"Yeah," said Al, slipping next to her and grabbing her hand.

"Good, I'll make some biscuits too."

Al pulled her toward the bedroom. "What are you doing?" she asked. "I just got here."

"I need a back rub," he said.

"Sure you do. I also brought some wine, maybe that'll loosen you up."

Al groaned and Janet laughed. "So that's what's wrong with you. Since when have you become a big drinker?"

"Since yesterday," he said, kicking off his shoes and tugging at his socks. "It was a bad day."

They both shed their clothes, Al down to nothing, Janet to brassiere and panties. He lay down on the bed and she climbed on top of him, straddling the backs of his thighs. Immediately she began to knead the top of his shoulders. Al moaned, "That's good."

Janet continued to rub his shoulders and neck and ran two fingers on the edges of his spine. "Why was it so bad?" she asked.

"I made a stupid mistake and I lost a bundle and I've just got this feeling that things are being stacked against me."

"Is there anything you can do about it?"

"Sure, I'm trying, but it just doesn't seem worth it anymore. I just don't get excited about anything."

She reached underneath him. "Uh huh."

"That's not what I meant, smart ass. I make my money, but I'm not reaching anything. You know when you're a kid, you feel like you're heading somewhere? Well now, I don't know where I'm going. I always thought that money bought freedom. Shit, it's made me a prisoner."

"Then give it to me," said Janet. "If I had your money, life would be a lot simpler."

"What would you do?" asked Al as she started to scratch his back.

"Well, first of all, I'd quit Roxies. Believe me, being a personality girl wasn't my goal out of the womb. Then, I'd probably open up a restaurant, not a diner, mind you, but a big restaurant, like the Chez Paree or Fritzels."

"There you have it," said Al. "You know what you'd do. Me, I've got—or had—the money, and I don't know what to do. All I know is that this business is killing me."

"That's because you don't live right, Al. You live like a hermit in this apartment and the only people that you ever see are Sandy and

Gene and the rest of your boys. You need to go out to dinner. You need to go to the theater. You need to enjoy life."

"Great, that's just what I need—attention. Sorry, babe, my uncle told me years ago, 'If you paint your face in public, eventually somebody's gonna call you a clown.' Lay low and lay off, that's me." He sighed and rolled over. "I'll never be able to do anything here. I'm thinking that it's time for me to get out of here."

Janet sat motionless. "Where would you go?"

"I don't know. I'm thinking Florida."

"What would you do there?"

"Anything but make book. Maybe I'd import cigars, give Poochie a run for his money."

"Why Florida?"

"The sun, the beaches. I don't know."

"I've never been to Florida."

"Maybe you'd come visit me."

"Maybe I could go with you."

Al looked up. Janet unsnapped her brassiere, shrugged her shoulders so that it fell in front of her. Her breasts stood at attention. "That's not fair," said Al, caressing her. "You know our arrangement."

"Of course I do. Miss Janet pleasures Mr. Al. No emotion exchanged, only sex and money. Miss Janet maintains her place at Roxies, conning drunks into spending more money, sucking up for a few dollars or a glass of booze, and God forbid that Miss Janet feel her age creeping up or try to make something more of herself."

Janet had been lost in thought, hearing her own obituary. Al reached for her face. "Sorry kiddo. I've got enough problems just worrying about what I'm gonna do."

She drew her head back, rolled her neck and closed her eyes. "Your problem isn't that you don't know what to do, Al," she said. "Your problem is that you don't know how to do it. You don't let anybody close to you. You don't participate. It's like your damn work, you want to stay right in the middle and let everybody else take the chances. You stay in your own cozy little world, not letting anybody else in, and that's got to be a lonely place."

"You think I'm lonely?" he asked, looping his fingers in the sides of her panties.

"I am," she replied. She lifted herself off him so that he could pull down her panties then she leaned forward, kicked them off with her feet. "And I'm getting too old for this."

Al pulled her to him, kissed her. He ran his hands up and down her body and brushed the hair from her face. "Hey, hey," he said. "It's just talk."

She began to kiss his cheeks and then his neck and chest. "It's just talk but you mean it. You're leaving."

"They may not let me," he said as she pulled him inside of her.

Hours later: phone calls from Gene, twenty grand laid off with Goldie, everything set up for the next office. Janet made dinner, fed it to him in bed, made him promise not to talk about Florida. She didn't know that he had tested the thought on her, really heard it himself for the first time. She curled up next to him and slept, while he turned on the television and watched the news. North Carolina beat Kansas by one in triple overtime. Gene confirmed a profit of $8,000. A good night's work, but chicken feed for the weekend.

Janet awoke at 2:00 A.M., dressed and let herself out while he slept. When she hit the elevator she opened her hand and counted it out: fifty dollars in grocery money from Al. The elevator door closed, muffling her sobs.

Frances took a heaping spoonful of mashed potatoes and slopped them onto Junior's plate. As she stepped over and began to serve Howie the Hat, Junior sliced off a quarter of an inch of butter and then cut up some of the fresh jalapeños that Frances bought especially for him and mixed them into the potatoes. A little salt and pepper and some more butter and it was ready.

"Damn, Hammer," said Wee Willie, who sat at the head of the opposite end of the table, "you keep eating them peppers and you're gonna turn your brown eye into a red eye."

Everyone at the table laughed as Junior sheepishly swallowed another spoonful of the mixture. Ever since he had knocked out

Crandy Williams, the air around the camp had lightened up, and the incident in the film room was nearly forgotten.

Junior cut up his steak, then dipped a piece into the potato mixture and ate it. His plate was covered with peppers, corn on the cob, a well-done porterhouse steak, the potatoes and a piece of cornbread. He also had a cold glass of iced tea and a bowl of cherries, bananas and pineapple. It was a feast prepared for a man who loved to eat.

Junior sat next to Osbie Jones, the old, colored cut man who would fix up his face, should it get cut up in the ring. Looking down to the opposite end of the table, past Howie the Hat and Spider Gomez and his sparring partners, he noticed Kid Spinelli. The Kid sat straight across from Aaron Green and was flanked by Wee Willie and Jack Albano. In front of the Kid sat a plate that made Junior want to laugh and Kid Spinelli want to cry. It was covered with celery. The only other thing on it was a half of a hard-boiled egg without the yolk, and a half a cup of soup.

"How am I supposed to survive on this?" asked Spinelli, banging his fist on the table. "This isn't even enough to keep my crab fleas alive."

"That's good," said Wee Willie. "You act like you're pregnant between fights, eating for two. Start eating for one and maybe you won't have to cut so much weight all of the time."

Frances came back out, carrying another plate of steaks. Junior worried that one day the old woman would try to carry too heavy a tray. She was old and her skin was dark and cracked, and she looked so frail that he thought that if she sneezed she might come apart.

"Who wants another?" she asked, stabbing a strip steak with her fork and gently placing it on Junior's plate. He smiled quickly, then took a mouthful of peppers and washed them down with milk.

Tico Hernandez, Spider Gomez's sparring partner and interpreter, started laughing.

"What're you laughing at, taco bender?" asked Kid Spinelli.

"Spider say that if Junior keep eating peppers like that he gonna have to sit in a bowl of ice cream."

"What else he got to say?" said Spinelli, ignoring everyone's laughter.

"He also say you too fat for middleweight, too weak for light heavy. He hope you like working in gas station."

"If he said that, how come I didn't see him talking?"

"Maybe your eyes as bad as the rest of you, gringo."

"Hey now," said Wee Willie. "Here we are, having a nice meal and you two are acting like kids. Quit that."

"Maybe you're having a nice meal," said Kid Spinelli, exaggerating his chomping on the celery. "But I'm starving here. You've got to give me some real food."

"You're right," said Wee Willie. "Frances, I'm gonna go back on my word now, but I'd be grateful if you'd bring Kid Spinelli the other half of that egg. He worked awful hard today and he deserves a reward."

Frances smiled and turned back toward the kitchen. "Well all right," she said. "But I'm not taking no 'sponsibility for his weight. He gonna keep eating, he ain't gonna lose no weight."

Kid Spinelli rolled his eyes and took another bite out of a stalk of celery. Aaron Green spoke up. "Uncle Willie, did you tell 'em about Friday?"

Wee Willie winked at his nephew and tapped his spoon on his plate. "Fellas," he said, rising. "You all been working mighty hard and you're gonna see it pays off. We got less than two weeks now before you fight and we gotta help sell some tickets. So, we gonna go to the Marigold Gardens for the fights on Friday. They'll introduce you all and let you take a bow."

Osbie Jones blew his nose and Junior jumped. *Introduce you. Take a bow.* Junior swallowed a bite of steak whole, coughed it back up.

"You okay, Hammer?" asked Aaron Green.

Junior's eyes watered. "Yeah, I just swallowed wrong."

"Happens to me all the time," said Osbie, leaning over his plate, peering straight into it. "Damn teeth ain't worth a shit anymore. Probably should have somebody chew the damn bananas for me."

"You gonna let us have a few beers at the fights?" asked Jack Albano, sliding back the folding chair and stretching his legs.

Wee Willie laughed as he sat back down. "The only beer you gonna get is if you can milk it from the Kid's celery."

"Aw shit," said Albano.

"Stay away from my food," said Kid Spinelli.

Junior sat, quiet. It wouldn't be that bad. A quick introduction and a bow in the ring, no questions. Mr. Lipranski would probably be there, doing some talking—he always showed him off like he was a new car and not a fighter. He could stay by Howie, who would be selling hats, and Jack, who would talk football with anybody. It wouldn't be so bad. He let out his breath and started on the fruit.

Two hours later, digesting the food and a film of Louis–Schmeling #2. He walked toward his room, stopped in front of Kid Spinelli's door. The Kid answered the first knock, started to talk until Junior shut him up with a napkin-wrapped package: corn on the cob, two peppers and a dry steak. The Kid kissed him full on the lips and backed into his room, attacked the corn like a high yellow hooker working for a dollar. Junior quickly danced down the hall, feeling like he'd just given a prisoner a hacksaw.

Tuesday, March 26

Al stepped out of the Buick and started across Rush Street. Halfway across he saw Poochie, who pretended not to see him, hailed a cab and sped off. He entered the High Roller and the owner, Tim Murphy, a short, squat Irishman, met him at the door and led him through the restaurant to a private room in the back. "How is your uncle, Al?" he asked, eyes shining.

"He's doing great, Timmy," said Al, noticing two of Angelo's men sitting at a table, facing the front door. One of the men turned and nodded, Al returning the nod. A little muscle never hurt. He changed his settle-up spot each week, but also believed that he could never be too careful.

"Timmy, I'm gonna have a little poker game going on back here, so keep me in mind if anything strange happens."

Timmy laughed, his belly jiggling and red nose running. "Al, I'm too old to bullshit. I spent many an hour with your uncle on settle-up day. So, give me the courtesy of a handshake, tip my waiters well and I'll make sure that you have your privacy."

He started to step out of the room and turned. "After I shut the door, you'll notice a peephole. That way, you only let those inside that you care to let inside. I'll have my waiters knock twice, and I'll start you off with some beer and sandwiches myself."

"Thanks," said Al, setting his briefcase on the oak table. He draped his suitcoat over a chair, sat down, opened the briefcase and began counting. $20,000 for Gamey Donato in envelope number one. $6,000 for Jimmy Spears in envelope number two. Stevie O . . . no shit, he owed $4,300. Zeppo Marx wanted to leave his winnings on account—good, maybe he could buy a laugh. $14,000 for Lionel Albertson, damn, it just didn't end.

Al finished filling the envelopes, put them back in the briefcase and took a cold bottle of beer from the bucket of ice that Timmy had placed in the middle of the table. He popped the top and took a quick swig. What a day. Two hours at the Southmoor National Bank that morning, pulling money from the safe deposit box and wiring funds. Indianapolis and Des Moines were big hits, while New York, Omaha, Milwaukee and Oklahoma City got their fill. He hadn't even counted the money left in his safe deposit box before leaving. A quick eyeball told him that it was a bit less than he took out. Twenty-eight years of bookmaking and half of it gone in one night.

There was a knock at the door and he peeked out; Sandy and Gene, nervously rapping. He let them in, Gene draping his coat over the back of a chair and sitting down, Sandy leaning against the wall in the back corner. Two more knocks and Timmy came in, carrying a tray of sandwiches and another bucket of beer.

"I saw a couple of Angelo's boys in the front room," said Gene, pulling out a deck of cards. "Did you call 'em?"

"Angelo offered and I accepted. I think it makes him feel like he's earning his street tax."

Gene shuffled the cards. "Don't you think it'll piss off some of the bettors? They probably don't want the recognition."

Al snorted. "First of all, they don't know them. Second of all, they wouldn't give a shit. All they want is their money."

Sandy worked a stick of gum, popped his knuckles like popcorn. Al and Gene started in on a game of gin. The first knock didn't come for a half hour. When it did, it was Jimmy Spears.

"Hey, hey," said Jimmy, shaking hands with Al and Gene and dropping his hat on the table. "Who's the gorilla?"

"That's Sandy, Jimmy. He's my driver. Sandy, say hello to Jimmy Spears."

"I know Mr. Spears," said Sandy, throwing his shoulders back, rolling his massive neck. "I humped furniture for him a few years ago."

Spears, pale and flabby with light, half-shut eyes, opened them in recognition. "Yeah, I remember you. You would never use a furniture dolly, always had to carry everything."

Sandy smiled, "Better workout."

"Better workout my ass. More damage to the furniture. That's why I fired you."

Sandy yawned. "You didn't fire me. I quit because your checks always bounced."

"Bounced, shmounced, you fucking circus freak. Throw on a fur coat so some hunter shoots your ass. Better yet, just take off your shirt. You probably look like a bear even without the coat."

Sandy closed his eyes and worked the gum. Spears glared at him, and turned on Al. "Just pay me off so I can get out of here, Al. I think you'd better be more careful who you hire."

"I'm just following your lead," said Al, handing Spears the envelope and leading him to the door. "And don't worry, I didn't pay you off with a check."

Spears didn't laugh as he replaced his Homburg. "Very funny. I'll talk to you tomorrow night. There's a fight I want." Spears left the room, slammed the door behind him.

"How many more?" asked Gene, as Al sat back down.

"Seven bookies and three bettors. I wired the rest this morning."

"Who's the third? I picture Gamey Donato and Ernie the florist."

"The Big A. He's flying through and said he wanted to drop on by for a while anyway. I guess he's got a friend that wants to start playing through me."

Al turned and looked up at Sandy through his reading glasses. "His checks really bounce?"

"Like Jane Russell's titties."

"I told you, Gene," said Al. "A guy will pay his bookie before his bills, his employees, his church, or his wife."

"Maybe because his employees, his church, and his wife won't have his legs broken," said Gene, eyeing his hand. "Did you ever stop to think that maybe Momo and Angelo make collecting a little easier for you?"

Al shook his head. "I've been booking for twenty-eight years and I've never had to break any legs to get my money."

"Maybe you just don't have the stomach for it."

Al shrugged. "I don't have the need for it. A man with a broken leg isn't going to continue to bet through you."

"But everybody else will pay you on time."

Al put his cards face down on the table. "This is a people business. It's a service business. It's no different than Poochie selling cigars. People can get the same cigars somewhere else, but they go to Poochie because they like him."

"Gin," said Gene, dropping his cards. "And that's a good example. Poochie owes you money and you ain't collecting. Maybe a couple of whacks to the head and Poochie would pay on time."

"Poochie's fine. He's always paid. His father bet through my uncle and he always paid. Poochie just needs a little time."

"Fuck him," said Gene, shuffling the cards. "I don't buy my cigars from Poochie."

"That's right, because you have a choice," said Al, emphatically. "If you liked Poochie and you trusted Poochie, you'd buy your cigars from him."

"I wouldn't buy a glass of beer from Poochie if my mouth was on fire."

Al shook his head. "You're missing the point. These guys could bet with somebody else, but they bet with me because they like me, they know that I'll pay and they trust me."

"Maybe, but it wouldn't be that easy for them to place big bets anywhere else."

"Of course it would, Gene, because if it wasn't me, it'd be somebody. We're all replaceable. The Big A is a big oil man. He could use a bookie in Oklahoma. Zeppo Marx is supposed to be a comedian, guys would love to say they take his action. We're all replaceable."

Al grabbed a ham sandwich. Sandy grabbed two. Gene cleaned his glasses, glanced at Al. We're all replaceable.

3:00 P.M.—six bookies and two bettors paid, only one of each to go. Gamey Donato came and went, swore that he wasn't bearding for anybody. He'd simply played a big-time hunch. Gene came back into the room after taking a piss, Herman Goetz in tow. Goetz wore padded heels, but they didn't help; he was jockey small. "How you doing, Herm?" asked Al, standing up to shake the little man's hand.

"Not so bad," said Herman, helping himself to a sandwich and sitting down. "These for everybody?"

Al nodded as Herman pecked at the sandwich, which appeared huge in his tiny hand. "Not a bad week," said Herman. "But my brother-in-law's killing me. He's afraid of his wife, so he runs down the street to a pay phone to call me. Problem is, he's always calling me right before the game starts, so I don't always have time to lay anything off if he's betting large."

"Tell him to call you earlier," said Gene.

"Already tried, he's one of them rich real estate guys and $2,000 is nothing to him. He thinks 'cause I make book and own the pool hall that it's nothing to me. Thank God for you guys. If I hadn't laid off that two grand, I'd be cleaned out again. Seeing how's I picked up the juice on some losses, I can buy a couple of new cues and a box of chalk."

"How's business?" asked Al.

"Pool business or my handbook?"

"Both."

"The pool hall's doing fine. I've got plenty of regulars that stop in and play and drink beer. I'm making a dime for every fifteen-cent glass," said Herman proudly, "and I'm doing all right with my book. I don't bet at all anymore, so's I'm staying up. Problem is my brother-in-law and my wife."

"What's with your wife?" asked Gene.

"My brother-in-law."

Al winced. "Your brother-in-law's making it with your wife? Isn't she his sister?"

The little man tightened his tie. Al thought that the collar of his shirt looked about the size of a cigar band. "Yeah, he's making it with her and no, she's not his sister. He married my sister. Go figure, the guy marries my sister, bangs my wife and he still can't get his bets in on time."

"What're you gonna do about him?" asked Gene. "I could probably arrange for a little help."

Al glared at Gene. Herman laughed. "What am I gonna do about him? Not a damn thing. This is the first bet he's won all year. Every time I've been stuck with one of his bets I've won, and frankly, if he keeps scoring with Margie, he'll keep her off my back. I need to score with my wife like I need a bad case of the clap."

They all laughed, except for Sandy, who just smiled as he continued working his gum. "You ever get stuck with one of his bets, you just call me," said Al. "Even if it's after the scheduled time, as long as the game hasn't actually started, I'll take your action."

Herman hopped to his feet. "You're the best, Al. I hope I don't get stuck with too much, but that sure takes a load off my ass. The pool hall just don't pay for two-thousand-dollar hits." He brushed crumbs off of his slacks and turned for the door. As he turned the handle, two knocks startled him.

"Open it," said Al.

Herman opened the door and squeezed by the waiter, who nodded at Al and picked up the empty sandwich tray. "Mr. Murphy asked me to pick this up and see if you needed any more food," he said.

"No," said Al.

"And," continued the waiter, "there's another gentleman waiting for you at the bar. I told him that you would have to let him in."

Al stepped out of the room and into the bar. The Big A sat at the bar, swallowing martinis like they were water. Few words, an envelope full of cash, a quick handshake. Al headed back toward the room when it hit him. No muscle. Momo's boys were already gone. They *knew* that he'd finished paying out.

Gene stepped out of the back room, turned off the lights, holding two buckets full of empty beer bottles. "Tough day, Al. Nothing worse than losing that much."

Al shook his head, questions nagging him. "You're wrong, Gene. When you're a bookie, there's one thing worse than losing a bundle—winning a bundle."

Winning brought attention, something no bookie needed. Somehow, he'd caught attention. Momo's boys *knew* that he'd finished paying out. Al paid Timmy Murphy for the food and beer, padded it for Timmy and the waiter. He watched Gene leave, told Sandy to pull the car up. Something was definitely wrong. He stepped out into a light rain, his whole world unraveling.

The Lip's footsteps pounded like drumbeats in the hallway of the office building. He always walked on his toes, leaning slightly forward, moving like a bowling ball. He studied the stenciled letters on each of the doors until he found the office that read, "Illinois State Athletic Commission." He opened the door and entered the sparsely furnished office, asked the receptionist for the Commissioner.

The reception area, three private offices and a conference room: Commissioner Willoughby strode out a moment later, looking fatherly with a pipe in his hand.

"Mr. Lipranski," said Willoughby, offering his hand. He was tall and lean, with thick brown hair flecked with gray. He sported a graying mustache, bushy eyebrows and a furrow in his brow that must have deepened during his days as a judge. The Lip took his hand and followed him into the conference room.

Two other men entered the conference room as the Commissioner asked the receptionist to bring in some sodas. Both men barely acknowledged the Lip, offered perfunctory greetings, acquiesced to Willoughby, who started the meeting.

"Mr. Lipranski," he said. "First of all I'd like to thank you for coming to Springfield. We're all a bit too busy to visit Chicago very often but we felt that this was quite an important meeting."

The Commissioner glanced through a pile of papers; no one spoke while he read. Occasionally he murmured, "Hmm," and finally he pushed the papers aside and looked up at the Lip. "Mind if I smoke?"

"Not at all," said the Lip, accepting a soda from the receptionist.

"Good," said Willoughby as he filled his pipe with tobacco, held a wooden match over it and drew the flame into the pipe. He continued. "My name is Jim, but in deference to my past, I'd prefer it if you called me Judge."

The Lip nodded as the Judge pointed at one man and then the next. "These gentlemen are also part of the Illinois State Athletic Commission: Alan Stankey and Lou Brown. Alan was my clerk for many years, and Lou has been with the boxing commission for over forty years."

The Lip locked eyes with each, noticed Stankey wince slightly at his introduction. "Mr. Lipranski," said the judge, "this fight is a critical fight not only for your fighters, but for the state of Illinois. As you know, the International Boxing Club is being sued for monopolizing championship bouts, including those at the Stadium. Thus, Mr. Norris and Mr. Wirtz have agreed to let you promote this fight, for a fee. This may not be a championship bout, Mr. Lipranski, but it could lead to one."

The Lip took a deep breath, his double-breasted suit straining. "Why do you say that?"

Willoughby smiled. "Because your fighter looks like he can become the next heavyweight champion of the world, and when he does, we want him fighting in Illinois."

The Lip laughed. "He's not my fighter. Don Hansen handles him. I just promote the fights."

It was the Judge's turn to laugh. "That's the age-old rap, sir, but I can assure you that we are aware that you actually manage your fighter. I can also assure you that we don't care. Your license is in order. Your card has been approved, and I don't foresee anything that will change that."

Alan Stankey spoke up. "There is one problem, Mr. Lipranski. Abe Rosen has requested that the commission have a representative handle the distribution of all funds. It seems that he's a bit concerned that if it's a small gate there may be some kind of misappropriation."

The Judge looked agitated as he drew on his pipe. Stankey stared, waiting for his words to sink in, and the Lip bit his tongue until he tasted blood. "There are *no* problems then, Mr. Stankey, but I'm curious if it's Mr. Rosen that is worried about the money or the I.B.C.?"

Stankey lost his words and the Judge interrupted. "It was a simple request by Mr. Rosen, Mr. Lipranski, and I agreed to it in terms of helping you. You have never promoted a fight of this magnitude, nor with more riding on it."

"You can say that again," muttered the Lip.

The Judge ignored him. "This is a tremendous opportunity for you and we want to do everything that we can to help. We've already told all of the local clubs to push it, and have used our influence with certain other groups that can help raise the attendance. Therefore, I think that you'll find that we're more than a governing body. We are also your advocate."

The Lip smirked. "I appreciate that. So what else do I need to do to comply?"

"We'll have representatives at the weigh-in and taping the hands before the fight. We'll go over all of the rules with you beforehand and meet with you again after the fight."

Lou Brown leaned forward, grasped the Lip's arm. "I seen your fighter," he said. He wore a simple sweater and rumpled slacks and had failed to shave the wispy hair from his face. He appeared to be in his early seventies, and the Lip knew that he was meeting a true fight aficionado. "The Long Count was thirty years ago this year, and I was there," he said, eyes gleaming. "Almost a hundred fifty thousand people at Soldier Field! It was amazing."

The Judge patted Brown on the shoulder. "Lou's seen it all, haven't you, Lou?"

"All of it. Everybody was here for that fight, Al Jolson, Charlie Chaplin. Heck, I sat next to Janet Gaynor. Or at least I think it was Janet Gaynor. Beauteeeful, just beauteeeful. Everybody was there. Tex Rickard didn't promote fights, he promoted events! Spectacles! That gate was almost three million. Can you imagine that? People was paying forty dollars a seat when that paid for a month of groceries!" His voice trailed off as he let go of the Lip's arm, pulled out a handkerchief and blew his nose. "Events. Spectacles."

The Judge smiled. "Anything else, fellows?"

"No," said Alan Stankey.

"Just 'Good luck!'" said Lou Brown, patting the Lip's hand.

The Judge motioned the two men out of the room and turned to the Lip. "I didn't bring you all of the way out here for a ten-minute meeting, Mr. Lipranski. There are some things going on that I want to discuss with you and frankly, I wanted to get a read on you."

"Well," said the Lip, "what kind of impression are you starting to form?"

The Judge tapped his pipe on an ashtray, refilled it and lit it. "I'm not quite sure. I've heard quite a few stories about you, convoluted at best. I also read the *Life* magazine account of your time in prison and I've also talked with Warden Kauffman."

The Lip interrupted. "Not searching for any positive characterizations, are you?"

"I'm not sure there are any. However, I really don't care. Loan shark, muscle, less than model prisoner, opportunist . . . it really doesn't matter. All that matters is that you're not connected. I won't tolerate any connections to organized crime."

"There is no organized crime," said the Lip, eyeing the Judge.

"And Orville Hodge was clean. Please. Sam Giancana, Tony Accardo, whomever, will not have a hand in the fight game in Illinois. If there are any major shifts in the odds, any hints of a fix, any scent of a problem . . . if I even hear one man yell, 'Apple,' you will never promote a fight in these United States again and I'll have the state's attorney investigate your every move. You see, there are some advantages to being a retired judge."

The Judge stood up, opened the door for the Lip. "Thank you again for coming, Mr. Lipranski. I assume that we are clear on protocol and I want to thank you in advance for your cooperation."

The Lip gave him a sweaty, limp hand when the Judge reached for a shake. "You're welcome, in advance," he said. "Should I assume that I'll see you soon?"

"And often," said the Judge, showing him the hallway.

The Lip shuffled back down the quiet hallway, feeling eyes and ears all over him. Certain arrangements would have to remain hidden, no calls to the wrong parties. No monkey business meant that the gate would have to cover him. It was a sellout or the Chicago River.

Junior and Aaron Green walked slowly down the gravel road; the crisp night air gave them a chill. Junior wore a heavy, gray cotton sweatsuit, while Aaron wore a pair of corduroys, a thick, black sweater and knit hat. "Ain't your head cold, Hammer?" asked Aaron.

"Nah," replied Junior.

"Shoot, you keep your hair cut so close to your head, you always need a hat. Here, take my hat. My hair's bushy enough that I won't catch no cold."

Junior pushed the hat away and pulled the hood of his sweatshirt over his head. "How's that?"

"Just fine," said Aaron. "Man, you sure need someone to keep after you."

"No I don't. Me and Mama done just fine."

"What ever happened to your daddy?"

"Don't know. Mama says that he just didn't come home one day. He worked in the slaughterhouse and she went looking for him, but she never did find him. He just up and disappeared."

"Do you think he's dead?"

"I hope so, 'cause I wouldn't want to meet him if he left Mama and Rae and me. I'm not for certain what I might do to him."

They walked silently for a few minutes, then, when they could see the lights of the motel in the distance, Aaron picked up a rock and threw it. "So what you got inside of you, Hammer?"

"What you mean?"

"Well, Uncle Willie says that you got a lot inside of you. He says that you got something that drives you and something that scares you and either they is or ain't the same thing."

"Wee Willie's just talking. I got nothing that scares me."

"I don't believe you. That night we was watching films, you seemed like you was really hurting."

"I was just tired."

"I'll let it go," said Aaron, throwing another rock. "But Uncle Willie says that the other thing inside of you is a whole lot of anger. He says that it takes a lot to get it out, like when Crandy Williams tried to head-butt you, but when it does, look out!"

Junior raised his eyebrows and lifted his upper lip, snorted out of his nostrils. "Now what makes you say that?"

"I saw it for myself. Don't you try to fool me. When he pulled his head up real quick, trying to catch you, you went lights out! Damn, I hope ol' Tomcat tries something like that with you."

"You're just fooling yourself, Aaron. I don't lose my head in the ring. The worst thing a fighter can do is get all mad."

Aaron smiled, threw his arm around Junior. "So long as you don't get mad at me, I'll let you go on believing that. Uncle Willie says that you can be the best he's ever seen, and he's seen 'em all."

They reached the motel's parking lot and slipped between the cars, heading for their rooms. The lights from the motel glared off the windshields, and when Junior heard his name, he couldn't see who was calling him.

"Junior, over here."

Aaron put his hand in front of Junior's chest. "Some cat over there wants you," he said, pointing to the back row of cars. "But he don't look right. I think you better come on inside."

"Junior, it's Cleotis! I brung your sister out here to say hello."

Junior's stomach filled with acid and his mouth went dry. "It's all right, Aaron. It's just Cleotis and my sister."

Aaron looked concerned. "That boy don't look right."

Junior waved him away. "Go on inside. I'll come in and play some checkers in a minute."

Aaron grunted and walked toward the side entrance of the motel. He looked back once as Junior shuffled over toward the dark figure at the back of the parking lot.

"For a minute there I thought you wasn't coming, Junior. What's the matter, you don't like seeing old friends from the neighborhood?"

Junior stepped up close and could smell the muscatel. Cleotis leaned against an old, green Caddy, the back of his right foot pulled up behind him, planted against the door. He wore a long sleeved, green silk shirt with a three-carat diamond ring stuck in the front. Both arms bore gold chains and five fingers held rings. Junior noticed that Cleotis's fingernails were as long as a woman's.

Perched on Cleotis's head was a Tyrolean hat, with a feather pinned to the side. Cleotis noticed Junior staring at it. "You like the hat? It's Ivy League."

Cleotis cackled in delight as Junior peered into the car. "Where's Rae?"

"She ain't with me," said Cleotis, pulling a bottle of muscatel out of the front seat, drawing on it. "She had to work tonight."

"What kind of work she doing?" asked Junior, straightening up.

"A little of this and a little of that. Tonight I think she's baby-sitting."

"You're drunk."

"Not quite, but I will be. I just thought I'd come out here and say hello. So, hello."

Cleotis doubled over in laughter, slid across the door of the car, caught the door frame with his hand to stop from falling over.

"You better leave, Cleotis. My manager won't take kindly to me having visitors."

"What? Ain't you told him about your brothers from the old neighborhood? Shit, I'll bet he cain't wait to meet me." Cleotis stood up, staring off into the parking lot, extending his hand. "Sir, I'm Cleotis Gibson. I'm a regular entrepreneur, just like my man Junior. Only, instead of being a fighter, I'm a lover. I give my love to my ladies and they offer it all over town. Only twenty dollars, or two dollars if you're in Bronzeville. What's that you say, 'reefer'? Why, yes sir, I believe I've got some of that too, a buck fifty apiece or three for two dollars."

"Quit acting like that, Cleotis. I'd better get back inside. I got roadwork at four-thirty tomorrow morning."

"Oh, I don't want to mess up your schedule, Hammer. You go on inside. I just want to let you know that I'll be coming to see you soon."

"What you want?"

"What do I want?" asked Cleotis, moving close to Junior. "What do I want?"

Junior stepped back. Cleotis's eyes were yellow and he could see red veins bulging as Cleotis struggled to keep his voice low. "What do I want? I want you to understand that you owe me, nigger! I am the only thing keeping your sister alive! And me and you keep our dirty little secrets between us. You got that? You owe me and I'm gonna come back one of these nights and tell you how you're gonna pay me, and if I don't, you better come looking for me. 'Cause if I don't come to you, I'm gonna go to your mama. I remember Kansas City. Do you?"

Junior felt a spider creeping up his back. He stepped forward, babbled fear. "You don't got to do that, Cleotis. That was a mistake! I didn't know! Why you got to turn on me, now?"

"Turn on you," said Cleotis. "I ain't turning on you. I just cain't figure a man like me working so hard, when a dumb old boy like you gets a free ride. I ain't turning on you. I done turned on you. I remember Kansas City, boy, and so should you! You're a bug. And I aim to keep you in a jar."

Cleotis jumped into the front seat and slammed the door behind him. He peeled out, spraying gravel across the lot, dust rising. Junior shuddered. The spider continued up his back, stepping slowly; Junior wished he could jump out of his skin. But he stood in the parking lot, clouds of dust billowing around him, unable to scream.

Wednesday, March 27

Sandy squeezed the car through the gate and down the gravel driveway. As they passed the fourth open garage door, Al got out, surveyed the dilapidated buildings and stepped inside. Tanks were piled in the back of the garage, and the screen door leading to the office was open, so he let himself in.

Tom and Jerry, the exterminators, were the only tenants in the row who didn't run either a body shop or an engine repair shop. In fact, their neighbors often complained about the odor of the pesticides that they kept in their garage and the fact that they never treated any of the other units. Tom and Jerry figured that since they never asked any of their neighbors to work on their beat-up truck, they didn't need to offer free extermination.

Al reached across the counter and patted a bell that sat on top of a sign that read RING FOR CERVIX. Moments later, Tom came out of the bathroom, wiping his hands on a dirty rag.

"Cute," said Al, gesturing to the bell.

"Most of our customers don't get it," said Tom, throwing the rag behind the counter. He was tall and lean, elbows poking the long sleeves of his coveralls. His complexion was chalky white and he blinked rapidly, talked quiet. "Actually, usually it's our neighbors that visit here. Our customers just call."

"Did you get the phones set up?" asked Al.

"Yes, yes, yes," replied Tom, agitated. "Jerry's at the phone company now, talking to his girlfriend. The lines should be working before noon."

"So you guys splice the lines yourself and just have her activate them?"

Tom raised an eyebrow. "It's not quite that simple. We scale the telephone pole, split the wire, test for active lines, pull off of inactive lines, mark the codes, drag the lines to the apartments that you've selected, wire the phones and then Jerry has his girlfriend activate the lines. Does that sound like splicing the lines and activating them?"

Al pulled out his wallet and withdrew ten twenty-dollar bills. He handed them to Tom. "Here's your money. You want to hear a breakdown of what I go through to get it?"

"Point taken," said Tom. The screen door opened and Jerry entered. Jerry wore the same dark blue coveralls that Tom did, with the T&J EXTERMINATORS patch over the right breast pocket, but the physical similarities ended there. He was of medium height, but looked to weigh nearly three hundred pounds. His fingers, which he used to rifle through the bills that Tom had handed him, looked snake-bit swollen. He sweated and breathed heavily as he counted the money.

"This is good, Al. We need some more chemicals for tests, so this is good."

Al thought better, but asked, "What are you testing?"

Tom and Jerry looked at each other, stifling grins. "I'm afraid we can't say anything, yet," said Tom.

Jerry grunted. "If there's anybody we can trust, it's Al. Who's he gonna tell?"

"I guess you're right," said Tom, blinking.

"It's a foolproof rat poison, Al. So succulent that they can't resist, so deadly that they can't, well, live," said Jerry, eyes wide. The exterminators burst into laughter, pounded their forearms into each other's shoulders.

"You ever heard of anything like that?" asked Tom, proud.

"Gambling," said Al.

The exterminators shrieked, slapped Al's shoulders. "Then I guess we're kind of in the same business," said Jerry. "But seriously, this is going to revolutionize the business. Your typical rat poisons need to be disguised in, say, cheese. But this product will stand on its own. Thus, cutting down on the need for, say, cheese. Think strychnine-laced soda pop. So delicious, so thirst quenching, so . . . deadly."

"The wave of the future," said Al. "How did the installation go?"

"The wave of the future," repeated Tom, reaching underneath the counter, pulling out a jar full of a chalky, thick mixture.

"The installation went fine," answered Jerry. "What're you doing with that?"

Tom bristled. "I've got a new formula that I'm going to try out."

"What is it?"

"Just a little something that I whipped up."

"Not now," said Jerry, looking at Al out of the corner of his eye.

"Yes, now. I've waited for over two hours for you to get back and I'm going to test it now."

"All right, but Al's going to watch too," said Jerry.

Al started for the door. "Hey, go ahead without me. I've got a lot to do today."

Tom pleaded. "Al, you've just got to watch. This will only take a few minutes and I've been working on it for weeks. You get to see our handiwork with the phone lines, but you really don't know us. Please."

"All right," said Al, "but make it fast. I've got stuff to do."

Tom squealed and Jerry and Al followed him into the garage. He set the jar on the ground and took a stick, dipped it into the jar and spread some of the mixture on the floor. Then, he walked over to the far corner and came back with a caged rat. "Now, you two step back away so he isn't frightened of you. No, back further, under the garage door."

Al and Jerry stepped back and Tom set the cage in front of the spot and reached in front and opened the cage. The rat, who had been captive for days, sniffed around and then, timidly, stepped from the cage. He stared at the goo, sniffed the air for predators. Curious, he stepped toward the mixture and sniffed it. Tom suddenly lost his patience and stamped his foot and the startled rat leaped forward. He landed on all four feet in the center of the goo and attempted to run, but his feet were stuck. He struggled, tugged at his feet and shook his body, but he couldn't move. Finally, he bent forward and tried to bite through the mixture and set himself free. His face stuck.

Tom squealed again. "It's a hit!"

"Wow," said Jerry.

Al stared, dumbstruck.

"What do you think, guys? Isn't it marvelous?" asked Tom.

"I don't know what to say," said Jerry.

"Really tony," said Al, shaking his head. "What's the use?"

"What's the use?" replied Tom. "He can't move. He'll starve to death. Exterminated!"

Jerry stepped forward, embraced Tom, stared at the struggling rat.

"What'll you do with him?" asked Al.

"What do you mean? asked Tom. "He'll die soon."

"Is there poison in there?"

"No, but he can't get to any food."

"Yeah, then you're right, he'll die in a couple of days. But who wants a dead rat stuck to their floor?"

Tom slowly pulled away from Jerry. Both men stared at the rat, stricken. "Well," said Jerry, "maybe the stuff will dry and we can just chip him free with a shovel."

Tom nodded. "Yeah, it should dry in a day or so."

Al rolled his eyes. "Thank God you guys can wire phones."

Al left moments later; the exterminators stared at the exhausted rat, which had ceased struggling. "Screw it," he heard Jerry say as he flagged down Sandy. "Go get the cat."

The Lip shook his head as he and Don Hansen drove down the long driveway to the Tam O'Shanter Country Club. Early-season golfers dotted the course, wearing knickers, sweaters and caps. Their white knickers were dotted with mud, a testimony to the wet, sloppy fairways, impenetrable rough and slow greens. The trees were still without leaves and a crisp breeze forced many of the golfers to don windbreakers.

"Now there's one sport that I've never understood," said the Lip, watching the golfers struggle with the cold and wind. "How can it be fun trying to hit a little white ball?"

"You've hit it on the head, my friend," said Hansen, sliding the Rambler into a parking space. "And that's about all that you'd hit. It's not so easy trying to hit that little white ball."

"Who would want to? It's cold and rainy. There's a lot of other things I'd rather be doing."

"Have you ever found yourself on a date, pushing for a little bit more than you know you'll get?" asked Hansen, as he stepped out of the car and buttoned his sweater.

"Of course," said the Lip.

"Then you know how these golfers feel. Their girl isn't going to be really ready until May or June, but they just can't wait."

The Lip shrugged as he walked toward the entrance of the Country Club. Bushes guarded the perimeter and a handrail curved with the sidewalk, leading into the club. A caddie approached him as he opened the door. "Are you here to golf, sir?"

"Do I look like I'm here to golf?" asked the Lip, holding up his arms to emphasize the suit and tie, as Don Hansen strode up behind him.

"We're here to watch Tomcat Gordon train," said Hansen, resting a hand on the Lip's shoulder. The Lip turned and looked at him, glared—don't touch me.

"Downstairs and to your right," said the caddie.

The Lip and Hansen walked down the stairs, tracking mud on the deep red carpet. As they reached the bottom of the stairs, they heard whoops and hollers and saw two young clubhouse girls scoot down the hall. They followed the girls and were met at the end of the hall by a pimple-faced teenage boy, who sat in a folding chair behind a card table. "Admission is one dollar," said the youngster, dressed in a sleeveless sweater that had a Tam O'Shanter patch over the left breast.

"Never mind, Joe. They're with me," said Abe Rosen, striding up to the door. Rosen was in his early forties, slight and thin with short, thick brown hair, and wore suit pants held up by suspenders, a light-blue dress shirt, and a conservative tie.

"Abe," said the Lip, holding out his hand. "What's my cut of the door money?"

"Nothing in the contract about admission to training camp," said Rosen.

"I'll chalk it up to a learning experience," said the Lip, turning. "Do you know Don Hansen?"

"Pleasure," said Rosen, shaking Hansen's hand, making notes on a legal pad.

"Pleasure's mine," said Hansen. "I've heard a lot about your fighter."

Rosen ignored the comments. "I suppose that the Judge has already told you I want the gate to be monitored."

"He did," said the Lip. "Is that right?"

"Technically, yes," replied Rosen. "But it actually came from Tomcat's backers. Nothing implied. They've never been involved with a fight this big and they thought that we could all benefit by the involvement of an unbiased third party."

The Lip surveyed the room: speed bags, heavy bags, an eighteen-foot ring with bleachers set up on all sides, fighters skipping rope and working the bags, and Tomcat Gordon in the ring—shadowboxing as an Elvis Presley phonograph blared "Blue Suede Shoes." "You should've come to me before going to the commission. It made me look bad."

Rosen looked flustered, scratched notes on the pad. He obviously didn't like confrontation. "Yes, well, it wasn't actually me that went to the commission," he said, flipping the page and writing "commission" at the top. "It was one of the backers, who, as I've said before, prefers to remain anonymous."

Talk tough. Keep him in line. "Anonymous, my ass," said the Lip. "You tell Heimie, Kikey, whatever you want to call him, that they had better not do that again. Your fighter is nothing without Junior, and I control Junior, so this had better be the last of this crap." He brushed himself off, symbolically, and continued. "So, now that this is behind us, let's see what your boy's got."

Rosen started to rebut, thought better, led them through the crowd and gestured at three empty ringside chairs. They all sat down as the Presley song ended and Tomcat stopped shadowboxing and turned in circles, flexing his pectoral muscles one at a time at the crowd, hands hanging low, a huge grin crossing his face. His muscular body was well defined and glistened with sweat. His crew-cut blond hair bristled and sweat streamed off his head. Suddenly he crouched over and began throwing quick combinations, gliding across the ring. On cue, somebody popped on another record and Presley began belting "Jailhouse Rock."

"This is from that new movie, isn't it?" asked Don Hansen.

"Sure is," replied Rosen. "Tomcat fashions himself the Elvis Presley of boxing. Hip, handsome, and gets the girls."

"This guy still sounds like a shine to me," said the Lip, acknowledging the song. "But this is a nice little production. How have your crowds been?"

Rosen beamed. "We nearly have to turn them away. The girls love Tomcat. They fill the place themselves."

The Lip inspected the crowd. Rosen was right. The typical fight fans had been nearly overrun by teenage girls, who sat at the edge of their chairs offering Tomcat rapt attention. Some popped gum and others giggled, but most simply stared at the fighter, eyes wide, breathing through their young mouths like they were afraid that they would forget to breathe if they closed them. Tomcat continued to dance, blew kisses as the song finished and he headed toward the men.

"Quite a show, Tomcat," said the Lip as the fighter leaned over the ropes and touched a glove to the Lip's hand. "You sing, too?"

"Sure do, man," said Tomcat, missing the humor. His voice was soft for a big man, with a slight twang that the Lip figured he'd picked up after he heard his first Presley tune. "They say I've got a future when I give up boxing."

"Well, don't worry," countered the Lip. "I still think that you've even got a future in boxing."

Tomcat nodded, catching the joke. "You're a funny guy, Mr. Lipranski. I might hire you as my opening act."

The Lip laughed, catching Hansen with one eye. Hansen laughed too. "Let's just worry about your show with Junior Hamilton," said the Lip. "You don't survive that, you'll be singing for your supper."

Tomcat snorted, leaned closer, spoke softer. "I can't lose," he said. "My entourage wouldn't like it." He stood up straight, waving at the crowd. "Girls, show's over. Come to Tomcat."

Squeals. Girls rushed the ring. The Lip and Don Hansen stood back, marveling. Abe Rosen motioned another kid over, hawking 8" × 10" photos of Tomcat, twenty-five cents apiece including an autograph. Tomcat nuzzled heads, kissed cheeks and offered hugs, occasionally snuck a hand around to cup a budding breast.

The Lip stared, half of the equation filled. Sell love or sell hate.

They left the room, stopped at the bar upstairs for a few beers and shot a game of pool. The Lip had a good buzz going by the time they drove off the property. Just before they hit the gate he had Hansen pull over and he jumped out, hustled across a fairway and unzipped. He took a leak on the 18th green as a foursome stared at him, too shocked to say anything. "Hole in one!" yelled the Lip as he zipped up and scurried back to the car, happier than he'd been in years.

Junior sat between Kid Spinelli and Howie the Hat. The three of them shared the couch in the motel lounge while the others watching the fights on ABC sat in lounge chairs or on the floor. The scene with Cleotis had shaken him and he'd ducked Aaron Green, who'd confronted him before his roadwork. He'd lied to Aaron, told him that he was exhausted and then had gone straight to bed, put off Cleotis as an old family friend looking for tickets. The roadwork had been horrible, the lack of sleep and pounds of stress pushed him to the back of the pack and Wee Willie had chewed on him like a tough piece of jerky.

"Apple, apple," yelled Osbie Jones from behind Junior as the two heavyweights in the ring clinched. "You're a bum, Timmons!"

Kid Spinelli hooked an arm over Junior's shoulder. "Anybody'd know a fixed fight it'd be him. That guy looks old enough to have worked David's corner."

"David who?" asked Junior.

"David. David and Goliath, David. Bible David."

"Oh," said Junior, looking back at the screen. Spinelli continued, asked him if he'd ever read the Bible. Junior should've said, "No, I haven't *read* the Bible, but Mama read it all to me." Junior should've said, "I know the story of David and the stories of Mary Magdelene, Ruth, Samson, and Judas." Junior should've told him how Mama had made him learn all of the stories of the Bible, talked about their meaning and how a good Christian lives. But he didn't. He didn't want to fight no more. Didn't want to think about the bad stuff. He fell back on another standby. He thought about Mama.

Apple pie. Apple pie steaming on the hot plate, nearly burying the smell of boiling diapers that ran up and down the hall. His eyes burned and his nose still smarted from the other fighter's first punch, but he'd won. He'd won his first fight!

"That was so nice of Mr. Daniels to let me bake this pie at their house today. He's gonna be real proud when I tell him that you won."

Mama stood up to cut him another piece. Her arms were the size of rolling pins and all of her jiggled when she moved. Junior didn't understand it; they never had enough to eat, but he and Mama were both so big. Mama always said that it was just in the jeans.

"Son," said Mama as she put another piece of pie in front of him. "How come all of the other boys wear a robe before the fight, but you don't?"

I don't have one because we can't afford it, Mama, he thought. We pay eight dollars a week to share this room. We've got an icebox, a bed and that hotplate. We share a stove and bathroom with the neighbors. You work all day and sometimes the night and Mr. Daniels pays you twenty-five dollars a week and if you didn't hurt your back, you'd probably still be running a shirt press at night. I don't have one because we just cannot afford it.

"Don't want one. I don't like how they feel."

"So you tried 'em on?"

Darn. "Just for fun. Really, I don't like 'em. They feel like a dress."

Mama laughed. "Don't tell me you been trying on dresses too!"

They both laughed as Mama leaned across the table and kissed him on the forehead. "Nothing to worry 'bout. You are the man of this house and I'm so proud of you. You always make your Mama proud."

Frances sat down next to him and put her hand on his leg, startling him. He blinked twice and looked at her. "I said, would you like some apple pie?"

Junior looked at her and then back at the television, composed himself.

"I'm sorry," she said. "I didn't realize that you were watching so intently. I just thought that you might like some pie."

Kid Spinelli's eyes pleaded with Junior, but he didn't notice. "No thank you, ma'am. I'm still awful full from supper."

Frances stood up, wiped her hands on her apron. "Well, there's plenty left if you'd like some. Say, Mr. Spinelli," she said, smiling.

"Yes, ma'am?" asked the Kid, beaming.

"Would you like me to salt and pepper some celery for you?"

Kid Spinelli looked straight at the television, frowning in disgust. Frances turned to leave, barely heard him whisper, "Yes, ma'am."

Junior watched the action on the screen, tried to focus on the fighter's moves. One carried his hands too low. The other had a nice jab but telegraphed his follow-up punches. I'd stick and move to the left, thought Junior. Get him going in a rhythm, following me. Keep that jab in front of him, annoying him. Don't let it up. Keep the jab flicking, annoying, then stop, come hard with the right.

"What you weigh?" said Osbie Jones, leaning toward Junior. "How much?"

Junior lifted his eyebrows, blinked his eyelids. "Two twenty, two twenty-five."

"Yeah, you're a big one. Jeffries was two-twenty, Willard went anywheres from two-thirty to two-forty-five. And Primo Carnera. Damn, he went from two-sixty all the way up to two hundred and seventy pounds."

"Was Billy Conn the smallest heavyweight contender ever?" asked Aaron Green. "You always hear about how small he was compared to Joe Louis."

"No," said Osbie. "I believe that was Charley Mitchell back in the mid eighteen-nineties. He only weighed a hundred and fifty-eight pounds when he fought Jim Corbett. Corbett had him by twenty-six pounds. But Carnera had Sharkey by near sixty pounds, and Willard had Dempsey by sixty pounds. You know what happened there. Dempsey knocked him out in the fourth round in Toledo. Took off a few pounds of teeth too."

"It ain't how much he weighs that makes a fighter great," said Kid Spinelli. "It's how much his punches weigh."

"Or how he takes a punch," offered Aaron Green.

"It's a whole bunch of things," said Osbie. "A man's got to be able to punch and take a punch, but he's also got to make his opponent miss, and when he lands a punch it had better make an effect. Like Joe Louis's left hook, or Marciano's uppercut. Get out of the way!"

"Was Marciano the hardest hitter?" asked Green.

"One of 'em," replied Osbie, blowing his nose into a handkerchief. "But what made him so interesting is that he had these tiny little hands. You'd think that those hands wouldn't hurt a man, but he used 'em like ice picks, poking and chopping. Now Clubber Jones, he had the biggest hands I've ever seen. That man held a pitcher of beer, it looked like he was holding a mug."

"Why do you think they called him Clubber?" said Kid Spinelli.

"It weren't because of his hands," said Osbie, chuckling. "It's because he was muscle for some old Greek cop. This cop, he had somebody that he couldn't get at, he'd have Clubber work him over. Always used a big old wood club. A man ought to watch out for Clubber Jones's club."

"The only club I'd watch out for is the Bud Billiken Club," said Kid Spinelli.

Aaron Green glared at Spinelli.

"What's your record?" asked Osbie, looking at Junior.

"Thirty-seven and oh," said Junior.

"And how long you been fighting?"

"Near six years now, since I was seventeen."

"You may have started late, son," said Osbie, leaning over and slapping Junior's knee. "But you got it. Look at these two," he continued, nodding at the screen. "They probably got twenty years of fighting between 'em, amateurs and all, but they ain't got what you got in one fingernail."

Osbie patted Junior's knee and then leaned back into the over-stuffed chair, kicked out the footrest. Junior thanked him, then turned back to the television and tuned out the conversations, the yells, everything.

Frances brought Kid Spinelli a plate of celery. He nodded and started in on it. Osbie stretched, said his goodnights, and left the room. The other fighters filed off and only Kid Spinelli, Aaron Green and Junior remained. Aaron got up and changed the channels on the television, swore under his breath when he found Bishop Fulton J. Sheen's show on in place of Uncle Miltie.

Kid Spinelli began to eat the celery—slowly. Aaron tucked his head into the side of the couch, began to sleep. Junior watched the screen—remembered.

The afternoon of his second fight; Mama was working late at the Danielses'. Junior gathered his gear: handwraps, mouthpiece, shorts, supporter and cup. He threw them all in the laundry bag and was nearly out the door when he saw it, draped on the chair. He walked over softly, picked it up, marveled. It was black, with gold trim and gold letters. He dropped the bag, slipped his arms into the sleeves. It fit perfect!

He slipped it off and spun it around. The gold letters screamed at him: JUNIOR THE HAMMER HAMILTON.

He folded the robe, placed it in the bag and ran out the door, ready to kiss the world.

Aaron and Kid Spinelli stood up, quietly. Kid Spinelli looked down at Junior, sprawled on the couch. "Let's let the big man sleep."

Thursday, March 28

Al woke to the ringing of the phone. Confused. What time? 5:00 A.M. Who the fuck? He answered the phone, fell back into the pillows, turned on the light to help focus. "Yeah."

"Al, it's Gene. I just got a call from Johnny Spector. Tommy got arrested last night."

A jolt. "Shit. How'd it happen?"

"I guess the cops kicked in the door around 8:30. Everybody else had left and Tommy was cleaning up, disconnecting phones. Three cops came in, busted him, and confiscated the phones. There were no slips left. Thank God, I took 'em when I left."

"They take any bets?"

"Huh?"

"Remember last year, when Red Murphy got busted. He said they sat around for an hour, answering his phones, giving out fake betting lines. He had to honor the bets and he lost his ass."

"I didn't hear anything like that," said Gene. "All I got outta Johnny was what I told you. He said that Tommy called him because he wanted to get the results of the Gillette fight."

"God bless him," said Al. "He's in jail and all he can think about is the bets. We spring him, I'll give him a raise. How do you think they found us?"

"I've thought about that. I'd say either Old Bones or those wacky exterminators spilled."

"I can't see the exterminators," said Al. "They love their work too much. And Old Bones has been around forever. He worked for my uncle and he's been with me since the beginning. No, I'd say either they got wind of Old Bones from somebody else and followed him, or whoever Tom and Jerry use at the phone company got burned. I'll check on them this morning."

"What do you want me to do?"

"Call Old Bones and see if everything's all right. Don't even say anything about getting busted. I'm gonna call Burt Cordell right now and get Tommy sprung. It'll probably just be a fine for not buying the fifty-dollar gambling stamp and not reporting where he was operating. Tommy wouldn't have said anything about us."

Al hung up and called Burt Cordell. The attorney answered the phone on the first ring, no surprise in his voice. Al told him to bail out Tommy, grease any palms, pay a bogus fine or offer a donation to the policemen's ball. Ask around and try to get a feel on how the bust went down. Any information was good information. Burt grunted affirmation, no emotion. All business. He'd take care of it.

Al hung up again and sunk back into the pillows, pulling up the covers and staring at the ceiling. Coincidence? No layoff action from Kansas City. Unable to lay off on the West Coast. Middled. A visit from Momo and Angelo. Tommy Spector busted.

The cops couldn't have gotten their information from the inside. If they had, they'd have busted them earlier in the evening, when everybody was there and they could collect the betting slips, increase their haul. No, it had to come from the outside. Probably somebody at the phone company or just plain bad luck—somebody wandering by the office, paying too much attention to the phone calls. A quick check with Tom and Jerry should help fill in the blanks. He hoped there wasn't a problem with them. He could always set up a couple of offices for a while, splitting the chances, but it would be nearly impossible to get new phone guys on such short notice—Friday night's fights always brought in a bundle. His source for new blood would have to be Angelo, and that was one call that he didn't want to make, although he sure felt like saying, "Thanks for the protection."

He peeled back the covers and got out of bed. A handful of downers wouldn't have put him back to sleep.

The Lip woke up dry, chugged water from the ice bucket in the room. He and Don Hansen had been out late the night before, guzzling beer at Club Alabam, ogling strippers at Aloha and the Flamingo on Toothpick Row. He'd gotten back to the hotel late, post

2:00 A.M., he thought, and had found Gilda sleeping in his bed. The night clerk had let her in. He'd sat on the edge of the bed next to her, pulled back the covers and stared at her skin: dark and smooth. He'd placed his hand in the middle of her back, slowly worked the sheets down and patted her ass awake. She had responded and kept him up the rest of the night.

Lunchtime, 1:00 P.M.: he chugged coffee and read the paper in the hotel coffee shop. Gilda still slept.

He ordered another coffee and plowed toward the sports section. Ads: John Ruskin Cigars—6 cents, Ancient Age Bourbon, Gilbey's vodka and Schlitz beer. Buggies at Sportsman's Park at 8:00 P.M. A two-cent liquor tax raise: $1.02 per gallon. $7.95 for a dress shirt at Marshall Field's, $2.00 for men's stretch hose.

The sports section: editorial—Nelson Fox would be the Sox's only All Star. No hope for the Cubs this year. There, two columns over: A picture of Tomcat being mobbed by girls. The caption: TOMCAT PROWLS AS FIGHT FANS SWOON.

The Lip read:

BEHIND THE NEWS
by Dally Richardson
Thursday, March 28

Tomcat Gordon, in town and training at George May's chic Tam O'Shanter, is attracting fight fans of the feminine variety. Gordon—blond, bold and burly—entertains his following by shadowboxing to Elvis Presley tunes and flexing his pecs like a burlesque queen. But no tassels for the Tomcat! No, fight fans, he's quite serious about the other aspects of his training. He appears to be in great shape as he tunes up for his April 6 bout at the Stadium with undefeated Junior "The Hammer" Hamilton.

Gordon, 26–3, has been slated as an 8–5 underdog, but he's caught the fancy of the Windy City women. Nearly two hundred of them turned out yesterday to watch their blond Adonis train, and the Alley Cat didn't disappoint them. He pummeled his sparring partners, danced across the ring like Mr. Bojangles and even offered to sing for the crowd. After the workout, he milled through the crowd, signing autographs and letting the fems touch their favorite feline. Oh, to be a passionate, pubescent pugilist!

There are still seats left for the fight, which will be this city's biggest heavyweight fight since last November, when Floyd Patterson knocked out Archie Moore in the fifth round. Another novelty: this fight isn't being promoted by the I.B.C. Rather, it's being promoted by novice promoter Robert Lipranski. See you at ringside, ladies!

The Lip seethed as he swallowed his coffee, canceled his order and took the elevator back up to his room. Another novelty. Novice promoter. He wanted to pop Dally Richardson's eyes out.

Gilda was still in bed when he entered the room. She didn't even roll over, and he could tell by her breathing that she was still asleep. She'd kept him up all night. What right did she have to sleep? He threw back the covers, grabbed her hips and pulled her toward him, her face rubbing the sheets hard as it slid off of the pillows. "What the—?" she cried angrily, cocking her head toward him.

"Time to get up," he said. He dropped his pants, burst out of his boxer shorts. He tore her panties away in one motion, ran a hand between her legs and entered her. She woke up quickly, a twenty-six-year-old with a thirty-five-year-old's libido. Moist skin slapped. Thrusts and pulls, brief touches to be remembered later. They panted, moaned, *shrieked*.

The Lip got up and stepped into the bathroom, anger subsiding. He left the door open, showered, slipped a towel around his waist and peeked out. "Aren't you going to get up?" he asked.

Gilda held the sheets tightly around her shoulders. She sat up and looked at him, her brow furrowing. "What is it with you?"

"What do you mean?" he asked.

"You don't just barge in here and take me like that."

"Didn't you like it?"

"Couldn't you tell? I must be as demented as you. Just try a little gentility next time. I like a little variety too, but I'm nobody's grudge fuck."

"Sorry, babe, something I read. I got a little carried away. I just realized that I've been doing myself a disservice. It's not just about selling the fight. It's about selling me. I've got to become a brand name for big fights."

"What's that supposed to mean?"

"What it means is that I need to make sure that when people see my name associated with a fight, it isn't just a fight, it's an event. A spectacle."

Gilda slipped in behind him and stepped into the shower. He pushed the door open further, so that the steam could escape and the mirror could remain clear enough for him to shave. He dipped the brush into the shaving cream, dabbed it onto his face. His eyes were red. Dark eyebrows and thirty-six hours of growth made him look menacing.

Tex Rickard promoted events. Spectacles. 150,000 people at Soldier Field. Tex Rickard had charm, charisma, *his boater.* "Gilda, come here," he said.

She stepped out of the shower, dripping. She bent over, drying her hair with a towel. "What do you want?" she asked, standing up straight, her moist body covered in goose bumps.

"A shave."

"Do you want me to shave the back of your neck?"

"No"

"What then?"

"My head."

Junior skipped rope. The round ended and activity ceased, but he kept on skipping, smiling and laughing. He'd slept on the couch until 4:00 A.M., finished with a half hour more in his room. He'd still been up before everyone, slipped into the kitchen unnoticed.

He'd snuck into Kid Spinelli's room, left a muffin on his chest. The Kid had seen him as they had started their roadwork, smiled at him like he was the Madonna.

He skipped rope. Another round ended. He kept skipping, smiling, running on fear-induced adrenaline. *Nothing* would stop the fight.

Friday, March 29

The cat curled up on the corner of the counter and purred as Jerry stroked it with one hand. The room reeked of chemicals and Al's eyes watered. It was midmorning and he'd rather have been a million other places, but he'd wanted to make sure that the exterminators were on the up and up. It hadn't been a drop in the bucket to bail out Tommy Spector, and Burt Cordell would probably charge him a bundle, starting with a bill for the few moments that they had spent on the phone.

"No, it's like I told you on the phone yesterday morning, Al. If you got busted, it wasn't because of us. We're professionals," said Jerry, as he nibbled on a powdered doughnut. His greasy hands left dark spots on the doughnut. He licked his fingers. "I talked to my girlfriend and she hasn't heard a peep, and Tom and I wired your new phones this morning. There was nobody around and nobody followed us."

"Where's Tom?" asked Al, his stomach turning as he watched Jerry polish off the doughnut.

"I don't know. As soon as we finished setting up the phones he left. He's in a fight with his sister, so he probably went home to scream at her some more. They still live together."

Al paid him and climbed back into his car. Sandy drove him home, mumbling the entire drive about the movie *Around the World in 80 Days*. It had been playing for a year and Sandy had probably seen it fifteen times. "Man, that David Niven's got class," he said, looking at Al in the mirror.

Al didn't acknowledge the comment. He pulled out a handkerchief and blew his nose. He still smelled the pesticides. Jerry had been on the up and up. That meant that it was either somebody following Old Bones or a fluke. But he didn't believe in flukes. The odds didn't support them.

Sandy pulled the car into the driveway and Al got out, told him to pick him back up at four o'clock. As he entered the building, the doorman beckoned him over. "Somebody dropped this for you, Mr. Kelly," he said as he handed Al an envelope.

Al took the elevator up and went into his apartment. He threw his topcoat over a chair, sat down on the couch and opened the envelope. Inside was a note written on a piece of yellow legal paper. It read, "Call me at SO 5-4430, Angelo."

Al put his topcoat back on, left the building and walked down the street to a pay phone. He dropped a coin into the phone and spun the dial. Moments later, a man answered. "Yeah."

"It's Al."

"Hold on."

Al heard someone in the background ask who it was, and then he heard his name repeated, followed by a laugh.

"Al," said Angelo. "They just dropped that note about fifteen minutes ago."

"Who's they?" asked Al.

"A couple of my guys, nobody important. What're you doing tonight?"

"Working. There's a lot of fights tonight."

"Well, let Gene handle the office tonight. You get your phones all set up?"

"Yeah."

"You could've called me, you know."

"I know. I should've called you after Jimmy got busted. Thanks for the protection."

"I know. You've got a right to be hot. That's what I want to talk to you about. I want you to meet me tonight at Vic D'Antonio's house. You know where it is, over on the South Side?"

"Yeah, I met Momo over there a few years ago. What are we going to talk about?"

"Lots of things. We'll shoot a little pool, have a couple of beers. Show up around 6:30. Vic's wife, Mimi, makes a mean batch of city chickens. Maybe there'll be some left for you."

Angelo hung up on him. The message implied: be there—no

choice. He could go to the office, get things going. Gene could run things, and he'd be back before they closed up for the night. Maybe not too bad, considering the bust. Then again, there was no guarantee that he'd be coming back.

He stepped out of the phone booth and pulled his coat close, cinching the belt tight. It was cold, getting colder. A strong breeze painted his face red. He walked home, his face stinging.

The Lip stepped out of the closet. "What do you think?" he asked.

Gilda shook her head. "You look like you've just survived a date with the electric chair."

"Don't you like it?"

"Tell me, who shaves his head for no reason?"

"There's a big reason," said the Lip as he completed a Windsor knot, pulled his collar down and tweaked his tie. "Recognition."

"You'll be recognized all right," said Gilda.

The Lip turned and looked into the full-length mirror on the back of the door. He wore a double-breasted black tuxedo, a pair of black dress shoes, a heavily starched white cotton shirt and a red and black spotted bow tie. The look was smart, bordered on class. But the coup de grace was the clean, bald head. He clenched his teeth, watched the muscles in his temple flex. "Are you set for tonight?"

"Yes, although I don't mind telling you that I'm not quite comfortable."

"You'll be fine."

"If I didn't want to get out of my parents' house so damn bad, I wouldn't do it. Ghosts or you, not much of a choice. You're taking me with you, right?"

"Yep. And if this works out like I think, there'll be some dough in it for you."

"How much?"

"I won't know until fight time. Enough to get you started somewhere else, so just be a good girl and help me out."

"I'm not particularly good. If I was, I surely wouldn't be caught up in this odd little romance."

The Lip stepped behind her and ran his hands over her shoulders and over her green dress. He cupped her breasts and kissed her on the back of the neck. "You're inadvertently drawn to me. Is that what you're telling me?"

"Well, it couldn't be conscious, now, could it?"

The Lip laughed and the phone rang. He answered it on the second ring, recognized Herb Bradley's voice and told him to come up to the room. Moments later, there was a knock at the door.

Gilda sat on the edge of the bed, leaned back and crossed her legs as the Lip opened the door. Herb Bradley started to speak, saw the Lip's head and stopped. He stood there, motionless, while Gilda and the Lip roared with laughter.

The projector hummed as Junior stretched his legs. The room was dark. The film of the Jack Johnson–Jess Willard fight provided the only light and flashed images on the walls. Junior was lost in thought when a voice rose above the sound of the projector.

"Is that you, Hammer?"

It was Wee Willie. He flicked the light on and Junior reached up and stopped the projector. "What're you doing in here, Hammer?"

"Just watching some film."

"Ain't you got enough of that man? You'll never know why he was smiling. Probably just knocked silly, or thinking 'bout all the money he got for throwing the fight."

Junior disagreed but didn't say anything.

Wee Willie pulled out a chair from the row in front of Junior and turned it around, so that he could face him, and sat down. "Here, this is for you," he said, handing Junior a black derby.

"What's this for?" asked Junior.

"I bought it from Howie the Hat. Probably paid too much, but it reminded me of that hat that Jack Johnson was wearing in that picture you keep in your gym bag. I thought you might wear it tonight. You know, the other guys think you look like him."

Junior smiled, wearily. "Thank you. I'll sure wear it."

"Are you going like that?"

"Well, I guess I could put on that suit you bought me in Lincoln."

"I'd appreciate it. Mr. Lipranski's pretty fired up on showing you off tonight, and I think he might be a little upset if you showed up in a sweater."

"I'll go change," said Junior, standing.

Wee Willie put a hand on his shoulder and pushed him back down into the seat. "There ain't no hurry. We got plenty of time. We don't get much time to just sit and talk, and I got a few things that I want to tell you."

"Okay," said Junior. He folded his hands in his lap and tapped heels on the floor.

"Hammer, you've got about the best stuff that I've ever seen."

"Thanks."

"I mean it. But you got to understand that you're gonna have to give up a lot to get where you're going. You've got to give up most women. You give up your privacy and you give up a lot of your time. Are you ready to do that?"

Junior squeezed his hands together so that Wee Willie couldn't see them shake. Knowing that his voice would betray him, he simply nodded his head.

"Well, those things kind of take care of themselves. You never really get used to it, but it becomes part of a new routine. You got a woman, Hammer?"

Junior jerked, shook his head.

"You love anybody?"

"Mama," said Junior with a strong voice.

Wee Willie lifted a brow. "Well, that's nice. I had a woman once, Hammer. I was married real young in life, right when I was still fighting amateurs. Then, the man that run the gym that I trained at told me that he thought I could fight pro. He told me that he thought that I could be the next lightweight champion of the world!" He clapped his hands at the memory, his face shining. "I did. I fell in love with those words, and I started to live for 'em. I worked hard, every day. I trained all the time, ate right and ran and ran. And I stopped paying attention to Clarice. She just didn't exist no more. I'd come home too tired to make love and I'd get up so early for road-work that she couldn't get up with me. It got so bad for her that she up and moved to another room so that I wouldn't wake her. Pretty soon we was hardly talking anymore, and then one day she just left. At that time, like I said, I was in love with those words, and I hardly noticed that she was gone. I never did win the championship, and I've thought of that woman every day since I retired. And you know what? If I could do it all over again, I'd do everything the same. You see, Hammer, I'm a flawed man. I saw myself as a champion and I'd have done anything to win it."

Wee Willie looked down at the floor and then slowly raised his eyes and looked at Junior. Junior stared back and for the first time, he realized that Wee Willie was old, real old. "I don't think you're flawed, Hammer. Maybe you'll succeed because it means less. Maybe that desire weighed me down. You're not flawed, Hammer, so I don't feel bad about what I'm gonna say. It ain't gonna weigh you down and you ain't gonna lay awake at night thinking about what I'm about to say. Hammer, you are going to be the next heavyweight champion of the world."

Sandy pulled in front of the house and parked on the street. "Are you sure you're gonna be okay, Al?" he asked.

"I'll be fine. They're not gonna whack me. Just in case, you covered?"

Sandy pulled the gun out from under his sweater and set it on the front seat. "Taught by the Boy Scouts. You're not out in forty-five minutes, I'll come in."

Al patted him on the shoulder and got out. He walked up the sidewalk, staring at the house. It was a typical suburban home: red-brick with a shingled roof, chimney, cream-colored curtains drawn, a knocker on the front door and a green welcome mat laid out on the porch. He ignored the knocker and rapped his knuckles on the door.

The door opened and a pretty, petite brunette answered. She wore her hair up and her pink and white polka-dot dress was partly covered by the white apron that she wore. Teddy bears cavorted on the front of the apron.

"Won't you come in?" she asked, opening the door. Her voice was sweet and childlike and a huge grin split her face.

"Thanks," said Al, stepping inside. "Is Vic here?"

She said that he was and that he'd be down in a minute, and ushered Al to a seat in the living room. He sat down on the couch and glanced around: bowling trophies over the fireplace, family pictures on the coffee and end tables, a painting of a sad clown visible from the hallway. "Hello, sir," said a small voice.

Al glanced down. A young boy had crawled from behind the couch. He wore blue slacks, a red and white striped shirt and a cowboy hat that was cocked forward and nearly covered his short, blond hair. A dish towel was wrapped around his neck and a pistol was holstered at his side.

"Hello," said Al. "Are you after some Indians?"

"No," said the young boy. "I just robbed a bank and I'm hiding out."

"Who are you hiding from?" asked Al, pulling the boy up so that he stood in front of him.

"The bad guys, of course. The posse."

A booming laugh filled the room and Vic D'Antonio stepped in. He wore a white T-shirt, a pair of long, orange Bermuda shorts, dark socks and lace-up shoes. His thick wavy hair was uncombed and his zipper hung at half mast. "Taught him well, eh, Al?" He swatted the young boy's rear end. "Go kill the fucking Marshal."

"Now, let's go shoot some pool," said Vic, beckoning Al to follow.

"Is Angelo here?" asked Al.

"He's not going to make it," said Vic, not turning around.

"Then I'd better head out. I thought that I was going to see Angelo. I've got work to do."

Vic opened the door to the basement, stopped and turned. Al could see Vic's wife in the front room, staring at them with that same ridiculous grin on her face. "One game of pool and you're out of here. Angelo had a couple of things that he wanted me to go over with you."

"One game?"

"One game."

Vic bounded down the stairs, Al followed. Al took in the basement in a glance: L-shaped with thick, beige carpet, more clown pictures, a high ceiling with no tiles—I beams and cross beams still visible. No windows, a pool table around the corner, television set, couch and an easy chair in the main section. A canvas-covered heavy bag lay on its side in a corner of the room.

Vic stepped around the corner to the pool table as Al stopped to look at the television. "Newest model," said Vic. "I picked it up a couple of weeks ago from Kenny Young. He couldn't make good on his juice, so I took the tube instead."

Al walked over to the pool table as Vic bent down and started filling the rack with balls. He gripped the triangle with his forefingers, and used his thumb to nudge the eight-ball into the center. Then he placed his fingers between the backs of the balls and the triangle, forced them forward. Satisfied it was a tight rack, he tossed the triangle under the table and offered the break to Al.

Al took a pool cue from the rack on the wall, rubbed chalk on the tip and stepped around the corner to break. It was then that he saw him. Tom. Tom of Tom and Jerry. A chain wrapped around his waist and over his shoulders. He was *hanging* from the ceiling.

"Mother of God," said Al, his uncle's words escaping his lips in a whisper.

"This is the son of a bitch that set you up," said Vic, snapping Tom's head back with the end of his cue. "He was jealous of his partner and that dame at the phone company, so he set you up, thinking that you'd think it was the phone broad. Stupid son of a bitch."

Al's hands shook as he held the cue in front of him. Tom hung from a hook screwed into an I beam in the ceiling. He was ashen white with batches of purple, crimson; eyes unblinking, face bloated, broken. He wasn't dead, but wasn't far from it. Al's mind played fast: Tom had fucked up royally, Vic was a raving psychopath, *he* might not get out alive.

"Come on, don't look so shook up," said Vic. "He's getting what he deserves. Fact is, it's kind of funny. The guy spends his life killing rats and he turns out to be one. Now, he's gonna find out how they feel."

Al glanced at the table, collected his thoughts.

"Break," said Vic, chalking his cue.

Al's hand shook as he positioned the cue ball at the head of the table. He aimed at the rack, forced himself not to look at Tom and shot his cue stick forward. The cue ball cracked the head ball, scattered the rest. The cue ball spun forward and caromed into the eight ball, which sliced off to the left, kissed a corner and fell into the corner pocket. Eight-ball break. Winner.

Al stepped from the table. "I guess that's it."

Vic D'Antonio was too angry to speak. Al walked away from the table, his entire body flinched, waited for it. He replaced his cue in the rack on the wall and walked to the stairs, never looking at Vic. He climbed the stairs, heard Vic swing his cue, hit Tom. Al flashed back; his mother beating dirt out of the rug on the clothesline. Tom wheezed, pleaded for help. Vic raged, calling Tom every name in the book.

Al stepped out into the hallway, heard Vic yell, "Your fault, you fucking rat!" He damn near fell, legs weak, glanced into the living room; Vic's wife and son, staring straight ahead, shit-eating clown grins painted on their faces. Al hit the door running.

The Marigold Garden, Broadway and Grace: 1,500 fight fans screamed at the top of their lungs while two Mex bantamweights beat each other senseless. The Lip sat ringside, along with Gilda, Don Hansen, his fighters, Tomcat Gordon and Abe Rosen, Wee Willie and Osbie Jones. Across the ring sat Dally Richardson and Mike Lantz, bored, scratching an occasional note to appear busy. The Lip watched Dally Richardson's eyes widen when he saw him. The writer reached over and swatted Mike Lantz. They both stared, began writing notes feverishly. The Lip grinned ear to ear.

The fight crowd sucked down warm beer in soggy paper cups, smoked cheap cigars and reveled in the gym where even Tony Zale had fought. The crowd was split between Mexicans, Negroes, and six hundred-plus white blue-collars who had ventured out to root for a washed-up heavyweight named Rocco Braun. Braun would fight right after the Mexicans, and Herb Bradley had arranged for the Lip and his group to enter the ring and promote the fight immediately before Braun fought an equally useless black heavy.

The two Mexicans battled in the ring and the Lip turned to Gilda. "What do you think?"

"I think that you're definitely in your element. These barbarians are ripe to be manipulated."

"Tone it down, babe. These guys just want to see a great fight, and that's what I plan on offering."

"That isn't all they want to see. I haven't felt this many eyes on me since my parents' funeral."

"Who can blame them? You look great."

"And this dress that you bought me is probably a size four. I wear a size six, and I have the feeling that was no accident." She crossed her legs, pulled a cigarette from her purse and lit it. "I just hope this is over soon. I could really use a whiskey sour right now."

The Lip laughed, patted her thigh and leaned over to talk to Herb Bradley. "Right after this fight, right?"

"Right. Dom Reggani is going to introduce you and you've got a couple of minutes to promote the fight. I'd do a quick introduction of each of the fighters, tell them there are seats still available and whatever you do, don't ask Junior to talk. I visited him this morning and I think if you ask him to say anything he might wet his pants right there in the ring."

"Don't worry," said the Lip, grinning. "I've got it all worked out."

The bell rang, and the two Mexican fighters bounced back to their respective corners. It had been an uneventful, defensive fight, with neither fighter landing much. Moments later, Dom Reggani, the ring announcer, called the two fighters to the center of the ring. He clasped both of their hands and looked out at the crowd. "Ladies and gentlemen, the judges have reached a decision. After five rounds, Judge Harband scores it 50 to 47. Judge Herzog scores it 50 to 45, and referee Ernest Balencio scores it 50 to 45 for the new Illinois State bantamweight champion, Jorge 'Speedy' Valachez!"

The crowd screamed. Cheers and hisses. The two fighters patted each other and returned to their corners, their trainers grabbed their stools and lifted the ropes so that the fighters could leave the ring.

"This is it," said the Lip.

"I think I'm going to throw up," whispered Gilda.

"You'll be fine," said the Lip. He squeezed her hand. "Think about a house with no memories."

Dom Reggani spoke into the mike in a deep baritone. "Ladies and gentlemen, one week and one day from tonight, the city of big shoulders will host another night of big punches! Not since last year when Floyd Patterson knocked out Archie Moore has our fair city hosted a prominent heavyweight fight, but one week and one night from tonight that will all change. Yes, ladies and gentlemen, next Saturday at the Stadium, promoter Robert J. Lipranski brings you a night of great boxing. A night of action. A night highlighted by the heavyweight fight between Tomcat Gordon and Junior 'The Hammer' Hamilton. Ladies and gentlemen, I bring you Robert J. Lipraaaaaaaaaaanski!"

The Lip stood up, waved his hands as the crowd roared. He stepped out to the end of the row and gestured for the rest of the entourage to follow him. Gilda stood and the crowd roared again, this time with whistles and catcalls. The Lip walked to the ring, hands raised high while the crowd digested the scene. The fighters mugged, Tomcat snapped his fingers and danced, but Junior simply shuffled toward the ring.

The Lip climbed into the ring first, while Gilda stepped off to the side. The rest of the fighters, Don Hansen, Abe Rosen, and Wee Willie all gathered in the center of the ring, waved at the crowd, acknowledged the waning applause. Junior was the last into the ring and as he stepped through the ropes he noticed Gilda walk over to the ring and carefully climb the steps. He held the ropes open for her and thought nothing of it when she grasped his hand and pulled herself into the ring. The Lip took the microphone from Dom Reggani and Gilda still held Junior's hand, felt it tremble while he fought to keep his composure. She glanced up at him briefly and saw that he stared into the crowd, his eyes darting back and forth, sweat gathering on his brow.

"Thank you, Dom," said the Lip, nodding at Dom Reggani. "Ladies and gentlemen, we have a real treat for you next week. We have four preliminary bouts followed by the most anticipated heavyweight bout in a number of years. The preliminary bouts feature some of the men that you see standing before you, such as Spider Gomez!" Spider stepped forward and bowed. "Kid Spinelli!" The Kid did the same, threw a couple of mock punches, stepped back in line. "Louis Brown and Howard Gregg." Howie the Hat and Louis Brown took one step forward, tipped their hats, and stepped back. "And of course, the main event."

The Lip motioned the two fighters forward and they stepped up beside him, Gilda still holding Junior's hand. Tomcat glanced down at it, frowned. Tomcat reached behind Gilda and tried to slip an arm around her waist, but she pulled tighter to Junior and felt him shake.

"September twenty-second, nineteen twenty-seven. Tunney defeats Dempsey in the long count. Nineteen thirty-seven, Joe Louis knocks out James J. Braddock in the eighth round. Forty-nine, Ezzard Charles defeats Jersey Joe Walcott, and then in fifty-one Charles beats Joey Maxim. In fifty-three, Rocky Marciano knocks out Walcott in the first round, and last year, Floyd Patterson wins the heavyweight championship of the world by knocking out Archie Moore in the fifth round. What did these fights have in common? They were heavyweight championship fights! What else? They were held in the city of the heavyweights! The greatest fight city in the world. The city that will continue to host the biggest and best of the heavyweights: Chicago!!!"

The crowd went ballistic and the Lip held his hands high until the cheers started to grow faint. "The fighter to my direct left," said the Lip, "needs no introduction. He's both a lover and a fighter! He's the blond bomber. He's twenty-six and three and in search of number twenty-seven. Ladies and gentlemen, Tomcat Gordon!"

Gordon stepped forward and blew kisses at the crowd, turned his waves into punches and threw several combinations. He danced around the ring, acknowledged the cheers from all four sides and then stepped over to the Lip and took the microphone from him. When Junior saw that he almost fainted.

Tomcat slung his right hip around and leaned over a bent leg. "I ain't-a-nothing but a Tomcat, winning all the time," he sang into the mike. The crowd screeched. "Thank you, thank you. Folks, I'd sure like to see you at the fight next week. I plan on sending my opponent here to Headache Hotel." The crowd laughed and the Lip grabbed back the microphone. Tomcat slid around Gilda and tried to slip an arm around her again, but she pulled away.

"And now," said the Lip. "One of Chicago's own."

Junior felt his head start to spin.

"He's worked for the railroad."

His legs went rubber.

"He supports his mother and sister."

His heart seemed ready to burst through his chest.

"He's undefeated in thirty-seven fights!"

The lights blinded him and Junior squinted through the clouds of smoke, thought he saw *her.*

"He's an artist. He's a dancer. He slings HAMMERS!!"

A current shot through his body. He shook, seizure bad.

"He's Junior, The Hammer, Hamilllllllllton!!!!"

Gilda faked a faint, fell forward fast. Junior caught her out of the corner of his eye, caught her mid-fall. She leaned up, threw her arms around his neck and kissed him. Junior straightened up, pulled her with him. She broke free and saw the terror in his eyes.

No movement. Stunned silence. A fat man in the front row leaped into the aisle and threw his beer into the ring. "You fucking shine!"

Pandemonium. Beer and food showered the ring. The fighters jumped through the ropes and ran for the locker room. Junior turned and looked at Gilda, his face wretched in astonishment and horror. Suddenly he felt Howie the Hat and Louis Brown throw their arms around him. They led him through the ropes where Jack Albano waited, pushed people away. Albano slugged a man in the forehead, rammed another into a corner-post face first. Howie the Hat cleared a path with his massive arms and they led Junior to the locker room.

Wee Willie rushed up behind the Lip, grabbed him, and spun him around. "You ain't getting away with this. You just lost your fighter!"

"I don't know what you're talking about," said the Lip, Gilda hiding behind him.

"You know exactly what I'm talking about. And you, Miss. You're dancing with the Devil."

Wee Willie sprang from the ring and jogged to the locker room.

Dom Reggani and two of his boys grabbed Gilda and led her away. The Lip stood in the center of the ring while beer cups flew. "And we still have tickets available. Tickets range from five dollars to thirty-five dollars, and the ringside seats ensure you of being as close as you can get to what will prove to be the greatest fight in this city's illustrious history!"

Dom Reggani grabbed the microphone from the Lip and canceled the last fight. The Lip stood in the center of the ring, beaming. Sell love or sell hate. Why not both?

BEHIND THE NEWS
by Dally Richardson
Saturday, March 30

Violence was scheduled, but pandemonium broke out! Five bouts were scheduled at the Marigold Gardens last night, but Negro heavyweight contender Junior "The Hammer" Hamilton opted to utilize the spotlight to showcase his love for an unidentified white woman, and the crowd, stoked to the gills on cold beer and a fierce bantamweight bout, voiced their displeasure by filling the ring with beer cups, half-eaten hot dogs and copies of our competitor's newspaper!

Hamilton, who stewed and fidgeted while he waited for his chance to neck with the comely Caucasian, ran from the ring and left his honey to the protection of chrome-domed fight promoter Robert J. Lipranski and ring announcer Dom Reggani. "I'm not sure what happened," said Lipranski. "I introduced him and the next thing I knew he was in a lip lock with the lady. Junior's a good kid, but I can assure you of this—anything that started last night will be settled in the ring next Saturday!"

Tomcat Gordon, reached after the melee, acknowledged that he was shocked by the spectacle and promised to take it out on Hamilton in the ring. "I thought that it was pretty low class," said Gordon. "I think that he was just trying to show me up, as I'm a real favorite of the ladies. But I'll teach him some manners next Saturday."

Gordon refused to comment on a rumor that the woman was his girlfriend.

Promoter Lipranski reminded this reporter that there are good seats still available.

Monday, April 1

A vacant lot at 4918 Campbell Street. Early morning. Just as close to sundown as sunup. Jack Taylor looked at the man and made mental notes: gray business suit, black topcoat, gray hat and a gaping hole in his forehead left by the .45-caliber bullet that had been plugged through the back of his skull. He searched the crowd, recognized the acting chief of detectives, a few of the plainclothesmen, and the chief coroner's investigator. Finally, he caught Leonard Funk's eye and he jerked his head up, beckoning him over.

"They've got a lot already, Lieutenant," said Funk as he strode up next to Jack. "The man's name is Leon Marcus. He's a former board chairman of the Southmoor Bank and Trust Company and was prominent in the Orville Hodge scandal. He's under federal indictment and was scheduled to go to trial in September. It seems that he had dinner at a friend's house last night and when he left five or six men jumped him, threw him into a dark-colored Chevy and drove him here, dumped him out, and killed him."

They both glanced at the body, which was surrounded by investigators. "Killed here, or dumped?" asked Jack.

"They found a .45 casing next to him. The blood pattern indicates an assault on the spot."

"Okay," said Jack, closing his eyes and pinching the bridge of his nose. "I want the area canvassed. I also want Glover and Osborne to visit the friend. Who is it?"

"A real estate developer named Alfred Rado."

"Right. Have them bring him downtown for a full statement. If he's married, bring the wife too. I want descriptions of the men and a better description of the car. 'Dark Chevy' isn't going to cut it. I see Skelton going over the body. He find anything else?"

"I'd say so," said Funk, kneeling down. "His pockets were filled. He carried a lot of cash, traveler's checks, cashier's checks, an uncanceled check, and some receipts."

"Sounds like he was a walking bank himself."

"Irrefutable. The uncanceled check was for three hundred thousand, and there was a receipt from Sam Giancana."

"Makes our job easy."

"Possibly, but I wouldn't recommend jumping to conclusions. Too many alternatives. Under indictment, carrying loads of cash, leaving a friend's house. They don't indicate a quick solution."

Jack smirked: "Leonard, there's only one thing wrong with your logic: the Feds, state government officials and real estate executives don't generally kill people. Mobsters do. You can have a couple of the boys head up to Menard and talk to Hodge, but it probably won't do any good. Have Phillips take impressions of those tire marks and have the lab technicians check an auto found at 3020 S. Wallace Street. I heard on the way over that they found a jumper on its ignition. And above all else, let's find Sam Giancana."

Leonard smiled, moved behind the wheelchair and started to push. "Don't bother," said Jack, gripping the wheels. He started to roll the wheels and the sleeves of his suit coat strained against his massive arms. "Does anything else about this stick out to you, Leonard?"

Leonard fell in beside him. "Frankly, yes. It actually reminds me of Clem Graver, the Republican leader in the fifteenth senatorial district and twenty-first ward committeeman. Four years ago, he was kidnapped by three men from a garage near his home as he was putting his car away. The case was unsolved."

"Any others?"

"Well," said Funk, scratching his chin. "Axel Greenberg was shot to death in December of nineteen fifty-five, but since he was a financial adviser to the Capone gang, I wouldn't classify it unsolved. In that same vein, Cherry Nose Gioe and Frank Diamond were murdered in the summer of fifty-four and Needle Nose Labriola and James Weinberg were found in the trunk of a car in March of that year. Actually," continued Funk, raising his eyebrows, "I can see your point. It would seem that Mr. Giancana would be the prime suspect."

"Yes and no," said Jack as they reached the van. "He wouldn't have any direct involvement. He would delegate it to one of his boys, who would pass it down. You know the old saying, 'Shit flows downhill.' In this case, I'm sure that if we work our way uphill, we'll find old Momo there holding the handles of a dirty wheelbarrow."

"Quite descriptive," said Leonard.

Leonard stepped in front of him, opened the side doors, slid out a ramp and locked it into a notch in the van's floor. Jack wheeled behind the ramp and was poised to roll inside when the acting chief of detectives, Spencer Bowen, stopped him.

"Any ideas?" asked Bowen, bending over to talk to Jack. A camel's hair topcoat covered his expensive suit, and he looked disgusted when he noticed that his wing tips had gathered mud at the crime scene.

"Giancana's our man," said Jack, attempting to hide his distaste for the man by staring at the ramp. "He may not have even been at the crime scene, but he pulled the trigger."

"Maybe so," said Bowen, stepping forward to look at his reflection in the van's sideview mirror. "But we need the shooter and whoever else was in that car. This man is an ordinary citizen, and the mayor is going to want this cleared up to the public's satisfaction."

"We'll do our best," said Jack, "but I'll warn you right now that there may be more to come."

"What's that supposed to mean?" asked Bowen, as he licked a finger and ran it across each of his eyebrows.

"Leonard," said Jack, spinning the chair to face his friend.

"Well, sir," said Funk. "There has been quite a shakeup in the syndicate recently. Tony Accardo stepped aside, and Sam Giancana is running their day-to-day operations, including prostitution, gambling, and extortion, and the necessary functions associated with said vice, such as strong-arm tactics and murder. In that regard, he has elevated some of his own people, such as Angelo Carpacci and Vic D'Antonio. Jack is implying that these men are quite possibly out to make a name for themselves, so that when Paul Ricca is released from prison, he doesn't simply take over for Giancana."

Bowen regarded both Jack and Leonard Funk. He noticed that, while Funk seemed educated and intelligent, he also wore suspenders with a belt and was quite unkempt. Even Funk's thin, sandy hair, he noted, seemed to have been combed with his hand.

"Thank you for that update, Mr. Funk. I appreciate your concern, gentlemen, so consider it noted. However, as I said just moments ago, I want the shooter and the other men that were in that car. Do anything that you must to bring them in, and frankly, I don't care if they are alive. Finally," he said, brushing the sleeves of his topcoat, "is there anything that I can do for you?"

Jack smiled and Bowen bent over his wheelchair. "Yes, Lieutenant?"

"Just two things," said Jack, smiling at the obvious discomfort that Bowen felt when around him. "First of all, we'll need free rein to question several people that won't be directly involved with the case, but that might be able to offer some help."

"Of course," said Bowen. "Why would that be a problem?"

"Some of them may be kind of highfalutin. You know, this guy was a banker and he had just finished dinner at some real estate developer's house. I just want the mayor to know that we may be talking with some influential voters."

Bowen's lips formed a curt smile. "Public safety is the mayor's number one concern, not voters. What is the second thing?"

Jack matched his curt smile. "I need you to stop bending over when you talk to me. I have this bad habit of biting anybody that gets close to me."

Bowen let out a grunt and straightened up. "Forgive me, Lieutenant. I just thought that a man in your situation might appreciate a sympathetic gesture."

Bowen turned and walked off before Jack could reply. Jack shook his head and then wheeled himself up the ramp, spun his wheelchair so that he could face forward, locked the brakes on the chair and secured it with the belts that were bolted to the floor. Leonard climbed in the driver's seat and Jack smiled at him and then turned away.

"Quite an asshole, eh?" remarked Leonard as he started the van.

"Yep," said Jack.

They pulled out onto the main street and drove in silence. Jack stared out the windshield as Leonard maneuvered into traffic. Jack ran a thumb across the dimple in his chin. "The mystery here isn't really who killed Mr. Marcus," he said. He glanced in the rearview mirror at the crowd of people gathered at the scene. "That's just one of the questions, like, 'How did this banker get involved with the syndicate and why was someone allowed to kill him?' No, the mystery is this, Leonard: what's going to happen next?"

Al woke to the ringing of the phone. 5:00 A.M. Not again. Who the fuck? "Yeah," he muttered as he cradled the phone between his shoulder and the pillow.

"My turn this time." Burt Cordell. "Don't go to your safe deposit box. The bank's founder was murdered last night."

"Shit," said Al. "I may need to go there. What does some banker's murder have to do with me?"

"Nothing and everything," said Cordell. "There are extenuating circumstances. The banker was involved with Orville Hodge. My sources tell me the Feds are going to be all over that bank. The last thing that you need is for somebody to find out how much money you have in the safe deposit box and start asking questions."

"There's not as much as there used to be."

"Whatever. Attention is something that you have never wished to accumulate and I don't think that it's a good time to start."

"You're right," said Al. "This has just come at a bad time. What happened to the banker?"

"Abducted and killed. They're looking for Giancana."

Al sat up fast. "Why Momo?"

"The banker had a receipt from him for a loan payment. If Giancana set it up, he picked the wrong guy. They left the banker loaded with cash, checks and their boss's name."

"If it was Sam," said Al, "two things have already happened. One, he's hiding, and two, a grave has already been marked for whoever pulled off that hit. You think I don't like attention. Momo fucking hates it."

"Then tell him to stop banging Phyllis McGuire. I'll be at my office if you need anything."

Cordell hung up. Al replaced the phone on the nightstand and rolled onto his back, looked at the ceiling. Another travesty. Now if he took a big hit, he couldn't pay, and that was trouble. Taking another big hit was doubtful, but with no reserve, he'd be gambling, and he never gambled. Then again, if he went to Angelo for money, he wouldn't be gambling; the outcome was clear: he'd be trapped into working directly for the syndicate, making book to pay off juice and the loan. Screw it. He'd find another way. Or he'd take the chance. He slipped out of bed and headed for the bathroom, hoping that his bladder wasn't becoming addicted to the 5:00 A.M. wakeup calls.

The Lip held up his hand and beckoned the waitress to the table. "More coffee, hon, and bring me a pitcher of ice water."

The waitress scurried away. The Lip could tell that she was afraid of him, and that pleased him. His new look drew stares and whispers and he knew that with the extent of his hangover, he had to look absolutely sinister. When the waitress brought him a pot of coffee and a pitcher of ice water he looked up from his newspaper, caught her eye and said, "Boo." She jumped back and then rushed to the kitchen.

The Lip laughed and then returned to the paper. He was still chuckling as he read the headline: MARCUS MURDERED! The first paragraph choked the laugh.

> Leon Marcus, former chairman of the Southmoor Bank and Trust, was abducted and murdered late last night. Marcus, a figure in the Orville Hodge scandal, had been visiting real estate developer Alfred Rado and was abducted by a group of men as he left Rado's home. His body was found a short time later at a vacant lot at 4918 Campbell.

"Son of a bitch," muttered the Lip. The Southmoor Bank and Trust was where the money for the fight was being held. That meant scrutiny. Just what he didn't need. Things had been going great: pre-fight publicity had grown hot, due in no small part to the events at the Marigold Garden. No word from Wee Willie, so the kid must've taken it better than expected. No matter. Junior was bound by contract. A meeting was scheduled with the radio and television representatives: if he was lucky, he could milk them for another $25,000. Herb Bradley had leaked a story to the newspapers; another mild explosion set to draw a crowd. Attendance probably pushing 17,000—getting close.

He finished the newspaper, chugged the rest of his coffee and drank the ice water straight from the pitcher. He spilled some water on his slacks and immediately thought of Gilda. He hadn't seen her since Saturday night. He'd stopped by the hotel bar and Ramon had told him that she'd been fired. Management didn't want her kind scaring off customers. He'd driven out to her house, but no one had answered his knock. He knew her type: attracted to the danger. She'd sulk for a while and then come back.

The waitress slipped his bill onto the table and scampered back to the kitchen. The Lip wadded up the newspaper, slipped fifty cents onto the table to cover two eggs, toast and coffee and left the restaurant. As he rode the elevator up to his floor, he hummed a Harry Belafonte tune that he'd heard the night before at the Club Alabam. The hell with some murdered banker. He'd make the money legitimately. Or he'd learn to swim.

Junior jogged down the gravel road, a few hundred yards ahead of the pack; Wee Willie was in a car, driving behind them. Junior replayed Saturday night. The fights, Gilda kissing him, the crowd; it seemed like a nightmare. It was all a blur until Wee Willie slapped his face in the locker room. They'd been by themselves, given space by the others. Wee Willie had looked on the verge of tears. Their conversation, verbatim: "Hammer," Wee Willie had said. "I should've told you this a long time ago, but I didn't find out till after we was signed with Lipranski. Word has it, him and your uncle sold horse in the joint. Lipranski and your uncle was partners. But that ain't the worst of it. Some say he had your uncle killed and that whole bit with holding up the body was just show. Some say your uncle owed him money so Lipranski set him up. I don't know if it's true, Hammer, but I should've told you before. I'm sorry, Hammer, but I told you: I'm a flawed man. I can taste that championship like it's fresh baked bread, but I don't want it no more, not after what happened tonight! That man's evil. He set that whole thing up, like he set up your uncle."

Junior had simply looked down at the floor. He had to have the fight. They all did. Mama did. Mama had worked all of her life and it was time for her to rest. Maybe that stuff about Mr. Lipranski was true. Junior knew his uncle had been busted for selling junk in the first place, so the fact that he'd start up in prison was no surprise. Even if it was true, it didn't really matter. Mr. Lipranski, Mr. Hansen, even Wee Willie, all thought that they were using him, but Junior knew better. *He* was using *them*. They were setting up the fight, showing him more money than he ever figured to see. He had to have the fight. Mama had to have the fight. Nothing else mattered.

He'd slowly raised his head. Wee Willie had fear in his eyes. "We're going ahead with the fight, Willie. I don't care about Mr. Lipranski or my uncle. I don't care nothing 'bout no crazy white woman and I don't care nothin' 'bout you. I'm fightin' for Mama. Not you; not me; not my uncle; not Mr. Lipranski. Mama. So you got a problem with Mr. Lipranski, you talk to him for your own self. Leave me out of it. This is my fight, not yours. You do anything to mess it up, you got to answer to me."

Wee Willie had slapped him. It wasn't hard; just enough to sting, but it hurt more than he'd let on. He'd stared at Wee Willie, watched his lips flutter and his mouth fail to form any words. He'd stood up, shaken his head and started for the door. As he'd opened the door he'd turned to Willie and said, "You lost your woman 'cause you wanted this so bad. Why'd you think it'd be easier this time?"

Jack wheeled up the ramp and past two young uniformed cops. He heard one say, "You see the the arms on that crip?"

The other young cop quieted his friend. "Shut up. That's Lieutenant Taylor. If he heard you say that he'd jerk your head off."

Inside the police station, Jack maneuvered his wheelchair next to the stairs. He stopped near the first step, reached behind him and pulled a strap out of the pouch on the back of the chair and looped it under his legs and over his shoulders. Once it was over his shoulders, he fastened it with the buckle and leaned forward. An extra handrail had been constructed that ran up the middle of the staircase. Jack grabbed it with one hand and grasped the side rail with his other hand. He then rocked forward and perched himself, like a gymnast, between the rails. Leonard Funk stepped in behind him and pulled his chair back into a corner and he felt eyes upon him as he started to climb the stairs: all of his weight supported by his arms. He moved up the stairs quickly, pumping his arms forward, his lower body held in a sitting position by the belt. He heard hushed voices marvel at his strength and he smiled inside, knowing that going down the stairs, fighting off his own momentum, was much trickier. When he reached the top of the staircase, he launched himself straight up in the air, turned to face down the steps, and then sat in his spare wheelchair as one of the men slipped it underneath him.

"Jack," said Leonard, huffing as he reached the last step. "I think that my stomach fills with a quart of acid every time that you perform that last move."

Jack laughed and rolled into the heart of the station. Everyone was busy, so after a few perfunctory greetings, he wheeled into his office. Leonard followed him and sat down, taking off his hat and slipping his topcoat over one arm.

"You set up interviews with Mr. Rado yet?" asked Jack.

"Yes," replied Leonard. "He and his wife will be down here at three o'clock. George told me the lab technicians have already checked the car that was found with the jumper on its ignition. It checks out. It's the murder vehicle."

"Great," said Jack, glancing at the pile of papers on his desk. "Have George concentrate on the vehicle. I'd like you to run a check on Marcus and the Rados and prepare for their interview. I'm going to take a few minutes and catch up on some paperwork and then I'll meet you in the interrogation room and we can compare notes."

Leonard nodded, stood up, and left the room.

Jack sat back and looked around his office. His desk was covered with papers, envelopes, and a picture of his parents. The walls were covered with plaques and commendations: the most the department had ever seen. A pair of boxing gloves sat in one corner, an old football in another. The cleaning crew must've moved things around, but he finally found it, resting against a chair on the other side of the desk: the picture of him and Ronnie. He wheeled around, picked it up.

He stared at the picture: black-and-white, he and Ronnie on their first day on the force, no grins—faces filled with pride and resolve. It had taken six years, but they had finally been paired up and had been partners for twelve years before it happened.

A stakeout: a wire room on North Clark Street. A tip told them that Sam Giancana was holding an invitation-only craps game that night. No cooperation from the ranks; a few even told them to stay the hell away. Rumors of corrupt cops guarding the place. Just before midnight the room lit up. Ronnie went up the front steps, Jack up the fire escape. No way to yell to Ronnie that there was no noise— something wasn't right. He tripped on the last step, watched through a back window as Ronnie burst through the front door and caught a full round from a sawed-off directly in the face. He'd screamed, kicked in the back door and started firing, found himself flying, floating, landing on his back in the middle of the alley. Nobody called it in. He wasn't found for three hours. A wino had stumbled across him, flagged down a squad car, begged for a reward.

Ronnie was dead, no living relatives. Jack was paralyzed from the waist down. His parents cared for him for the next two years. Rehabilitation was slow: he built up his arms and chest with rage and the resolve that he would find out who set them up and kill him. The mayor stepped in on his behalf, offered him a desk job. Jack told him that he wanted Internal Affairs. Word came down—no; he was too consumed with vengeance. They kicked him a desk job in Homicide. Two years later, he'd proven that he could handle a full case load. On the side, he investigated *it*. The rumors proved true. Corrupt cops guarded spots for Giancana and Tony Accardo. He spent every available moment trying to identify the bad cops. He researched the tip. Finally, Jim Brody offered to help.

Brody was an old-timer, not too bright, with a beer gut and a taste for strip joints. Jack didn't like him, but needed some help. One night Brody called and told him that he'd found an informant.

He'd stashed him in the back room of a vacant house on the South Side. Jack met him there just after sundown.

Brody had met him outside the house, smiled, told him that they were about to solve the case. He'd helped Jack inside the house, and headed to the back room to get the informant. He'd come out alone, told Jack that there was a problem. Jack had reached forward to pull himself up to the table and asked what the problem was. Brody responded with a crowbar across his arms, breaking them both just below the elbows. "You're the problem," he said, laughing. "You're bad for business."

Brody had swung the crowbar like a baseball bat, sent Jack to the floor. The crowbar had clanged on the wood floor and Brody had continued to laugh as he went back to the back room. He'd returned moments later, carrying a blowtorch and a pair of wire cutters. He'd bellowed with laughter at the sight of Jack, crawling to the door, dragging himself, dead lower body and broken arms, *with his elbows*. Brody had set the blowtorch down, bent over to roll Jack onto his back, when Jack swung the crowbar. He'd taken out Brody's legs and the big man had hit the floor like an anchor. Jack was on him immediately; choked him to death with just his hands.

Jack set the picture on the front of his desk, took one last look at Ronnie.

The Rados arrived early. The two young cops ushered them up the stairs. Jack rolled out to greet them, heard one cop ask the other if he'd changed in the year since he'd been back. "Yeah," said the other. "He's gotten tougher."

Al tried to put numbers together, couldn't come up with anything. Regardless, another big hit and he'd have to go to Angelo. His only other option, not an option: limit the bets that he accepted until things cooled off. If a man couldn't count on his bookie, he got another bookie. Bettors, he knew, took as long as they could to pay off, but when they won, they wanted their money immediately. Any glitches and they would look for another shop. Facts were facts. Men like Jimmy Spears, even Poochie, had other options. He had to offer dependability.

He rode the trolley south on State Street, got off and walked east. He'd decided to pick up a gift for Janet; pacify her until he made a decision. She was a good girl, and he cared for her, but didn't know how deep it went. He'd only loved one woman in his life, and that had been his mother. That died when he had walked into Preston Daniels's office and seen her high heels peeking out from behind his desk. Daniels had looked up, his face flushed. His expression never changed; he'd dismissed Al by simply ignoring him. That night he'd had it out with his mother. Screams, things thrown, the lines that lived with him forever: "I only married your father because I was pregnant. The only nice thing that he ever did for me was die. I'm upgrading, and you're not part of the deal."

It had been thirty-four years since that night, but Al still felt a shiver when he thought back on it. The years had taught him that his mother had been scared. She was beautiful and intelligent, but had never fended for herself. Preston Daniels was the richest man in Chicago and had offered her a place in life that she felt that she deserved, and she couldn't see any other way to attain it. Al hadn't spoken to her since a chance encounter on the street, and neither had even attempted to contact the other. He regarded his uncle as his only family.

He entered Marshall Field's and lost himself in a crowd. Thirty-four years. A lot had happened in thirty-four years. He'd quit the newspaper the day after his fight with his mother; started working for Uncle Pat. He'd booked at school, spent his free time handicapping games, realized that the real money was on the other side. Uncle Pat set him up with his first handbook, bankrolled any losses. He'd been successful; *risen.* After a few years, the real bettors started coming to him, and he made sure that he paid off the winners immediately, let the losers play until fear forced them to pay. Bobby Lipranski had sharked money to the Polacks, gone ballistic on a *friend,* and spent time at Stateville. Al kept rising, became one of the biggest layoff bookies in the Midwest. The Lip did his time, came out, and started hustling fights.

He stopped in front of the jewelry counter and looked at gold bracelets. A leggy saleswoman modeled a few for him, came on to him, licked her red lips when he paid cash for a gold S-link bracelet.

He left the building and walked over to Michigan Avenue, enjoying the stretch. He didn't get out much; not a lot of people that he cared to run into. He continued walking north, decided to wait to get a cab until he reached Lake Shore Drive.

The walk relieved some of the tension of the past few days. He hadn't told anyone about Tom, and had felt his heart rattle like a machine gun when Jerry had called to report that he couldn't find him. There was real pain in Jerry's voice, but Al had done his best to convince him that he knew nothing of his friend's whereabouts. Danger surrounded that whole situation. If he let on that he knew what happened, either the law or Vic D'Antonio would be all over him. Vic had counted on that, and Al hadn't disappointed him.

Now, that banker had been murdered and he couldn't go to his safe deposit box. Chances were minimal that he would have to, but, as he'd learned by that damn North Carolina–Michigan State game, he had to plan for even the most remote possibility. He'd drop his house limit, coach his boys to keep the book as balanced as possible, and spend the afternoon on the phone with Goldie and some of the other layoff bookies, making sure that they could bail him out of any jam. He didn't anticipate that he would see any heavy action until Saturday's fight, but now that the black man had gone crazy and made out with that white woman in public, he knew he'd see a bundle bet on the outcome.

A breeze whipped the wind off of the lake and Al deposited the gift in his coat pocket and put on a pair of gloves. A gust nearly blew his fedora off, and when he grabbed it, he raised his other hand and hailed a cab. A cab quickly pulled over and he got in and instructed the driver to drive to 880 North Lake Shore Drive. The cab shot east onto the drive, and Al stared out the window, mesmerized by the activity of the Great Lake. The view from his apartment seemed to be all lake, but from the street, he was captivated by the constant movement of the waves, the tranquillity of the motion. He continued to stare as they drove on. Losses mounting. Tom murdered; a point delivered. A dead banker. Water. Tranquillity. Florida was starting to sound better and better.

• • •

Herb Bradley's office: the Lip on the phone, behind the desk; Herb sitting like a flunkie in his own office. The Lip cradled the phone, jotted notes with an ink pen. "I can't guarantee a championship fight within the next three fights, Mr. Cohen. What I can guarantee is that after this fight, Junior will be a marquee attraction. This fight may be a sellout, and his next three will be even bigger."

The Lip listened: Gary Cohen of the network. The Lip was fighting for more radio/television money; Cohen wanted something in return. "Okay," said the Lip. "I can give you a three-fight deal, but I can't guarantee a championship fight. That's not up to me. I'd have to get Floyd Patterson's people to sign, and I don't know how long that will take. Then again, just look at the other contenders. Who's he going to fight, the Olympian, Pete Rademacher? He's only been fighting professionally for around a year."

Herb Bradley held up a newspaper, pointed at the headline: FIGHT TURNS INTO GRUDGE MATCH!

"Mr. Cohen, this fight has captured the public's attention. I'm not just proposing that you capitalize on that; I'm proposing that you become our partner in promoting Junior. A three-fight deal, including the fight with Tomcat. Yes, I realize that you've already paid for this fight. It's only another fifty thousand! You'd be guaranteed the three biggest fights of the year! Fight fans won't even remember Floyd Patterson when this is done. Junior is going to be the biggest fighter since Marciano, and I wouldn't be surprised if the Rock came out of retirement for a shot at Junior. Yes, of course you'd get the first shot at that fight. Okay, now we're talking. Sure, sure, but I need the money as soon as possible. Junior will look at it as a show of confidence, and I can assure you that when you join his team, he's as loyal as a Cubs fan. Great. Send the papers to the hotel. I'll sign them and get them back right away. Now, when do we get the check?"

The Lip hung up and shook hands with Herb Bradley. "Well, we just took in another fifty grand. Junior and I will sign any papers. Let's keep this quiet and have any check sent to me personally. I don't want anything going to that dirty bank."

"Attendance is going strong. I'm figuring around eighteen thousand," said Bradley.

"Not good enough. I need a sellout. Can you imagine selling out a non-championship fight? When does Dally's column appear?"

"It'll run on Wednesday. You know, Mike Lantz is going to be pissed if Dally gets all of the scoops."

"I can't help that. Dally's paper has all of the readers. Tell Mike that we'll give him an exclusive interview after the fight."

"You'll do that?"

"Hell no, but tell him that we will."

"Things aren't going bad for us right now, Lip."

"No," said the Lip, pulling a couple of fresh cigars out of Bradley's humidor and handing one to him. "But I keep waiting for someone to say it."

"Say what?" asked Bradley, as he accepted the cigar.

"April Fool."

Joe Louis Gym. Noises: fighters spraying air out of their nostrils, grunts from Kid Spinelli as Aaron Green slams a medicine ball into his stomach, speed bags rattling, heavy bags being beaten, Junior and Howie the Hat exchanging punches in the ring.

"Stick and move, Hammer," yelled Wee Willie as he slapped the canvas floor of the ring. "Tomcat's lighter than the Hat. You've got to move faster!"

Junior peered out from under his headgear, his hands up around his face, elbows tucked into his ribcage. He slipped a right from the Hat and shot a left hook into his ribs. He finished off a combination with a left to the head, and the Hat staggered back as the bell rang.

Junior walked to the corner and leaned against the rope, facing Wee Willie. "Work on your footwork this round," said Wee Willie. "Tomcat's a stalker, so make him come to you, but don't let him cut off the ring. If he starts to cut it off, just stick and move!"

Junior turned around as Aaron Green returned from giving the Hat his instructions and placed Junior's mouthpiece back in his mouth. Aaron slipped out of the ring just before the bell rang.

Junior was surprised about how good he felt. Fear had started to give way to confidence. Threatened with the loss of the fight, he'd fought back! The Hat lumbered toward him, hands starting to fall, exposing his face. Junior skipped to his left, peppered the Hat with jabs. He started to dance and move, popped a jab and then suddenly stopped and split the Hat's defense with a jab and a right uppercut. "Stick and move!" yelled Wee Willie, but Junior didn't hear him. He worked on instinct, snapped the Hat's head back with quick jabs, worked for an opening. The Hat lifted his right hand to catch a jab and Junior replied with a hook to the body, forced air out of the Hat like he'd sat on a whoopie cushion. The Hat's eyes opened in surprise and Junior followed up top with a left hook to the side of his head. The Hat slumped forward and Junior straightened him up with an uppercut, then followed with a straight left that sent the Hat's mouthpiece across the ring.

"Time," yelled Wee Willie. The Hat staggered to his corner, blood rushing from his mouth. Aaron Green stepped into the ring as Wee Willie stared at Junior.

"Check this out," said Aaron as he walked past Junior. He held up the mouthpiece: two teeth imbedded in the plastic. "No more corn on the cob for Howie."

Junior walked to the corner. Strange. He still felt good. Real good.

Tuesday, April 2

No damn elevator; Jack sat in the lobby of the bank, tried to cool down, ignored the people who stared at him. Leonard was upstairs, searching for information on the Sunrise Club, an old whorehouse in Schiller Park that Momo had purchased, courtesy of a mortgage held by the dead banker, Leon Marcus. The banker must've been blackmailing Giancana: purely a money issue; the banker had kept an uncanceled check for $300,000 in his pocket—a reminder of how close he'd been. Alternatives just didn't pan out. Orville Hodge, the former state auditor who had cashed over $600,000 in fraudulent state warrants at Marcus's bank, was doing time. The fact that Marcus was due to stand trial in September for misapplying the bank's federally insured funds gave credence to the theory that he was killed to stop him from talking, but that solution fit Momo Giancana, not a state auditor. The oil man who had written Marcus the check for $300,000 was dead, and the other characters in his life just didn't fit the script. It had to be Giancana. The question was, who pulled the trigger?

Jack finished his coffee and set the empty cup in his lap. He rubbed his brow and ran through Giancana's men. Jackie Cerone, Fifi Buccieri, Mad Sam DeStefano, Willie Potatoes—the list seemed endless, and each man had more men underneath him. Screw it. Wipe 'em all out and you'd get the killer.

He noticed that his colostomy bag was full, wheeled over and asked the receptionist for the location of the closest bathroom. She pointed down a hall and Jack rolled away. When he hit the bathroom door he nearly screamed in anger: one bathroom door gave way to a second door. There was no way to maneuver his chair inside. He wheeled back toward the staircase, furious. Leonard Funk stood waiting. Thank God.

"The FDIC has the place flooded. I'll come back later."

"Let's hit it," said Jack, already rolling toward the front door.

Leonard stepped outside behind Jack and helped him down the steps, then walked briskly to the van. He pulled out the ramp and stood aside while Jack wheeled himself inside. "Hold on for a minute, Leonard," said Jack as rolled out of view. Minutes later, Jack wheeled back, asked Leonard to step aside and heaved a coffee cup full of waste out the side door. Piss on all of them: the assholes in the bank, Sam Giancana and a banker stupid enough to blackmail the syndicate.

Al scanned the newspaper while he waited for Janet. Not a bad Monday night; made a little on the heavyweight fight in New York. The German, Willi Besmanoff, had won a decision over Bob Baker. Locals had played a lot: foreigners brought out their hate money.

He sat in a corner booth at the High Roller. Not exactly Booth One at the Pump Room, but not bad. Timmy Murphy brought him a bottle of beer and slid into the booth next to him. "Not here to pay off today, are you?" asked Murphy.

"Kind of," said Al, leaning on the table. "A little 'thank you' lunch for a broad."

"Say, Al, who do you like in the fight Saturday?"

"I like 'em both."

"I thought you'd say that," said Murphy. "I like the colored kid, but I've got to tell you, he sure isn't popular."

"You mean the thing with that white woman the other night?"

Murphy nodded. "And there's an article in this morning's paper that says he's a real bum."

"Hmm," said Al. He hadn't seen the article, but he could already see the Lip's fingerprints all over the fight. "I guess it really doesn't matter what he's like, as long as he's a decent fighter."

"Spoken like a pro. You take the action. Me, I need someone to root for. That Tomcat's a little boisterous for me, but I'll probably pull for him."

"Why pull when you can play. Just give me a call."

Murphy laughed, then rose from his seat. "I hope this is your lady."

Janet: killer green patterned sweater and black skirt. Tight in all of the right places. "Janet, Timmy Murphy," said Al.

Timmy took her hand and helped her into the booth. "I'm the proprietor of this establishment and a long-time friend of Mr. Kelly. Therefore, you can consider me a long-time friend, also." He bowed slightly and smiled.

"Well, Mr. Murphy, if your chef is as talented at his work as you are as a host, we're in for quite a meal."

Murphy laughed. "May I offer the young lady some wine or a drink?"

"You may offer the lady anything that keeps you referring to her as 'young,' although a cup of coffee will suffice."

"Then coffee it shall be," said Murphy. "But I'd be remiss if I didn't come back and give you the same offer a bit later on."

"And I'd be remiss if I didn't thank you in advance for a nice glass of after-lunch chardonnay."

"Very good," said Murphy.

Al watched him walk away. "He's just like your uncle," said Janet.

"Full of blarney, eh?"

"But nice blarney. He's one of the few men that's made me feel that he enjoyed offering a compliment."

Al moved around the booth and drew her near. "You look great," he said as he threw an arm around her.

"Nice try, but you're not one of them."

Al pushed his lower lip over his upper lip. "I tried."

"Don't worry, Al. You show your appreciation in other ways."

"Such as?"

"In bed. In my bank account."

"And with gifts."

"No, I don't think that you've ever given me a gift."

"Well, then this is a first," said Al. He reached under the table, withdrew a gift-wrapped package and handed it to her.

Janet looked at the small box, then raised an eyebrow as she started to unwrap it. "I don't hear it ticking, so I'm assuming it's not some kind of going-away present."

She withdrew a small jewelry box and gasped when she opened it. "It's lovely," she said as she held the bracelet in the air. "Oh, Al, it's beautiful."

"It's no going-away present," said Al. "I've decided that I'm not going anywhere. I guess I've just had a bad few days."

Janet turned to face him and kissed him. "That's the best present I've ever received, and I don't mean the bracelet. I knew there was something special about coming to lunch with you today. Do you realize this is the first time that we've ever had lunch together?"

"C'mon," replied Al, smirking. "We had corned beef sandwiches just last week."

"You ran out and got them and we ate them in bed. What I mean is, you've never taken me out for lunch before. We've only had dinner out a few times."

"That's me, doll. In my world it just doesn't pay to draw attention." Janet picked up a menu, so Al did the same, and pretended to read it. "You didn't say anything to anybody about me leaving, did you?"

"Of course not," said Janet. "I hoped that you were just thinking out loud."

"I guess I was," he said. "Hey, try the rib-eye sandwich. It's fantastic."

They ate lunch, left, and finished the afternoon in bed. All bases covered: Janet was happy and wouldn't tip his hand. If he decided to go, he knew that it would be complicated; he couldn't just up and leave. He'd have to work it out with Momo, and that meant money. But Momo was in hiding and Angelo was jockeying. The timing was all wrong, but he just couldn't shake the feeling. Al laughed silently to himself while Janet cleaned up in the bathroom. Making book for twenty-eight years, and he was about to play a gut feeling. He shook his head in amazement. Twenty-eight years and he was no wiser than the players who paid him.

The Lip sang as he read. "Luck be a lady tonight. Luck let this be a profitable fight." It was already mid-afternoon, but he'd been out late the night before and had just gotten up. The hot shower and shave had worked wonders, and he felt refreshed as he picked up the newspaper that had been slipped underneath his door. He dropped back on the bed and his white terrycloth robe fell open.

He flipped through the paper until he found the sports section. "Yeah, baby!" he yelled.

The headline was pure Dally: COLORED CONTESTANT COVETS CONFLICT!

BEHIND THE NEWS

By Dally Richardson

Tuesday, April 2

It seems that Junior "The Hammer" Hamilton enjoys conflict, whether it be inside or outside of the ring. After witnessing Hamilton incite the fight crowd on Saturday night by dallying (and I hate to have my name even associated with such behavior) with his white girlfriend, this reporter put on his gloves, pulled out his shovel, and started to dig. Behavior like Hamilton's isn't conceived overnight, and I wasn't surprised to find that he has a history of erratic, even violent behavior.

Six years ago "The Hammer" worked for the railroad. One day his crew was sent to dig up old track, but Hamilton, prone to bouts of laziness, stayed behind. The crew foreman, who has since died, proceeded to chastise Hamilton, who knocked him to the ground. A passerby, fearful that the huge Negro was going to seriously injure the small foreman, leaped out of his car and attempted to calm Hamilton. But "The Hammer" was ready to pound, and pound he did, nearly killing passerby Allie Jennings. Jennings, who has since left the area, told this reporter that he begged and pleaded for his life, but that Hamilton simply laughed and kept hitting him. He finally stopped when he just got too tired to continue. Hamilton was immediately fired from his job, but, having found the release for all of his jungle instincts, he fought his way into the prize-fight profession.

"I knew he'd had some trouble," observed clean-craniumed promoter Robert J. Lipranski. "But I didn't realize that it was that bad. A man with Junior's skill could've killed that man. Frankly, I'm worried for Tomcat Gordon. He may be the public's pick, but that won't save him in the ring."

Lipranski said no charges were ever filed and that Hamilton hadn't been in a fight outside of the ring since he began promoting Hamilton's fights two years ago. "Until Saturday night, I hadn't seen Junior provoke anyone or anything."

I'll have more on Hamilton as the week goes on, but suffice it to say that, although journalistic integrity dictates that I withhold bias, I'm going to have a hard time forgetting that one contestant in Saturday night's heavyweight bout is a thug. Hamilton will receive 20 percent of the gate, but let's hope that's not all he gets. A lesson in civility would be appropriate.

The Lip scratched himself. Everything was going perfectly. In fact, he'd have to start taking a bigger cut of Junior's share—say 50/50 or, shit, 60/40. Yeah, with all of the work he'd done, 60/40 was about right. Junior could never get that kind of press on his own.

A knock at the door. "Yeah." Gilda opened it, stepped inside.

She wore a fur coat, and the stole around her neck made her eyes glisten. Her lips were painted red and were locked in a mischievous half grin.

"You're like an early morning drink."

"Bad for you but hard to give up. Your parents' house that bad?"

"I'm here, aren't I?"

The Lip sat up, opened his arms.

"First, a few ultimatums," she said.

"Such as?"

"Number one," she said, closing the door behind her and dropping her coat in a chair. "From now on, keep me, but keep me out of your business." She kicked off her shoes, put one leg up on the chair and began to roll down her stocking. "Number two: let the press know that I'm not Junior's girlfriend and that the whole thing was some kind of accident."

The Lip shrugged. "After the fight."

"I knew that you'd say that, and as long as you take care of me for a while, that's fine." She removed the other stocking, reached behind and unzipped her dress. She wiggled free and it slipped into a heap at her feet. She reached back behind again and unclasped her bra. She fell free and laughed as the Lip drew his breath.

"I can tell that you're glad to see me," she said, nodding.

The Lip glanced down between his legs. She was right. "A few ultimatums means at least three and that's only two," he said, devouring her with his eyes. "What's the third?"

She stepped over to the bed, pulled his robe open further, grasped him in her hand and bent over. "Don't move."

"Your sister's here," said Aaron Green, waking Junior from his late afternoon nap.

Junior shut his eyes tight and then opened them wide, attempting to wake up. "Where is she?"

"In the lobby."

"She all right?"

"More than all right. You've got one hot-looking sister, man."

"She's too old for you."

"I'm thirteen!" shouted Aaron, eyes wide. He turned and started down the hall. "Ain't no girl too old for me now."

Junior shook his head and rolled off the bed. Who would have figured his sister for a jabber? As a girl, she'd spent most of her time with her mother or at church, but somewhere, somehow, something changed. She'd started hanging out with a group of smeckers, then moved on to the needles. It had broken his mother's heart, and Junior had wanted to strangle Rae for that. She moved out not long after and they didn't see much of her, but she'd started hanging with Cleotis and he knew what that meant: hooking and jabbing. A "hi yaller." He'd gone after Cleotis, found him and threatened him. Didn't matter—Rae clung to Cleotis like shit to a dog's ass.

He threw on a T-shirt, slipped into a pair of sweatpants and laced up his tennis shoes. He walked down the hall, spotted Rae. A long, flowered white dress peeked out underneath a fake fur coat. Pumps made her appear taller, and she swayed a bit as she beckoned for him to follow her outside.

"Wait up, Rae," said Junior as he stepped outside.

She continued ahead, moved around the side of the building. She stood next to a drain pipe, oblivious to the puddle of water that crept over her shoes. Her eyes swam.

"Rae, what you doing here?"

She smiled, opened her arms.

Junior stepped forward, but a figure cut him off and slipped into Rae's embrace.

"Ha, ha!"

Rae and the man spun around. The Tyrolean hat, yellow eyes, and mouth not quite full of teeth. Cleotis. "Say, Junior, we thought we'd pay the celebrity a visit."

Junior bit his upper lip, stepped forward. "What you want with me this time?"

"This time? I just wanted you to see your sister, let your mama know that I'm taking care of her."

"She high?"

"Most of them ladies she was hanging with is dead. You better be happy I took an interest in Rae."

"You done a lot for me and Rae, all right."

Cleotis cupped one of Rae's breasts and she nibbled on his ear. He smirked at Junior, but his eyes narrowed. "That paper said you gonna make twenty percent of this fight. That's a lot of money."

"Not that much. I gotta pay everybody out of that, and Mr. Lipranski uses some to pay bills."

"Don't play stupid with me, nigger. I talked with some cats downtown say they think you gonna make eighty thousand for this fight. Even if you pay out most of that and pay taxes, you're still gonna make at least twenty grand. I can't even imagine that. Most people living on a couple of thousand dollars a year, tops, and a dumb old nigger like you's gonna make twenty grand. Something 'bout that just don't seem fair."

Junior stammered. "Don't think it's gonna be that much."

"What do you mean, you 'don't think'? Ain't you got a clue how much you aim to make?"

"Willie and Mr. Lipranski's in charge of that. I gotta worry 'bout the fight."

"You are dumb. They're charging thirty dollars for balcony seats. Shit, I get a shoeshine for a quarter or a glass of beer for fifteen cents and somebody's gonna pay thirty dollars to watch you fight? Them boys gonna lay you out for the money. Oh well, fuck you. You're the dummy, always was."

"N–n . . . now, you don't have no reason to talk to me like that," said Junior. Rae stumbled, Cleotis caught her.

"There you see it, dummy. I'm taking care of your sister. She ain't got me here, she falls."

"Told you, I'm done with her. She's her own problem."

"Well," said Cleotis, running a long fingernail across his nose. "I'll bet your mama won't think like that."

"What you mean?" asked Junior, his voice rising.

"What I mean is, I don't get fifteen thousand from you after the fight, I'm gonna go have me a talk with your mama. Tell her you don't care 'bout Rae no more. Tell her you don't show me no respect like you should. Tell her 'bout Kansas City."

Junior froze. Cleotis propped Rae up against a car, stepped

inches from Junior. "Now you listen to me, dummy. You gonna pay me that money or I'm gonna go have a talk with your mama. I shoulda done it a long time ago, but I used to like you. Now, you think you're Mr. Big Shot and that you're better than me, but you're not. You a spineless, stupid dummy and you gonna pay me or your mama's gonna find out about Kansas City and your sister's gonna be on her own. I'm sicka covering for your ass. You gonna pay me and that's that."

Junior slid against the brick wall, didn't hear Cleotis bark at his sister as they sped off: "Shit. You had one piece of talent in your body, I'da told him you was pregnant."

Didn't see Cleotis slap his sister across the face: force of habit.

Didn't hear Cleotis say, "Thinkin' 'bout it, maybe I'll tell him I had you scraped, get a little more money. Milk that dumb boy."

Junior didn't hear Cleotis, didn't see him, didn't see her, 'cause he was too busy scrambling, thinking: How would he ever explain it to Mama?

Wednesday, April 3

Jack hoisted himself through one last pull-up and dropped into his wheelchair. The brakes on the chair were set and it didn't budge as he fell into it.

His biceps ached; his fifth set of one hundred pull-ups had been nearly impossible to finish. Since the accident, his lower body had practically wasted away, but his upper body seemed to attract all of the bulk that he was losing. His arms were bigger than his legs and after his exercises, his biceps knotted like they'd been cast in iron. His torso was lean but taut, and the angry scars from the shotgun blast seemed to testify to his invincibility. His body stated it in bold: he was all muscle, violence and sheer, impenetrable will.

Post attack number one: Jack's parents had cared for him for two years; his dad forced him to stop feeling sorry for himself and take action; his mother fed him love. His dad fashioned the harness that

Jack wore around his neck to hold his legs in place when he lifted himself; constantly tinkered with his wheelchair—perfected it for a man of action; helped Jack find a house close by and retrofitted it for a paraplegic. His mom weaned him off of bouts of self-pity and booze, taught him to cook for himself, showed him the gift of reading. She hammered it home: the man of action needed to become a man of intellect; his mind would always be stronger than his body. Jack listened to them both, loved them more than ever. He learned the lessons. He fed his mind, looked for solutions rather than problems, realized that he could accomplish *anything*!

Post attack number two: he hadn't been saved by his intellect, but by muscle and rage. He continued to read, thanked God for letting him go back to work and for giving him Leonard Funk, did more pull-ups and dips than most men thought possible. An aide came in during the evening to help out around the apartment. His parents stopped by to offer him love and support. He spent more and more time on the job, consumed with catching criminals, Sam Giancana. His days were filled, but his nights, his nights were hell.

Two images haunted his sleep, but he couldn't say which was the dream and which was the nightmare. In one, he simply got up out of bed and walked. He never noticed the first steps, but then, suddenly, he would remember that he couldn't walk and he'd be overcome by a sudden giddiness and he would step forward gingerly, faster and faster until he was running and leaping and then . . . he would wake up. The first time, he cried like a baby, but the next time, he fought back the tears and willed himself back to sleep, praying softly to return to the dream.

The other dream was even more vivid. He would be sleeping, when out of nowhere he would see the house. It was sundown but the sun would suddenly drop from the sky and he would find himself inside the house. He knew it was coming, but he could never react quickly enough. The crowbar would smash his forearms and then crush his jaw so quickly that his eyes hung in place, catching a quick glimpse of Jim Brody as he smiled gleefully. "You, you're the problem!"

He would find himself on the ground, feel the skin from his elbows peel off on the hardwood floor, scream to himself that he wouldn't let the weight from his useless lower body kill him. He would see the crowbar and force himself to stay conscious, grab it and hide it underneath him. Brody would step out, bend to roll him over and Jack would be panic stricken, petrified that he wouldn't get the crowbar out in time. But he would. He would. And then the nightmare began, because as he choked Brody to death, he didn't feel the pain rack his forearms, didn't see Brody's eyes bulge from the sockets, he didn't notice his heart beat so hard that it nearly burst from his body. All that he was aware of were the screams, *his*, as he willed his hands together and choked the rage from the depths of his soul. He would wake up exhausted, his arms limp at his sides, and each time, he would gather himself, run his hands over his chest and across his neck, making sure that he hadn't been choking *himself*.

Jack spun his wheelchair around and headed to the bathroom. Once inside, he rolled under the sink that his dad had fashioned for him and washed his face and hands. He looked at himself in the mirror as he brushed his hair; his face was wide with a strong, dimpled chin, heavy cheekbones, dark brown eyebrows and brown eyes. He was forty-two years old, but his hair was still thick; if it hadn't been cut so short, it would still curl.

There was a rap at the door and Leonard Funk let himself inside. Jack had given him a key. It made it easier, but also showed Leonard how much he trusted him.

"Are you almost ready, Jack?" asked Leonard.

"Sure," replied Jack. "Just let me grab some fruit for the drive." Moments later he rolled into the kitchen wearing a sportcoat and red patterned tie and reached up onto the counter and grabbed a couple of bananas and an apple.

They left moments later, Leonard locking the door behind them. As they drove to the station, Jack ate an apple and Leonard hummed classical music. Then they went through their morning ritual, reiterating what they had learned the day before and questioning their day's activities. By the time they had reached the station, they'd agreed that they would visit the Rados at their home, search the bank and its back offices, and put out an APB on Sam Giancana.

They entered the station house and Jack immediately looped the belt under his legs, strapped it behind his neck and headed upstairs. Leonard parked the wheelchair in the coatroom and then followed him.

Jack stopped halfway up the staircase, balanced between the handrails. "Good morning, Acting Chief of Detectives Bowen," he said as Spencer Bowen passed him on his way out. Bowen nodded impertinently, didn't acknowledge Leonard's follow-up greeting.

"Must not be getting any," said Jack as he dropped into his wheelchair, unfastened the harness and slipped it into the backpack that was attached to the back of his seat.

"I believe he's married," said Leonard.

"That's my point."

"Captain wants to see you two right away," said a clerk as he walked by, balancing a pile of file folders.

Jack rolled into Captain Rogers's office, followed by Leonard. Rogers lifted his head slightly, then went back to reading the report on his desk. Jack yawned as Leonard sat down in a chair across from the Captain's desk and picked up a newspaper.

"Put that down, Funk," said Rogers. He pushed the file aside and rubbed the back of his neck. His tie was loosened and the short sleeves of his dress shirt were already damp with perspiration. He leaned back, lit a cigarette, took a puff, exhaled. "You two are off the Marcus murder."

"What?" said Jack and Leonard, simultaneously.

"It's a numbers game. We've got nearly two thirds of the department on it and we've got other work to do. I'm sorry."

Leonard shook his head, stared at his feet. Jack felt the veins in his neck inflate, his jaws clench. "That's bullshit and you know it."

"What did you say, Taylor?"

"I said that's bullshit and you know it. Don't try to feed me that crap."

Rogers took another puff and looked at the ceiling. He held the pose for a moment, then ground out the cigarette in an ashtray and looked straight at Jack. "Your manners need a lot of work, Jack. The mayor's office wants you off the case. They don't want to be second-guessed. This is the murder of a prominent citizen and there's gonna be scrutiny. They're afraid if you're involved, there will be the wrong kind of attention."

"But I'm the best that you've got, Dan, and you know it."

"I do know it. I also know that this case is already solved. It was one of Sam Giancana's boys. We've got a lot of other cases that aren't so easy to figure out. Yeah, I'm under orders from the mayor, but I also want these other cases solved."

Leonard interrupted. "If you're so sure that Giancana is involved, then that's more the reason to keep us on. Nobody knows him or his operation like we do, and if we can connect him to the murder, then we may be able to send him to prison."

"Nice try, Funk. You know as well as I do there's no way we'll ever tie him to the murder. We're bringing him in for questioning, but I'm not holding my breath."

"Any other reasons, Captain?" asked Jack.

"The mayor also thinks that this might be too personal for you."

Jack fought rage. "You mean Spencer Bowen thinks it might be too personal for me? Why, because Giancana's the reason that I'm in this chair? You think that might affect my reasoning?"

"You're already making me glad that you're off this case, Taylor. Just talking about it and you're ready to blow. Now, I've given you all of the time on this that I'm gonna. Go get the file on last night's murder from Andy Scott and get started."

Jack rolled out the door, steaming. Funk stopped in the doorway, couldn't resist. "What type of case so vitally needs our attention?"

"Hooker snuff."

Jack rolled toward his office, digested "Hooker snuff." He spun around the corner, nearly ran into a fat man, offered an inaudible apology and almost missed the man's words as he mumbled, "You want something on Sam Giancana, maybe we can help each other."

Jack stopped in his tracks, grabbed the man's sleeve, motioned toward his office and put a finger to his lips. "Shhhhh."

The lunch crowd always surprised Al. They didn't offer much more than cold sandwiches and burgers, but the tavern always drew a nice crowd. He finished sweeping behind the bar, tapped another keg of beer, grabbed a couple of burgers and some fries and sat down across from his uncle in a corner booth.

"So you've earned your month's pay again, I see," said his uncle as Al gave him a plate of food.

"I'm co-owner and assistant manager, so I've got to do something," said Al. "But you should be happy that I come in here. I never even stop in anymore at Roxies," he said.

"So what did Tommy Spector say about his arrest last week?" asked Pat between bites.

"He thinks it was a fluke. There was nobody else there and the cops didn't make much of it. They didn't try to answer phones or anything. They just cleaned out the rest of the stuff and busted him. He thinks maybe one of the neighbors thought that the apartment hadn't been rented and that a bunch of us had broken in and were using it for free."

Pat shook his head. "Nonsense. Have you checked any other possible leaks? Your phone guys, Old Bones?"

Al's stomach went queasy. "Yeah. They're all fine. I don't buy his version either, but it wasn't that big of a deal. If somebody really wanted to screw me, they would've busted the place when we were all there and the lines were humming."

"What do you think happened?" asked Pat, taking a swig of beer and wiping the corners of his mouth with a napkin.

"There's a lot happening and I think it was somehow connected. Think about it: first I get middled, then Tommy Spector gets busted, then this banker gets murdered."

Pat interrupted. "What the hell does some banker's murder have to do with you?"

"Nothing and everything," said Al, repeating Burt Cordell's line. "It was a message to a whole bunch of guys, not just me. The message said, 'You fuck with us, you wind up dead.' That's why we got busted—to send a message. The message for me was, 'We protect you and we can stop at any time.'"

"Who was sending that message and why?"

Al put his elbows on the table and put his face in his hands, rubbing his forehead. "Here's the way I figure it. Angelo's trying to work his way up the ladder. When I got middled, he came to me and offered to bankroll me. He was shocked when I didn't accept. But that also told him something. It told him that I could afford it and that I could still operate. You get where I'm heading?"

Pat nodded. "He thinks that you're making too much money. He realized that if you could get hit that hard and still operate, then they're missing an opportunity."

Al opened his hands in emphasis. "Right. Now how can Angelo impress Momo? Make him more money. He figures that I'm making a lot of money, so if he can force me to be dependent on them, or better yet, get me in the hole, then he can make more money off of me."

"You'd better be careful, son," said Pat thoughtfully. "The next message might be stated a little more clearly. Have you any idea what you're going to do?"

"I've got some ideas, Uncle. Don't worry about me. As long as I pay the street tax and play the game right, they won't kill me. A good bookie's clients are hard to maintain and they know it. They kill me, they lose all of my clients. No, as long as I play along, I'll be okay."

"You've given me no better answer than I could've made up myself," said Pat, frustration crossing his face. "What are you going to do?"

"I've got some time. The newspaper said that Momo's in hiding, and I can't imagine that Angelo's gonna put any more pressure on me until this whole banker thing blows over. I'll bide my time for a while, but I'm thinking of some things."

"Well, I hope that you'll be kind enough to fill me in when you make up your mind. I made book and ran a Chicago wheel for over forty-seven years, and I had more than my share of run-ins with the boys. I may be a seventy-three-year-old saloon keeper in your mind, but I've a wealth of experience. So, when you decide to open up, look me back up."

Al flashed on Vic's basement.

Pat got up to leave and he grabbed his arm. "Pat, don't be like that. I haven't made any definite plans, and I'll come to you before I do, but right now, it's best if I keep some things to myself. It's just like handicapping, remember? If you start looking for everyone's opinion, pretty soon you outthink yourself."

"Now, you've got me more worried than ever," said Pat, leaning over the table.

"Why?"

"Because you're beginning to talk like a bettor."

Roxies was jammed. B-girls clung to men, coaxing them into buying more drinks; men dressed in suits and ties guzzled twenty-five-cent beers and paid seventy-five cents for bad whiskey. Don Hansen and Herb Bradley looked over the Lip's shoulders as he threw the dice, halfway through a game of 26.

"I still don't get it," said Bradley.

Hansen shook his head, noticed a hot mixess behind the bar. He smiled and raised an eyebrow, then turned to Bradley. "Get this—his point is five. The player gets ten dice and has thirteen rolls or a hundred and thirty chances to hit his point twenty-six times. If he hits it twenty-six times or more, then he's paid a dollar for every twenty-five cents. If he hits it thirty-three times or more, then he gets paid two dollars for every quarter bet. If he hits it less than eleven times, he gets paid a buck for every quarter, and if he hits it thirteen times, then he gets fifty cents for a quarter bet. But, and it's a big but, if he hits it twelve times or between fourteen and twenty-five times, then he loses the bet."

"How many times has the Lip hit five?"

"He's hit it nineteen times and he has two rolls left."

The Lip shook the dice in his hand, nodded to the dice girl, and flung the dice down the table. They kissed, caromed off the end of the table and came to rest: four dice settled with five spots showing. "Yeah!" yelled the Lip.

"Player has twenty-three. He needs at least three fives on this last roll," said the dice girl as she scooped up the dice and pushed them to him.

The Lip rolled his head, stretching his neck. "C'mon baby," he said as he flung the dice again. This time they crashed into the far end of the table, jumped back nearly a foot, and stopped. "Shit!" yelled the Lip. No fives showed.

"Sorry," said the dice girl as she passed the dice to the next shooter.

The Lip threw an arm around Hansen and Bradley. "Let's belly up to the bar. If that's the worst thing that happens to me over the next few days, then I'm a lucky man."

The rectangular bar stood in the middle of the room. Patrons ringed it and four bartenders worked from the center; bottles of scotch, bourbon, whiskey, and vodka were stacked on shelves, glistening under the lights of the bar. The rest of the room was dark and smoky. The Lip pulled three cigars from his breast pocket and handed them out. Don Hansen leaned over the bar, caught the eye of the bartender, and waved her over.

"What do you suggest tonight?" asked Hansen, brushing his white hair back.

"What are you in the mood for?" asked the bartender.

"That's a loaded question."

"Are you a loaded patron?"

Hansen laughed. "The mixess is quite clever."

"The mixter has a long way to go."

The Lip interrupted. "Three boilermakers, Canadian Ace."

The bartender nodded and went to fill the order. "She's not bad," said Hansen. "I have to give credit to the management."

"Give credit where it's due," said the Lip. "Al owns this joint and he knows the secrets to running a good club: great cooze gets them in, cold booze keeps them in."

"Your buddy Al the bookie owns this place?" asked Hansen.

"Yeah, this and a piece of his Uncle Pat's place."

Herb Bradley cut in. "Maybe we shouldn't be here. It wouldn't look good if you ran into him."

"Never happen," said the Lip, puffing on his cigar. "He's a fucking hermit, never goes out. We've got a better chance of running into President Eisenhower."

"Then why did you pick this place?" asked Hansen as he accepted their drinks from the bartender. He threw four singles onto the bar, told her to keep the change. Her look said it all, sarcastic, "Thanks, big spender."

"I don't know," said the Lip. "I guess I just felt like checking out the old haunts."

The Lip held his shot high. "Here's to a sellout."

They dropped the whiskey into their mugs of beer and quickly chugged the frothing mixture. Herb Bradley didn't quite finish his, held the glass up high again, and said, "Here's to a great fight."

The Lip grabbed his arm before he could swill. "Drink it down, Herb, but remember this, it's not the size of the tiger in the fight and it's not the size of the fight in the tiger. It's the size of the crowd at the fight."

They all laughed. Bradley tried to finish his drink, spilled most of it down his chin.

"What all have we got to do between now and the fight, Lip?" asked Bradley, wiping his chin with his coat sleeve.

"A lot. First of all, you're responsible for keeping us in the press. I want feature articles every day, and get Tomcat on the radio. Also, I want press at the weigh-ins and all of the fighters' measurements, weights and records published the day of the fight. People eat that shit up." He turned to Don Hansen. "You and I have got to call all of the fighters' managers on the under-card and make sure they're set. Have you got the boys to set up the ring?"

"Sure," said Hansen.

He tried to continue, but the Lip interrupted. "And make sure the ring girls are stacked. We're getting them from Trocadero, but that wop manager may try to hold out on us. In fact, make sure that a couple of them lose their tops between rounds. It won't hurt us for future fights."

"There are nudity laws," said Bradley.

Hansen nodded toward the doorway, smiled. "And you may not have to worry about future fights."

"What?" asked the Lip, turning to face the door.

A tall, lanky bouncer pushed a dark figure. The figure didn't budge. The Lip jumped off of his stool and charged through the crowd like a rhino. "Get the fuck out of my way," he yelled as he pushed two men to the side. They turned in anger, thought better when they gauged his size. He made his way to the front door and grabbed the bouncer by the back of the hair. "You got a problem up here, buddy?"

The bouncer tried to spin, saw that the Lip was bigger and obviously stronger. "Mister, you don't let go of my hair, you're gonna regret it."

"I do let go of your hair, you're gonna regret it. The man that you're hassling here is about to become the next heavyweight champion of the world. I let go of you, he's liable to warm up with you."

The bouncer went limp; fear made his voice quiver. "We can't let him in here, you should know that." He looked at Junior: hat pulled down near his eyes, scarf wrapped around his neck, wool topcoat popping like he wore shoulder pads.

The Lip let go of the man, pushed him into the wall. "You've got a room on the second floor, behind the liquor closet. We're going back there."

"How did . . . ?" The bouncer stopped, realized that if the Lip knew about the back room, he didn't want to know how.

"Make it quick, and let him out the back door when you're done."

The Lip grabbed Junior's shoulder, led him through the bar, up the stairs, and into the back room. Once inside the room, he locked the door, sat down on the couch. Junior stood, hands in his pockets.

"What are you doing here, Junior?"

Junior lowered his head. "I went by your hotel. The lady there told me you was here; said she was sorry for what happened."

"I didn't ask how you knew I was here, I asked what you're doing here."

Junior stood up straight, looked the Lip in the eye. "Me and you been due for a talk for a while."

The Lip returned the stare, crossed his legs, and put out his cigar in an ashtray on the end table. He stared at the ashtray, let his eyes slowly walk toward Junior. The first things that he saw were his shoes: tan, leather work boots—steel toes jutting through worn leather. His eyes worked their way up, didn't notice any bulges shrieking "gun," caught Junior's eyes and couldn't find fear. "What's on your mind, Junior?"

"I know what you was doing with me and that woman. You just trying to sell tickets. I'm no dummy."

"I don't know what you're talking about."

Junior took two steps forward, pulled his hands out of his pockets. The Lip leaned back into the couch, knew that if Junior came at him his only chance would be to wrestle the big Negro to the ground. He was a bit heavier than Junior and just as strong, but he'd never match his quickness. He'd seen enough of Junior in the ring. If he wanted to, Junior could beat him to death with his fists.

"Are you coming at me, Junior?"

Junior shrugged. "No. I need a favor from you, but I want you to know that I'm no dummy. I got things figured out. I just know that the more tickets that sell, the more money I get."

The Lip let out his breath. "That's right. Everything that I've done is for us. I don't think you're a dummy. That's why I won't tell you that everything that I've done is for you. If it didn't benefit me, then I wouldn't be doing it. But that's the beauty of our relationship: our interests are aligned. Anything that I do that benefits me also benefits you."

Junior snorted. "You tell that same thing to my uncle?"

The Lip's eyes went narrow. "You got something to say?"

"Willie told me what he heard 'bout you and my uncle. But you know what? I didn't care. I never believed you two years ago when you told me that you and my uncle was friends. My uncle never gave a hoot about me when he was out of prison, so why would he change when he was inside? All I believed was that you could get me fights that Willie and his friends couldn't. Any fool can see that colored fighters mostly fight other colored fighters. So, Mr. Lipranski, I needed you to get me fights, and that's it. But things gonna change when I win this one."

The Lip sat up, body tingling. "How's that?"

"I win this fight, all of the big promoters gonna want me. I won't need you, you gonna need me."

The Lip stood up. "Listen, kid. I don't know what's on your mind, but we're a great team. We're looking at a sellout! Can you believe that, a non-championship fight and it's going to sell out! Nobody else could've done that for you, nobody!"

The Lip started to pace. Junior leaned against the wall, wrinkled his brow. "How much money do you figure I'm gonna make, including all of the money that you owe me?"

The Lip stopped, thought. "If it sells out, you could make nearly a hundred thousand. That's before taxes and paying Willie and your entourage. Realistically, you'll take home about thirty thousand. That's more money than a lot of guys make in their entire life and one hell of a lot more than you ever would've made without me."

Junior bit his upper lip. "You want to keep promotin' me after this fight?"

"Of course."

"Then there's one thing I need you to do for me."

The Lip stepped closer. "What?"

"I want you to put a bet on me."

The Lip laughed. Relief. "Sure, kid. Is that all that you wanted? You didn't need to go through all of that just to get me to put a bet on you. How much do you want? A grand or two? Consider it done."

"All of it."

The Lip blinked rapidly, shook his head. "All of what?"

"All of it. Put thirty thousand on me."

The Lip stared at Junior. He couldn't speak. Thirty thousand dollars! More than he had. Betting on credit would be nearly impossible.

"That's a hell of a lot of money, kid. What if you get hurt or he slips in a lucky punch?"

"Ain't gonna happen. All of it. On me."

Only one way. He had to do it. His voice was nearly inaudible. "Sure, kid. Anything you say. But this squares us. You're with me for the long run. I'll have a contract drawn up—you've gotta sign."

Junior nodded.

They went out the door and down the back steps. The door opened to an alley behind the bar and when they stepped outside the cold night air made them both shiver.

Junior turned to leave. He walked several paces, then turned to face the Lip. "You know your way back?" asked the Lip.

"Sure," said Junior.

"Then what is it?"

Junior forced his hands into his pockets, buried his chin under the front of his jacket. "You really kill my uncle?"

The Lip stared at him, turned, walked back inside, and slammed the door behind him.

Junior jogged back toward the train. He was proud of himself for acting tough. Mr. Lipranski had actually looked worried when he stepped toward him! He hadn't known how scared Junior had been. Damn, Junior thought, maybe that was how everybody else did it. They was scared, but just acted tough. Funny thing was, Mr. Lipranski'd never know that he wasn't afraid of fighting him, wasn't afraid of *what* he'd do. The only thing that he'd been afraid of was hearing Mr. Lipranski say "No." If that would've happened, he didn't know what he'd have done. But Mr. Lipranski had said "Yes," so he was set. Now all he had to do was whip Tomcat Gordon and everything would be okay. He'd pay off Cleotis, move Mama. Money was the answer to it all.

He stopped, looked at the platform. The elevated train sat motionless. A cluster of people moved toward the open doors; their puffs of breath caught momentarily under the lights, then disappeared into the cold night air. The train started to move and he slowly walked toward it, stopped right before he reached the platform.

The train pulled away and Junior let it get a few hundred yards in front of him before he began to jog. He pulled his coat up taut near his neck, buttoned the top buttons and jammed the edges of the scarf inside the top of the coat. He slipped on the gloves that Mama had given him and concentrated on the train's taillights. Soon, his steps found a rhythm and he found himself breathing in unison with the sounds of the train.

He'd always found jogging peaceful, and that night it didn't start any differently. His arms, legs and lungs seemed to work in harmony. He stopped noticing the steps, barely felt his feet hit the ground. His thoughts wandered. Maybe that was right! Maybe other people was scared, too. Maybe they just faked it. Everybody had to have things that haunted them: things they didn't want nobody else to know. By God, Mr. Lipranski surely had things that he didn't want nobody else to know, and Wee Willie too. That's right! Wee Willie hadn't told him about his wife for years; that had to eat him up. And Mr. Lipranski sure didn't tell him everything about Uncle Henry. No, seemed like everybody had secrets. He had a secret and nobody would have to know. The money would solve that. Kansas City could stay buried. Forever. He flashed on it, for the last time.

It was a big fight, his first fight against a white man. He wasn't supposed to win; even Lipranski had been nervous. But someone forgot to tell Junior, and he'd knocked the man out two minutes into the seventh round.

Later that night, Cleotis, Rae and a group of people that he didn't know. A party at an apartment in the bottoms; booze, smack, and ladies dressed for the night. He tried to convince himself that he'd gone to watch after Rae, but he was still high from the fight and didn't want the night to end.

Cleotis had handed him his first drink. It was sweet but hard, and everyone had laughed when he gagged. The second one hadn't been much better, but they got easier as the night wore on.

Cleotis wasn't such a bad guy after all. He kept telling people how great Junior had been, knocking out the white man in front of the white crowd. "Was a man, tonight," he kept saying. "Was a man tonight!"

Everyone in bright colors, needles and reefer floating around the room. Rae and the others jabbed right in front of him, swayed to the music. Sweet Mary Jane! Nobody seemed to mind that he wouldn't touch any.

A pretty girl in a yellow dress, lips shining, lipstick stains on her teeth. "C'mon, baby, c'mon." A back room, he felt her push him inside. Darkness, he stumbled onto the bed. A figure came to him. Lips, hands, a tongue: a woman. His hands all over her, hers unzipping him. Her hips rose, cotton brushed against him. Heat. Good heat. He fell into motion.

So this is what it's like. Must be doing it right, she's panting, moving.

He roared. The door opened. The lights came on. Cleotis looked at him. He looked at the bed.

"And I thought I was in the wrong room," said Cleotis as Junior screamed.

• • •

It was nearly 4:00 A.M. and Wee Willie and Aaron Green stood out-side the motel, bundled in heavy coats, eyes peeled toward the road.

"This just ain't like the Hammer," said Aaron.

"Ain't nothing like that boy," said Wee Willie, looping an arm over Aaron's shoulder. "That boy's got some problems; a lot to learn."

"What kind of problems?"

"I'm not exactly sure. He don't tell nobody, but you can see 'em coming out."

"I wish there was something we could," said Aaron. "I like him. He's not only a great fighter, he's really nice."

"Maybe that's part of it, boy, me trying to turn a nice boy into a fighter."

"No," said Aaron, pulling free and turning to face Willie. "You're a nice man and you were a great fighter!"

Wee Willie sighed, started to say something, stopped. Aaron's eyes were as wide as china plates, "Hammer!" he screamed.

Willie turned quickly, saw the figure buckle against the motel sign. They ran to him. Aaron fell to the ground and threw his arms around him. "Hammer, you shouldn't have done that. Where've you been?"

Junior looked at Aaron, then up at Wee Willie. He couldn't speak. He dropped his head back and gulped air.

"Help me get him to his feet," said Wee Willie.

They started to lift Junior, heard him shriek as he got to his feet. Then they noticed them: his work boots, tan, leather, steel toes pop-ping out, *sopped in blood.*

"Climb up under his other arm, Aaron," said Wee Willie as he draped Junior's right arm over his shoulder. "We'll get him inside and get them boots off."

"Jesus, Hammer, you had us scared. How far you run?" asked Aaron.

"Don't . . . know . . ." said Junior, between breaths.

"Where were you?" asked Aaron.

"Down . . . town . . ."

Wee Willie nearly stopped. Downtown. Nearly fifteen miles. A ten-mile run in the morning, four hours of exercises, sparring, bag work and then a fifteen-mile run at night! Madness!

They helped Junior into bed, slipped off his shoes, washed and bandaged his feet. They were cut and swollen and the steel insert in the front of the boots had jammed his toes back into their sockets. He'd be lucky if his feet healed at all before the fight. But that wasn't what Wee Willie was worried about. He helped Junior undress, sponged him off quickly with a washcloth, and then turned off the lights. He stood in the doorway one last moment, looked at Junior and wondered if he would survive the fight.

Leonard Funk set the sandwich, potato chips, and soda pop on the folding table next to Jack and pulled up a folding chair. Jack sat staring out a window: the blinds open just enough so that he could see anyone coming or going across the street.

"Why don't you eat your sandwich, Jack, and I'll take over for a while," said Leonard.

Jack turned, saw Leonard's mouth moving and took off the headset. "What did you say?"

"I said, why don't you eat your sandwich and I'll take over for a while."

"Better yet, I'll eat the sandwich with the headphones on and you can do the same with that other pair."

Leonard realized that arguing was pointless. He put on the headphones and started to eat his sandwich. There was no conversation on the line that he was hooked into, so he reflected on their morning. Jack had called him pre-6:00 A.M. and told him that he'd called in sick and that Leonard should be prepared to report in a bit late; they had something to do. Jack had prepped him on the way: the fat man that had stopped him on the way out of Captain Rogers's office was named Jerry Pinkley. He ran an exterminating business and his partner had disappeared. Pinkley knew that it wasn't a revolution by the roaches, so he thought that the disappearance might have something to do with their side job—hooking up telephones for a bookie named Al Kelly. Pinkley was sure that Kelly had nothing to do with his partner's disappearance, but knew how the game was played: Kelly answered to somebody and that somebody answered to Sam Giancana.

"That's our play," Jack had said. "This guy Jerry said that he could hook us into the phones that he hooked up for the bookie. We're patched into any calls on the line, incoming or outgoing. It's a long shot, but who knows? Maybe we'll hear something about this guy Tom or the banker, Marcus."

Leonard had tried to reason with Jack, told him that they'd never pin anything on Giancana, because he always delegated. He'd suggested that they arrest the bookie, attempt to coerce his assistance. Jack had laughed. "What would we do?" he'd asked. "Arrest him because he didn't pay fifty dollars for a gambling stamp, failed to report the address of his business and turn over ten percent of his gross receipts? C'mon, Leonard. They've put out an APB on Giancana, and he'll eventually turn himself in. I want to listen in on this guy to see if we can bring Momo in before he turns himself in."

Leonard had resisted, said that it was a one-in-a-million shot. Jack's retort was priceless: "That's why we do it. Something about listening in on a bookie with only a one-in-a-million shot at hearing something worthwhile appeals to my sense of irony."

Jack used a mop handle to push the blinds open a bit further, then let them fall back into place. "You don't need to hang around here, Leonard. There's only a couple of fights tonight, so I don't suppose they'll have anybody on these lines for a while."

"Have you heard any conversations yet?" asked Leonard as he gathered the wrappers from their sandwiches and put them inside the bag.

"I think there's only one guy there. He called somebody a while ago and told him not to forget the salami. I guess they're figuring on a long night. Anything on that hooker snuff?"

"They still haven't been able to identify her, but one of the officers that discovered her thinks that she goes by the street name of Lucy. If it's her, then she works his beat, which encompasses the South Loop."

"What happened to her?"

"They found her in an alley with her throat cut. No purse, panties missing."

"A john rob her?"

"Maybe. More likely her pimp, wanted to make it look like a robbery. You know the statistics: if a married woman is murdered, chances are that it's her husband. If a prostitute is killed, chances are it's her pimp."

"Anything else on the Marcus murder?" asked Jack as he clasped his hands behind his head and then stretched his arms.

"They're having trouble finding the key to his safe deposit box and a so-called 'mystery room' adjoining his office on the second floor of the bank building."

Jack snorted. "And we're put on a hooker snuff. That still galls me. I promise you, someday I'm gonna bring Sam Giancana in. There's a big difference between him and Tony Accardo. Tony stayed as far away as possible; Momo gets too close to the flame."

"Well, if it's any consolation," said Leonard, "I think that we'll solve our case before anyone solves Mr. Marcus's murder."

"That and a new set of legs will get me a promotion," cracked Jack. "Now get on out of here. It's bad enough that I'm wasting the department's time here. You shouldn't be doing the same. No sense in both of us getting canned if they ever find out that I've got an illegal wiretap going."

Leonard rose, gave Jack a solemn look. "Are you sure that you know what you're doing?"

"Yeah," said Jack as picked up a headset. "I'm playing a hunch."

"You won't go over there alone?"

"Their room's on the second floor; I don't think I'd quite make it."

"And you'll be all right here, just sitting here, all by yourself, listening for God knows what?"

"Leonard," said Jack as he slipped the headset over his ears. "It's what I do every day."

Thursday, April 4

Al set his newspaper on the counter and walked back into his bedroom. He picked out a pair of gray slacks, white shirt, hand-painted tie and a houndstooth jacket and took his time putting them on—in no big hurry to get to the office.

The headlines screamed that the police were looking for Momo. That didn't make anything any easier. If Momo was in hiding, then Angelo would try and solidify his position and impress Giancana. That meant that the young mobster would do his best to drive him into a hole, and Al knew that meant trouble.

So far, no problems. He'd made a bit last night on fights out on the East Coast. He'd started to get some action on the fight: Junior an eight-to-five favorite to start; early money playing up Tomcat. Al had laughed when Pete Barnes told him that the early money favored Tomcat. He could've told him that before the phones ever started to ring; the real hate money always came in early.

The phone rang and Al picked it up on the third ring. "Yeah," he said. "Yeah, tell him I'll be right down." Poochie: probably begging to keep his account open.

A quick check of the time; four o'clock—time to head in. He grabbed a hat and topcoat from the hall closet, locked the door behind him, and headed to the elevator.

Poochie was waiting for him as Al walked out into the lobby. "Al, I hadda come by," he said, his wheezy voice sounding like a prolonged cough. "I got a few things I wanna talk over."

Al stepped out the front door, Poochie following. "Your account, Pooch?"

"Yeah."

"You're down sixteen thousand seven hundred now. That's the fourteen five you owed me and a twenty-two-hundred-dollar loss on Michigan State. What are you planning on doing?"

Poochie walked over and sat down on a bench at the corner bus stop. He motioned Al over. "I've got a whole shipment of cigars and cigarettes coming in this week. Primo cigars. My best sellers. I swear to you, by month's end, I'll pay up."

"By month's end? That's almost thirty days away, Poochie," hissed Al. "I'm taking a lot of grief for carrying you this far. Your limit was supposed to be seventy-five hundred and you've doubled that."

"C'mon, Al. You know I'm good for it," said Poochie, slapping Al's knee. His red nose ran, so he grabbed a handkerchief from his breast pocket and blew. "Just let me bet this fight. I win, I'll keep playing. I lose, I'll pay up and I'll quit."

"Now you're talking," said Al. He returned Poochie's slap to the leg. "You think I'm a great guy for letting you keep playing, but I'm not. I've got to tell you, the only reason a bookie lets a guy keep playing is because he's losing and we all know that sooner or later you're gonna pay."

Poochie shook his head vehemently. "No, Al, that ain't you. You let me keep betting 'cause you're a great guy. Hey, I'm bound to win some of it back!"

"No, you're not. There isn't any taking turns. The odds say that you don't ever have to win. All they say is that sometimes the favorite wins, sometimes the underdog wins, but there's no guarantee that you'll ever be on the winning side."

"Quit talking like that, Al. I know that you think you're looking out for me, but I can take care of myself. Shit, I'll let you in on a little secret. That colored fighter, Hamilton, his manager's a customer of mine. Good-looking white-haired guy, does great with the cooze. Anyway, he's ordering a box of his favorite maduros the other day and we started talking. He lays it on me: the Hamilton kid's a lock. He says he's betting everything he's got 'cause this kid's gonna kill that Tomcat Gordon. So there, Al, you remember you heard it from me first."

Al looked off into the distance, saw that the lake was angry; a storm was brewing. He turned to Poochie. "Yeah, thanks for the tip, Pooch. You can bet this fight. You win, I'll let you keep playing. You lose, you're done."

Poochie clapped him on the back. "Thanks, Al. I appreciate it. And watch for that Hamilton kid. He's a friggin' lock. A lock, I tell you."

They stood up and walked toward the parking lot. Poochie grabbed Al's arm and ushered him around the corner toward the back stalls. "I've got something to show you, Al, but I don't want you to be pissed. I ordered it before I hit this losing streak."

Curiosity bit. "What is it, Pooch?" asked Al.

Poochie guided him to the far side of the lot, lifted his finger and pointed. "There she is!" he yelled. He took out the keys out of his pocket, got in the driver's-side door, rolled down the window and yelled to Al as he backed out of the stall. "She's a beaut, eh?"

"She's a beaut, all right," said Al, trying to hide the sarcasm as he slowly shook his head.

"Can I give you a lift somewhere?"

Al motioned him away. "No, Sandy's on his way."

Al shook his head, closed his eyes and slowly opened them. No, it was no aberration. He fought a laugh, and instead watched, solemnly, as Poochie drove away, waving like mad from his brand-new, lime-green Edsel.

The Lip sat hunched over the coffee table in his hotel room. He ran down the checklist again, making sure that he'd accounted for everything. He muttered as he put a check mark next to each item. "Called the managers for all of the prelims; weigh-ins set for Friday at five thirty; doctor ringside—make sure to introduce him to the Judge; ring girls set; crew confirmed to put up ring, check on 'Robert J. Lipranski Productions' for the canvas." He stopped for a moment and laughed as a thought came to him. "Pure fucking genius. Have Herb Bradley plant a story that says I shaved my head to symbolize the struggle of the American Negro."

He laughed again and rocked back into his chair. The phone rang and he grabbed it. "Robert J. Lipranski Productions. Yes, Ramon, who is it?" The bartender, somebody wanted to see him. "Send them up. No, then what room? Is everything kosher? Okay."

Someone to see him in room 714. Probably the Judge or Gilda, playing out a fantasy. He settled on Gilda, straightened his tie, ignored the sportcoat, and left the room.

A quick elevator ride and a knock on the door of 714. That crazy bastard Vic D'Antonio answered the door, motioned the Lip inside. Three steps in he felt nauseous: Angelo Carpacci, Reg Lewis, and Lincoln Johnson, together. The syndicate and the powerful blacks together. It couldn't get worse. It was about to.

Lincoln Johnson rose up off the couch and offered a hand. "Mr. Lipranski," he said. "Thank you for coming to see us on short notice." He nodded toward Reg Lewis. "You remember Mr. Lewis."

"Sure," said the Lip as he gave Lewis a brief handshake.

"And it seems that we have a mutual friend—Mr. Carpacci."

Angelo laughed. "Nice haircut, Lip. The barber pissed off because you couldn't pay him?" Angelo and Vic laughed. The Lip ignored it. "What is this?" he asked no one in particular.

"This," said Lincoln Johnson as he sat back down on the couch, "is a meeting." His weight caused the couch's cushions to curl up around him. "Why else would we all be sitting here in suit and tie, waiting on you?"

"I don't know," said the Lip, "and that's what bothers me. What are you doing here and what does it have to do with these guys?" He pointed to Angelo and Vic.

"It seems like we may have a problem," said Lincoln Johnson. He looked at Angelo, who sat, legs crossed, twirling his pinkie ring. "A mutual friend introduced Mr. Carpacci and me, and it seems that we both have an interest in you."

The Lip's nostrils flared and he cracked his neck. "My business with Angelo is in the past."

"Your business may be," said Angelo, looking up, "but your payment isn't."

"You see," continued Johnson. "That's the problem. Mr. Carpacci and I have compared notes, and it seems that you owe him seventy thousand dollars, and, ironically, since you have done such a splendid job of promoting this fight, you may also wind up owing me a little over seventy thousand dollars."

The Lip looked around the suite, found an empty chair, pulled it over and sat down. Reg Lewis poured a glass of water and handed it to him. "Thanks," said the Lip as he accepted the water and tipped the glass. He bought a moment, played his options. A sellout meant a little over $70,000 for Johnson, only around $48,000 for him. That left him short on paying off Angelo. Obviously, Angelo was using him to leverage in. Where could he fit in? Easy answer, he couldn't. Play them against each other, stall for answers.

"I can't believe that you'd fall for that crap," said the Lip, staring at Lincoln Johnson. "I can't believe that you would even listen to his kind."

"What do you mean by that?" said Vic D'Antonio.

Angelo sneered. "Don't listen to him, Vic, he's just trying to get you burned up. He don't mean nothing."

"Sure, I do, Angelo," said the Lip. "I'm trying to do something for the black community, and these two can ruin it by bringing you in. I guess they've forgotten what your people did to Teddy Roe and the Jones brothers."

"You're out of line," said Vic D'Antonio. He lurched forward but Angelo grabbed his arm.

Angelo pushed Vic back toward his stool and turned to face the Lip. "I'd almost rather pay to see you two go at it. You've got to be in the two hundred fifty range, and Vic's a big guy. So what is it, big guy, you think you can talk us out of the room? You're wrong. Mr. Johnson and I have already held our discussions and we've made some decisions. Isn't that right, Mr. Johnson?"

"You are oh so correct, Mr. Carpacci," said Lincoln Johnson jovially. "But I can't help getting quite a kick out of Mr. Lipranski. It seems that he thinks that he can rile us up by bringing up the not-so-distant past, but he's missing the point. We're smart enough to learn from the past! Our acquaintances didn't take the time to find those points that would lead to a mutually beneficial business relationship. They spent too much time worrying about their differences. We, on the other hand, are less worried about our differences and more worried about finding profitable ventures."

Johnson clapped his hands together and slipped forward on the couch. "The problem here is that Mr. Lipranski is afraid that we're here to infringe upon his fight. Our job is to explain to him in non-threatening terms that we're only here to enhance his business interests. So, Mr. Carpacci, let's do it. Reg, run down the hall and grab us some sodas."

Reg Lewis shot him a perturbed glance and headed for the door. "Yeah, go with him, Vic," added Angelo.

Reg and Vic snorted and left the room. "Now," said Lincoln Johnson, "let's get down to business. Even if the fight is a sellout, you're going to wind up on the short end. It's impossible for you to pay back both Mr. Carpacci and myself. We've discussed it, and neither of us finds payment at a later date acceptable. So, do you have a solution?"

"No," said the Lip, leaning back into the chair. "But I imagine that you do."

"You're absolutely correct," added Johnson. "However, as I said before, it's our goal to find a mutually acceptable resolution to our problems. In that regard, I believe, we have been successful. Mr. Carpacci."

"Junior's gonna throw the fight," said Angelo.

The Lip nearly smacked his own palm onto his forehead. No shit. He should've seen it coming. Boxing's oldest solution. Problems: keeping it from Wee Willie, the Judge; convincing Junior. "It can't be done," sighed the Lip. "Neither Junior or his trainer will go for it."

"I thought your guy Hansen was his manager?" asked Angelo, agitated.

"He is, but only on paper. I choreograph Junior's moves, Willie Green is his trainer. He'll never go for it and neither will Junior."

"What makes you so sure?" asked Lincoln Johnson.

"Green is a fight guy. He's waited all of his life to train a champion, and Junior, well, let's just say he marches to his own drummer."

"There," said Johnson. "You've provided your own answers. If this Green wants a championship bad enough, he'll recognize that if they don't throw this fight, they'll never get the shot. It sounds like you're telling me that the Hamilton boy is a simpleton. How hard can he be to deal with?"

Angelo cut in. "No, I know what's going on here, Mr. Johnson. The Lip always wants to know what's in it for him. Just like in the pen, he was always looking out for himself."

The Lip glared. "If that's the way you see it, what is in it for me?"

Johnson laughed. "Now we're getting somewhere. If you can guarantee the outcome of this fight, I am willing to drop my cut to ten percent. That should leave you enough to pay back Mr. Carpacci."

"What are you kicking in?" asked the Lip, staring at Angelo.

"If you're asking me if I'm forgiving the seventy large, the answer is no. But, there's a lot that you can do if you know the outcome of a fight. Isn't your best friend a bookie?"

He felt beads of sweat pop on his scalp. Al. Shit, could he do it? No choices now, only answers designed to get out of the room alive. The Lip rocked, lifted a brow, couldn't help himself. "I should've figured that you cocksuckers would want to muscle in on my fight. Say Junior throws the fight; what about your coon parade?"

Lincoln Johnson lost his smile, snarled. "No one ever bothered to tell you that you didn't get your nickname because you're loquacious; you got it because you don't know when to keep your big mouth shut. Junior will still fight an exhibition in the park. You'll just have to convince him to fight well enough that people can see some promise in him. And since you've caused me to drop my cloak of respectability, I'll give it to you straight. If Junior Hamilton doesn't throw that fight, Mr. Carpacci and I are going to draw straws to see who gets to kill you."

The Lip shrugged. "You put it that way, I guess that it won't be too hard to fix after all."

Lincoln Johnson stood up, brushed himself off, and waved a hand in front of his face. He smiled, composed. "That's more like it," he said. "In fact, I don't want to know anything else about this. Let's just watch it unfold on Saturday night. However, I do caution you that it had better look authentic—say, the eighth round. You know, I understand that the I.B.C. is going to lose their court case, and there may be room for more fight promoters. Keep that in mind, Mr. Lipranski. There may be many more opportunities for you, and it'll be nice for you to have powerful partners."

Johnson opened the door, shook hands with the Lip, and let himself out. Reg Lewis and Vic D'Antonio walked up just as he was leaving and Lewis followed him down the hall.

The Lip brushed by Angelo, pushed Vic against the wall. "Watch it!" said Vic.

"Yeah, watch it," reiterated Angelo. "You need to get along with the help. Partners, shit. You're working for me now."

Junior rolled over onto his stomach and Osbie Jones went to work. "Bet you didn't know I gave massages, too. Well, you been in the fight game as long as I have and you get pretty good at darn near everything. Never any good at keeping time, though. I'd always get caught up in the fight, forget to ring the damn bell."

Junior tried to relax. Osbie worked up and down his spine, kneaded the deep muscle in his shoulders and back. No turning back: he was risking everything on the fight. He'd beat Tomcat, damn straight.

Osbie splashed oil on his hands, rubbed it into Junior's skin. "Looks like the Hammer's nearly asleep, there," said Wee Willie, entering the locker room. "Maybe I'll take his place when he's done."

"Not hardly," muttered Osbie. "This ain't part of no employment contract. I'm just helping the Hammer relax."

"Looks like you're doing a might fine job."

Junior didn't say a word, waited for Wee Willie to continue. "Osbie, soon as you're done, I'm gonna talk to Junior a little."

"Then I'm done," said Osbie. He wiped his hands on the back of the towel that hung around Junior's waist, slapped him on the ass and walked out of the room. "Get you some sleep tonight, you hear."

"Uh huh," murmured Junior.

"Sit up on that table, Hammer," said Wee Willie as he pulled up a stool.

Junior sat up, pulled the towel tight around his waist, and glanced down at his feet. They were swollen and bandaged but weren't hurt as badly as they had originally thought. His heels were blistered and his toes had been cut, but the balls of his feet, where he spent most of his time perched in the ring, were fine.

"How're your feet feeling?" asked Wee Willie.

"They's okay. Them steel toes rubbed my toes wrong, but I'm getting around all right."

"What were you doing downtown?"

"I seen Mr. Lipranski."

Wee Willie came to attention. "Why?"

"I had to talk to him about some things. Private things."

Wee Willie shook his head. "Hammer, I'm supposed to be your trainer. You don't have anything that's too private to tell me."

"I just don't want to. It's between me and Mr. Lipranski."

Wee Willie sighed. "If that's the way it's gonna be, then that's the way it's gonna be. But what ever made you run all of the way back here?"

"Don't know. I missed the train and just started running. It wasn't so bad."

"Wasn't so bad? Your damn feet look like they was drug behind that train! Hammer," said Wee Willie, dropping his voice, "Hammer, you've got some problems, and you've got to deal with them."

Junior looked at the floor.

"Look at me," said Wee Willie. "You've got to get over whatever's eating you. You're killing yourself. Nothing's worth that."

"I'm just tired," said Junior.

"Of course you are. You fatigued yourself way too much, but you ain't been right for a couple of months now. Ever since we came back from the fight in K.C. there's been something wrong with you. Damn, boy, that was the real start of your career!"

"Well," said Junior, swinging his legs. "Maybe it's just the fight. This is a big fight for me."

"It ain't the fight. Once you get in that ring, you've got plenty of confidence. No, don't you try and bullshit me. There's something bothering you, and if you don't want to tell me, that's your business. But I'll tell you something. You better figure out what it is and figure out what to do about it, 'cause we ain't going through this again. I know you won't give up this fight, but win or lose, if you don't get hold of yourself, I'm done with you."

"You're off there, Mr. Green. Ain't nothing wrong with me. Just that I'm fighting in front of my hometown now and if I win, Mr. Lipranski says I'll get a shot at the title."

"Mr. Lipranski wouldn't know a title if a queen gave him one. Maybe you will get your shot, but what's the cost gonna be? Remember what I told you? There's a thing called giving up too much. You may get that title, but there ain't gonna be none of you left to enjoy it."

"I know what you're doing, and I'm grateful," said Junior as he slid off the table. "But I'm fine. I'm gonna go sit in the steam with the Kid for a minute."

Junior hobbled off. Wee Willie yelled after him. "Hammer, I ain't read much, but I know one thing I read: 'To thy own self be true.' You can bullshit everyone else, but don't bullshit yourself. You better deal with your problems before the fight, or they'll deal with you!"

"What've you got for the fight in Detroit?"

"Herzog's seven to five."

"Give me 'Zog ten times."

The line went dead. Jack scribbled the note: Bettor took Detroit fighter Herzog ten times at seven to five odds. If his typical bet is ten dollars, then he bet seventy dollars to make fifty.

Jack set the pen on top of the note pad and grabbed another soda from the cooler that Leonard Funk had left. There was another sandwich left and he figured that he'd eat it before Leonard showed up to pick him up around eleven o'clock.

He returned his gaze out the window. Nobody had entered or exited the apartment building since 5:00 P.M. and it was nearly 10:00 P.M. A streetlight illuminated the street and he noted that there was no space at the curb for any more cars to park.

The conversations hadn't amounted to much. Jack figured that there had been a half dozen guys in the room, each with his own phone. Four had left the building, so only two remained. One of them had to be Al. That meant that only two lines remained open. Jack breathed a sigh of relief; they'd only tapped into two lines— when six lines had been open the odds on him hearing anything worthwhile were a million to one.

A line rang and Jack returned his attention to the headset.

"Yeah."

"It's Big A."

"Hold on. Let me get Al."

Al took the phone. "A?"

"Howdy, Al. Didn't you tell me that you're posting odds on that colored kid's fight on Saturday?"

"No names, A. He's an eight to five favorite."

"Sorry, your guy used your name, so I figured you didn't care. Anyway, I'll take the white kid twenty times at my usual. Did my friend ever call you?"

"He sure did."

"Who'd he take?"

"I never pass out that information."

"Smart man, pard, but I don't think that my friend and I are. From the way he was talking, I'll venture that he bet the same thing I did, but the other way. So I bet twenty thousand on the dog at eight to five odds, but paying you twenty percent juice. So, let's see, I make twenty-five thousand six hundred on my bet if I win, but you'll have that covered with somebody else's money. And you'll find thirty-two thousand dollars on the favorite to cover my twenty-five thousand six and leave you with a nice, tidy sixty-four hundred. Damn, I'm in the wrong business!"

Laughter erupted on both ends of the line. "It ain't that easy, A. But if it wasn't worth it, you wouldn't be calling me."

"You're right. I'll talk to you in a few."

"Good-bye."

The line went dead again. Jack nearly broke the pencil in half. Damn. He'd had Al Kelly on the line and the bookie hadn't said anything. He wished that he'd been able to interrupt the conversation, yell, "Where's Sam Giancana?!"

Sixty-four thousand in juice! Jack's eyes lit up; that kind of money meant that the syndicate was definitely involved—no bookie could operate on that level without blessings and protection. He bit his lip involuntarily. He couldn't shake the feeling—he was on to something.

A knock at the back door; Leonard walked in, briefcase in hand. "Any luck?"

"Not really," answered Jack. "They're taking a little bit of action on some out-of-town fights and they're already taking action on Saturday's heavyweight fight."

"Any mention of Mr. Giancana?"

"Not a peep. But I'll tell you this; this bookie is taking in serious cabbage. He's got to be in with Momo."

"Well, it's almost eleven. Do you want to call it a night?"

"Sure," said Jack. "But I want to be back here early tomorrow. You mind picking me up around five?"

Leonard shook his head. "I knew we should have fashioned a cot for you. Five it is."

Jack took off the headset and grabbed the sandwich from the cooler and set it in his lap. Leonard grabbed the cooler and they headed toward the back door.

Leonard reached in front of Jack and pulled open the door. Jack rammed his chair forward and the front wheels skipped over the doorsill. He pushed the wheels forward and rolled toward the van, stopped and turned back to Leonard. "Do you think that I take this too personally, Leonard?"

"How can one take one's job too personally? You were severely injured and attribute that to a syndicate kingpin. It's only right that you want to bring him in."

"That's the problem," said Jack, wheeling himself up the ramp.

"What?"

"I don't want to bring him in. I want to kill him."

Friday, April 5

His reading glasses slipped down his nose. Al pushed them back up and concentrated on the figures on the paper in front of him. He sat on a stool at his kitchen counter, a legal pad with notes and figures in front of him. The figures proved it: If a family of four could get by on $5,000 per year, he should be able to live for at least twenty years on what he had in the safe deposit box alone. Add in the money that he could get for selling Roxies and a little stipend each month from Pat for the income from the tavern, and he should be set. Two final, major nights: Junior Hamilton's Saturday night fight with Tomcat Gordon and the May 1 matchup between Sugar Ray Robinson and Gene Fullmer. Five hundred thousand in bets with a 4.5 percent hold added another $22,500 to his retirement fund. Barring a catastrophe, just over thirty days until Florida.

He wished that he could go to the bank, but the morning paper still blared the Marcus murder. The cops were still sifting through papers at the bank and had finally gotten into his secret room and safe deposit box the day before. Paperwork confirmed the loan to Momo, but smelled funny. The newspapers responded by putting his name in three-inch headlines. Not good for Momo, not good for Al. The subhead could've read, "Stay the fuck away."

Al poured himself a cup of coffee and sat down in an easy chair. He leaned back and let the footrest kick out; his knee was still swollen from all of the walking earlier in the week. He set the coffee cup down on an end table and leaned back into the chair.

Preliminary plans: odds set favoring Junior at 8 to 5, shift them at even a hint of trouble; set Uncle Pat straight, tell him only what he needed to know; keep Gene in the dark, he was getting too close to Angelo; watch Angelo, keep him happy.

Final plans: empty the safe deposit box on May 2, collect all debts and leave payoffs with Gene; leave Sam Giancana an envelope full of cash, a list of bettors and a plea for peace. If Giancana knew that he'd never talk and would always remain loyal, then there might be a way out. Ultimately, the payoff would have to be huge—one big, thick envelope.

Al slipped deeper into the chair, thought about the people in his life. He'd miss Pat, Sandy, Pete Barnes, some others. Gene, screw him, he'd sold out. Janet, that was another story—he didn't know how he'd feel. The coffee didn't work; he started to nod off, saw his mother's face flash, and came up out of the chair, '57, Chicago: time to leave it all behind.

A spasm in the middle of his back kicked the Lip awake. His head throbbed, mouth cotton dry, eyes on fire. He stumbled to the bathroom, drained, chugged two glasses of water and a half dozen aspirin, and dove back into bed.

He rolled onto his back and closed his eyes, but could still see them—Lincoln Johnson and Angelo, laughing. No fucking dream, a real-life nightmare. His 10 percent had vanished, no real money left in the fight, and the threat of partners in any future fights.

There had to be something that he could do! He'd turned the fight into an event! What had that moron at the Judge's office called it? A spectacle! His spectacle. He ran over the situation, played it all out, compared it to the other critical conflicts in which he'd persevered.

Two years ago—another impossible situation; constant thought had found the solution, his childhood beatings had allowed him to carry it out. He pulled a pillow around his head, flashed back to 1955, his last month at Stateville. He'd been running heroin with Henry Hamilton since he'd been in the joint. Angelo Carpacci would get it to a guard who would smuggle it in; he and Henry would split it, sell the capsules for $1.50 each. His last month, one last big shipment—enough junk to last the year—nearly a hundred grand in profit. Attention was high—the warden had visitors and didn't want to see anything go wrong. The shit had to be held—tight. Henry volunteered—he and his bitch, a young Puerto Rican with an ass like Bettie Page, swallowed one hundred balloons each; they'd eaten extra meals every day to stretch their stomachs.

The guard broke the news; Henry was going to screw him. He was being released early and was taking his balloons with him. The Puerto Rican hadn't known—he was being left behind with a stomach full of heroin and an anus that would only be used as an exit.

The prison yard: The Lip and Jake Cole had rushed Henry and Julia Martinez. Julia never knew what was coming down—the Lip's iron bar turned him veggie with a clip to the head. Henry spotted it sooner, slashed Jake's throat with a shiv, and came at the Lip.

The Lip had turned on him, caught him chin high with the bar and then turned his own shiv into his gut. The shots had rung out as Jake Cole staggered to the ground—bullets had made him dance like a puppet. The Lip had taken refuge behind Henry's body, slipped his hand into the back of Henry's pants to see if he'd shit out any of the balloons.

Rage had turned to fear as bullets skipped all around him. He'd lifted Henry's body to use as cover; the bullets had stopped and the *photographers* had started shooting. His picture ended up on the cover of *Life*, sentence reduced by weeks, a debt to Angelo that still needed to be repaid.

The Lip rolled over in bed and moaned. There had to be a way. He'd come too far. The fight was an event, a spectacle.

Gilda walked in carrying breakfast on a tray. "You'll have to get up, eventually."

"Why?" he asked, propping himself up with the pillows. He wore a white tank top and his boxer shorts peeked out over the top of the covers. Despite sitting in the middle of the bed, he seemed to be as wide as the headboard.

"Which sounds better, bedsores or sticky sheets?"

"Smart ass."

"You were quite drunk last night."

"I had reason."

"Which was?"

"I'm getting screwed on the fight."

Gilda sat on the edge of the bed and pushed a strawberry at his mouth. "Eat this and tell me what happened."

"Let's just say that some debts are being called in and that what started out as my gig has turned into somewhat of a partnership."

She handed him a cup of coffee and set a bowl of fruit in his lap. "Who are your new partners?"

"You don't want to know."

"Anything that you can do to keep them out?"

He frowned. "I'm racking my brain, baby. "

"Well, my father always said that the key to serenity is to know the difference between those things that you can change and those that you can't."

"Your father was either a drunk or a wimp."

Gilda glared, shot back, "He was neither, pig. He was happier than you'll ever be. He was a loving husband and a great father. Don't take your bad luck out on me."

The Lip leaped out of bed and began pacing the room, tasting stomach acid and rancid booze, his hair trigger-temper *primed*. "I'm not taking anything out on you. I'm just telling you that his line was bullshit. There's nothing that can't be changed if you want to change it! You don't like your life, you change it! You don't like where you live, you leave! You don't like your foster homes, getting knocked around, treated like dirt, you leave! You always look out for yourself. Can't change? That's bullshit. Everything changes."

The Lip leaped out of bed, every muscle in his body taut. "Can't change things, shit. I don't like this coffee, I throw it out!" He flung the cup of coffee into the wall, smashed it.

"I don't like this fruit, I get rid of it!" He heaved the tray across the room; fruit splattered on the curtains and carpet.

"I don't like getting screwed, so I killed the only two men that tried to screw me and you know what? I don't like the fucking I'm getting, I get rid of the woman I'm fucking!"

Gilda had backed into the corner. "I'm sorry."

The Lip's face went blank and he pointed to the door. "I know you are. Get out."

"But . . ."

"Get out! Get the fuck out!"

Gilda shrieked, tore the door open, and ran.

"Change, shit, you can change anything. I changed. I went back. I showed 'em. I gave 'em the Lip!"

The Lip walked toward the bathroom, stepped on a strawberry, and nearly slipped. "Fuck!" he screamed as he stepped through the door, bent over the stool, and threw up.

Junior watched Jack Johnson labor under the Cuban sun. He was enthralled with Johnson; the bald head, well-defined muscles, perfect blend of skill and power. He often wished that he was Johnson, confident and superior.

The film clattered on and Junior watched as Jess Willard lumbered after Johnson. Johnson peppered the big man with jabs and shuffled about the ring, flicking his jab to keep the big man at bay, following up with a right when Willard over-compensated to defend the jab.

"You sure look like him," said Aaron Green, slipping into the chair next to Junior. The film room was pitch black, save the light from the projector, but each could see the other smile and Junior looped an arm around Aaron's shoulder.

"Thank you, Little Chief."

"I'm not just saying that, I mean it. And Osbie says it too and so does Hat and Jack Albano."

"What does your uncle say?"

"Willie says that you look like you and he likes that just fine."

Junior smiled softly and turned back to the screen.

"Hammer, can I ask you something?"

"Sure."

"What you gonna do with all the money?"

"Ain't been no money yet. The money from this fight? I'm gonna buy my mama a new house."

Aaron smiled. "You gonna move her to one of them white neighborhoods?"

"I don't know. I guess I'll let her pick. I don't know nothing 'bout most places but where I'm from."

"Me neither. Uncle Willie says we're gonna buy a farm after you win the championship. He'll train fighters out there. Make it a fight camp. All it takes is money."

Junior nodded. "All it takes is money."

Money. Never had none. Money would buy Mama a new house, give her plenty of food, clothes to wear.

Clothes. The robe. Couldn't figure it out until that morning, finishing the roadwork. Snow falling and the wind whipping off the lake to slap people. Mama, waiting for the bus, shivering. Shivering . . . because she had made a robe for her son. Made it from the lining of her winter coat.

The movie's image was faint on the screen, nearly lost in the light. Jack Johnson was barely visible, lying on the canvas at the end of round 26, a smile seeming to appear on his face, one glove held up, protecting his eyes from the sun.

"Yep," said Junior. "I'm gonna buy my mama a new house."

• • •

"If you must know," said Leonard, "I pick the sesame seeds off of the bun because they get caught between my teeth. Do you want me picking at my teeth all day?"

"Better than what you usually pick at," said Jack. "So anyway," he continued, "this guy Al Kelly is a layoff bookie, and a smart one if the phone calls I've heard are any indication. But he's also acting kind of jumpy on the phone. Maybe he's spooked about his guy getting busted at their last office, or maybe he knows something about this phone guy's disappearance."

Leonard sat up straight. "God, I nearly forgot. We've talked about this bookie and Sam Giancana for the last hour and I've never even asked you about the other fellow. Is anyone looking for him? His partner seemed so distraught; I hope that we find him."

"Yeah, someone's looking for him. I put Andy Scott and Dave Walters on it. He's contacting the girlfriend and the family. I'm listening to this bookie and his pals to see if we hear anything. You know, since I'm tapping those phones without a warrant and listening in on my own time, there isn't much that I can do, officially, with the information."

"Then why are you listening? You that intent on pinning something on Sam Giancana?"

"I guess I am. But I'm listening because I think this bookie is going to spill something. One of his guys got busted not long ago and now one of his phone guys is missing. His protectors aren't protecting him. He's got to be nervous. I'm hoping that something happens and that we can flip him—get him to talk."

"Why would he talk?"

"It's amazing what someone will do when he's backed into a corner."

"You've said that before. I don't want to sound pessimistic, but I don't think that you're going to hear anything of any substance. I think that we would be better off concentrating on finding the exterminator."

"You know, after talking to his partner, I'm not sure that I want to find him."

"Why not?" asked Leonard as Jack set his napkin on his plate and rolled back from the table.

"Because," said Jack, as he turned and began to roll his chair toward the front door. "If we find him it's because we dug somewhere like Soldier Field. You just don't mess around with guys like this. He's dead, Leonard. He's dead."

"What odds have you got on the fight, G?" said Al, phone cradled between his cheek and shoulder, hacking off a piece of salami. "Then let me drop ten thousand on you for Tomcat Gordon. No, I've already got a bunch of plays and I'm trying to play this one a little conservative. No, no reason. Okay. Thanks a lot. I'll talk to you later. Lay low, G."

Al replaced the receiver and put a check mark on his note pad. An early layoff. No complications. A good feeling in his stomach.

Gene hung up his phone, looked up at Al. "Why you laying off so early?"

"The odds favoring Hamilton are eight to five. We need to have a lot more bets on Junior to cover any Tomcat losses. I'm not gonna get burned on this one."

Gene raised an eyebrow. "That's not you. You don't spook. Anything else going on?"

Al shot back acerbic: "How kind of you to ask. No, nothing else is going on. I just wanted to make sure that I can still lay off. The way the Lip's hyping this fight, we're gonna see a lot of action. I just want to make sure that everything's kosher."

"This salami kosher?" asked Pete Barnes, striding toward them, Hawaiian shirt untucked, gut lapping over his slacks.

"Different conversation, Pete," said Al. "What've you got so far?"

"So far, we've got forty-eight thousand on Hamilton, sixteen on Tomcat. K.C. called in a nickel on Junior, and we're getting a little bit of action on that middleweight from the South Side, Spinelli."

"The fat fuck might not make weight," said Gene.

"Where did you hear that?" asked Al.

"My brother eats up the fight game. He's been to both camps, watched them spar."

"What does he think about the fight?" Pete cut off a hunk of salami with a pocket knife, hung the remainder back near the window.

Gene started to answer, paused, spit it out: "He can't tell. He said that they both look great but that Junior looks a little spooked."

Al laughed. "You would be too if the Lip was pulling your strings."

"What's his story?" asked Pete.

"You weren't here when he was around?" asked Gene, giving Al that "Where the fuck has this guy been?" look.

"Of course I was," said Pete, frowning at Gene. "I just don't know much about him. Wasn't he breaking heads for a while?"

"He's done it all," replied Al. "He started out running bets, then he was a lookout, then he started sharking, ended up doing some time."

"That's what I remember," said Pete, excited. "He's a big son of a bitch, isn't he?"

Gene: "Big? He ain't tall, but the mother is big. I was there when he killed Davey Gronowski; they almost had to pull his arms out of their sockets to cuff him."

"I've seen him carry a keg of beer under each arm," added Al.

"No shit," muttered Pete as he stepped away, answered a ringing phone, and cradled it to his chest. "Were you two pretty good friends?"

"When we were kids," said Al. "We scalped tickets together, sold newspapers, that kind of thing."

"Good guy?" asked Pete.

"I don't know if I'd call him good," said Al, "but he always did right by me. It's funny, I've seen him screw people every way you can imagine, but he's never screwed me. But my uncle never trusted him. He always said, 'He's a monkey in a zoo and if you keep reaching between the bars, eventually he'll bite you.' Well, he never bit me and I guess I'm still watching him swing."

Gene took off his dark horn-rimmed glasses and ran a handkerchief over the lenses as Pete went back to his phone call. "How long you think we'll be here tonight?"

"Look around you," said Al.

They both glanced around the room: five men, excluding them, and each was on a phone. "The fight is thirty hours away and our phones are already buzzing. I'll bet we're here until at least eleven P.M."

"No you wouldn't," said Gene.

"No I wouldn't what?"

Five phones hung up simultaneously. Each man recorded the bet that he had just taken. Pete Barnes gagged on salami skin. Gene ignored it all, turned to Al, poker faced: "You wouldn't bet on it."

"Just watch the ears," said the Lip. "They're the only thing that holds my hat up anymore." The other patrons of the hotel's barbershop howled.

The Lip sat in the barber's chair, a white apron draped over him, his face clean-shaven and his scalp covered in shaving cream. Another patron was getting his hair cut and two men sat in chairs, awaiting their turn.

The Lip closed his eyes and leaned back. Two hours before the weigh-in, twenty-nine before the fight. The gate still going strong; just the thought of a sellout used to give him a hardon. But Angelo Carpacci and Lincoln Johnson had changed that. No profit in the fight; a big wager was his only shot.

He smelled the pipe's tobacco even before the Judge spoke. "Be careful with that man's head, please, barber. It seems to be full of interesting ideas."

"Welcome, Judge," said the Lip, smiling. "Aren't you a little early for the weigh-in?"

"I sure am, Mr. Lipranski, but I thought that you and I might have a nice chat before the evening's festivities. Have you got time for a cup of coffee or a bite to eat?"

The Lip looked up as the barber took a final swath and then cleaned his scalp off with a hot, wet towel. "Of course, Judge, anything for the Illinois State Athletic Commission."

The Judge set his suit coat on a chair and pulled out a pocket watch. "Well, it looks like we only have a little while before you'll want to head down to the main ballroom for the weigh-in. Why don't we just walk down to the hotel's coffee shop?"

The Lip stood up, ran a hand across his scalp, and admired himself in the mirror. "Great job, Hank."

The barber threw up his hands as if to say, "no big deal," and the Lip handed him two crisp dollar bills. "Keep the change."

• • •

Junior looked at the ceiling, hostage to an attempt at a late afternoon nap. His thoughts ran laps while his feet moved like windshield wipers.

Something not right. He'd started to feel better, stood up to Wee Willie and then Mr. Lipranski, but something still wasn't right. He put his hands underneath his head, closed his eyes, tried to find it.

The money from the fight, the bet, would take care of Mama, Cleotis. He could move Mama out of that dump, find her a nice, new place. He'd pay Cleotis, but what would stop Cleotis from coming back? That was it, he felt the uppercut to his stomach.

He sat up, dropped his feet to the floor, reached for his shoes.

The hell Mama been through and now this. First, Daddy didn't come home from the slaughterhouse, Rae started jabbing. Now, her only son done one of the dumbest things a man could do! All those years, Mama said, "Some people mistake quiet for dumb," and now he'd proved her wrong.

Junior stood up, shadowboxed, thought like a fighter. Man throws his jab, catch it, watch out for the cross. Stick and move, don't let him get near. Keep him off balance. Don't let him get set. Don't let him use his weapons. Don't let him use his . . .

Junior slapped his hands together, jogged in place, wondered if he could do it.

Al shook his head at the news: Poochie had just lost his shipment of cigars—a hijacking with no insurance. He glanced at Gene. "Poochie thinks he's playing the smart money this week. He's got a tip."

Gene laughed. "Poochie ain't played yet, and you know what? I do believe that the smart money comes in early on the prizefights. The other sports, I'm not so sure, but the smart money comes in early on the fights. What's the balance now?"

Pete Barnes waded through the slips, checked his notepad. "Now we've got seventy-six thousand on Junior, twenty-one thousand on Tomcat. We're still quoting the odds at eight to five, in favor of Junior."

"Move 'em to nine to five," said Al. "That should pick up the pace on Tomcat."

Gene came out of the john, drying his hands on his shirt. "Ain't it a bit early to move the odds, Al?"

Al raised an eyebrow. "It ain't early when it's my money, Gene. When it's your money, you can keep the line the same."

"Jeez, Al. I'm just saying it's not that far off balance. That don't seem like reason to move the line."

"Thank you for your sage advice. I'm moving it."

Pete Barnes walked the room, tapped each man on the shoulder, explained the shift while they held a hand over the phone. Several of the men looked at Al over their shoulder. He stood, looked at the betting slips, ignored the eyes.

"I see Gamey Donato hasn't played yet," said Al.

"So," replied Gene.

"So, do you think he'll beard another bet?"

"I told you, I talked to Gamey again after you paid him off. He said he wasn't bearding for anybody."

"I started taking bets when I was in grade school, Gene. I'm probably a better judge of human character than I am a bookie. Players just don't change their betting habits like that. Gamey usually plays for a few hundred dollars. All of a sudden he bets twenty large? Sorry, it just doesn't work that way."

Gene picked at his nose. "Why does it matter? He's good for it. If you know he's good for it, why do you care?"

"I care because I qualify anybody who plays through me. I don't want Gamey Donato judging a player's character. I want to do that myself. Let's say Gamey would've lost that money and I had to collect from him. Maybe the guy never pays Gamey, or maybe it's a group of guys and they don't pay him. Now, Gamey made the bet assuming that he could get their money, so maybe he doesn't have it to pay me, either. Then where am I?"

"He's good for it. You know that."

"I'm sure he is, that's why we paid him. But that's not the way I work. I qualify everybody myself. That way, I get in trouble, I've got no one to blame but myself. Gamey calls, you take his bet, but you tell him that I want to see him personally, come settle-up day."

Pete Barnes waddled over, huffing. "The action's turning. Tommy just took ten thousand on Tomcat at nine to five. If the shift in odds starts putting more on Tomcat, what do you want me to do?"

Al rubbed his lower lip with his hand. The layoff to Goldie had gone fine. The book would be a bit out of balance for a while, but should balance out by midday, fight day. Another layoff would show that he was spooked, a shift in the odds would scream it. "Hold steady. We aren't gonna shift the odds again unless we start getting way out of whack."

"Can you cover losses?" asked Gene.

Al didn't even turn to acknowledge him. "Of course I can. You can tell Angelo that I'm just fine."

"I wasn't asking for Angelo."

"Of course you weren't, Gene. But if you happen to see him, you can pass that on. I'm fine, just fine."

Gene tried to lighten it up. "Hey, it's Friday night in Chicago. Let's go chase some cooze together."

"Not tonight."

"C'mon, we can hit Rush Street or Toothpick Row. What do you say, me, you? Hey, Pete, want to run out for a few pops tonight?"

"No can do," said Pete Barnes, pulling on the bottom of his Hawaiian shirt. "I don't wash my lucky shirt tonight, you guys are gonna hate me tomorrow."

"I'm not heading out, either," said Al, pulling out a chair and sitting down at a table. "Tomorrow's a big day."

"You need to start getting out, Al," said Gene. "Nothing beats a Friday night in Chicago. Can I do anything to change your mind?"

"There is something that you can do."

Gene put a hand on Al's shoulder. "What's that, boss? Just name it."

Al glanced at Gene's hand, returned his attention to the betting slips. "Sit down and get on a phone."

The Lip stood at the bar, picking up shots for the table. Ramon, the bartender, lined up five shot glasses, filled each with Early Times bourbon. The Lip slammed one shot, thought back on his conversation with the Judge. No insinuations, straight smack: "Warden Kauffman tells me that you killed Henry Hamilton because he was attempting to leave the prison with a stomach full of your heroin. The warden said that he was the only man he'd ever seen die with a smile on his face. One of your stabs tore open a few of the balloons in his stomach and he was saturated with enough horse to keep a dirigible flying for years."

The gist of the message: I know who/what you are. The fight had better come off without a hitch.

"Your friends were in here yesterday," said Ramon, slapping the Lip from his thoughts.

"Who's that?"

"Mr. Johnson, Mr. Lewis."

"I saw 'em. What time were they here?"

"Mid-afternoon, say four o'clock."

Right after their visit, probably shared a laugh at his expense. The Lip pulled a fin from his money clip, set it on the bar. "Anybody else with them?"

"Two other men were there for a few minutes, but did not stay long."

"A skinny dago with greasy hair, a wild-looking gorilla with him?"

"That would be them."

"Anybody have anything interesting to say?"

"The two white men stood at the bar for a moment and asked me about you and Gilda."

"What did you say?"

Ramon pushed the full shot glasses to the Lip, wiped his hands dry with a bar towel. "I told them that she had worked here but that I didn't know you. They didn't find that very believable. In fact, the slender man said that if there was a bar here, you would've checked it out before looking at your room."

"He's got me there. What else did they say?"

"Not much. When they went back to the table, I heard your name a few times, but couldn't really hear much else. They seemed very interested in the fight."

"They would," said the Lip. "Keep your ears open, my friend."

"I shall," said Ramon.

The Lip returned to the table, set a shot in front of each man, slipped back into his seat. "Don, Herb, here's to another successful fight together. Dally, Mike, here's to great press!"

They swallowed their shots, quickly followed up with slugs of cold beer.

"So how's the gate?" asked Dally Richardson.

Herb Bradley spoke up. "It's great. There's an outside chance that we'll sell out."

"That would be a miracle," said Mike Lantz. "I don't remember the last non-championship bout that sold out, especially with the Fullmer-Robinson fight so close."

The Lip ran a finger along the rim of his icy beer mug. "You two have done a great job helping us and we appreciate it."

Mike Lantz looked annoyed. "Well, one of us had a lot of help."

"Fuck you," said Dally Richardson. "I dug for those stories myself."

"You don't even dig in your own backyard."

"Don't worry, Mike. You'll get the interview that I promised you."

Lantz smirked. Richardson and the Lip exchanged a quick glance: don't worry. "You bringing anybody to the fight, Mike?" asked the Lip.

The writer grimaced. "No."

"I've heard that you and your wife have had some trouble. I'm sorry about that."

Lantz gazed at his beer mug, embarrassed, shot Dally Richardson an annoyed look. "That's not quite accurate. We don't always get along, but that's normal."

Too many beers. Richardson laughed. "She seems to be getting along just fine with your brother."

"That's enough," said the Lip. "Mike, the reason that I asked is that I've got a seat open next to the ring girls, and I wanted to know if you want it. Nice-looking strippers. Friendly, too."

"Now you're talking," said Lantz. "But make sure that my colleague isn't anywhere near me. He's been known to copy my notes."

"If I copied your notes, I'd probably have the results of the fight wrong."

They sat at the table until nearly eleven o'clock. Mike Lantz and Herb Bradley cut out early. Dally Richardson finished two more rounds, thanked the Lip for the drinks, and went home. Only the Lip and Don Hansen remained.

"I'm heading over to Trocadero to meet a couple of babes. Want to go?" asked Hansen.

The Lip begged off. Hansen left and the Lip signed off on the bar tab.

He sat back down, toyed with his cigar, let the ash build. He weighed the decision. Only one way to make it work: shove a dagger into his best friend. He'd racked his brain, nearly prayed for an answer.

He eyed the pay phone, created reasons to stay away. One last time, he closed his eyes, thought back: scalping tickets, selling the papers on the off-ramp, bearding for the newsmen, drinks at Pat's, chasing the B-girls, living the life. . . .

Ashes fell from the cigar, dropped on the palm of his hand. He looked down, calm, dropped them onto the floor.

He found a pay phone, fished out a coin, dropped it in the phone and dialed. "Yeah, it's the Lip. Long time." He heard Al's voice in the background, made the pitch. "I need fifty thousand on Tomcat. Can you swing it? . . . I guess that you could say it's a lock. . . . Sure, Angelo knows. He set it up. . . . Feel free to use the information any way you want. . . . No, Al can't know. That would alert everybody, and if word gets out, I won't survive it."

He hung up the phone, shuffled back to the bar. "One more, Ramon. Make it a double."

The Lip polished off a double shot of Early Times, felt his knees shake, wondered what was happening to him. He wasn't bothered by fixing the fight, hurting Gilda, or abusing Junior. But Al, that was another story. Damn it, Al's money was the only way.

He glanced down at his hand, the palm was burned where the ashes had fallen. Compassion: shit, just enough to scare him.

He'd taken the elevated train south and walked the rest of the way. Everyone else at the fight camp had been in bed, save Kid Spinelli, who was gorging himself on a cake pan full of his wife's lasagna. The Kid had made weight and was celebrating by finishing off the entire pan himself. Watching him dance around the locker room had been the only thing that had made the weigh-in seem eventful.

Junior walked up the steps, stepped around the trashcans in the corridor, and nodded at one of the neighbors, washing clothes in the sink in the hallway. He turned the corner and sniffed the air—still smelled like gas. No matter how many times they called the gas company, it always smelled like gas.

Junior knocked quietly on the door, listened to Heddie scream at her kids down the hall. No answer, so he let himself inside. The room was so small that he couldn't seem to get air; he could feel heat from the hotplate that had been used earlier in the night.

"Mama?" he said into the darkness.

"Is that you, son?" she replied, coming up off of the couch, flicking the lamp. "What're you doing here? Ain't you fighting tomorrow?"

He stared at her a moment. Her housecoat was tattered and dirty, the kind of dirt that didn't come out. She wore a nightcap, too, but it had fallen into her lap and her hair was matted against her head. Her large eyes were bloodshot and her cheeks seemed to sag to the floor. She rubbed her eyes. "Didn't you hear me, son. What're you doing here?"

He ignored the question, sat down next to her at the far end of the couch. "Do you like it here, Mama?"

"Well," she said, as she sat up. "Can't say that I like it here, but it's fine for now."

"I never liked it here, Mama, 'cept for you. I hated the cold in the winter and the hot in the summer. I hated all of the dirt and bugs and rats. I hated hearing all of the yelling. Heck, I even hated seeing Mrs. Johnson's kids running 'round in their diapers."

Mama chuckled, softly. She leaned forward and patted Junior's hand. "Careful, she might just hear you."

"But you know what I hated the most, Mama? I hated that you had to work so hard and then come home to this place. It ain't right, Mama, and it's gonna change. I'm gonna make a lot of money from this fight tomorrow and I'm gonna buy you a new house."

Mama smiled. "You already told me that, son, but let's just see what happens. You've had all of them expenses and such so far. You know."

"I do know. I've already talked with Mr. Lipranski 'bout that. I'm gonna be paid a lot of money on this fight. Nothing's stopping that."

"But you didn't have to come here tonight to tell me that, Junior. What is it, son?"

Junior stared at the wall. His eyes wandered until he found the picture of Mama and him and Rae when they were kids. Everything was all right then. Even when Daddy left, everything was all right. What happened?

He closed his eyes and clenched his fists. "I've got to tell you some things, Mama. I did something. I didn't mean to, but I did something. I swear, Mama, I didn't mean to . . . but . . . it just happened."

Junior fought tears. He put his head in his hands and rocked forward, fought to get air, body shaking.

Mama leaned forward, patted his back. He moved into her arms and hugged her. She held him for moments, forever.

"Junior," she whispered into his ear. "There's nothing that you have to tell me. I already know."

He pulled back, shocked. "You know?"

"I know that, no matter what it was that you did, I'll still love you. You're a man now. You don't have to tell your mama everything. I don't want to know everything about you. Son," she said, grinning, "do you think I tell you everything?"

"I don't know."

"Well, I don't. And you know something else? I've made mistakes in my life, too. Marrying your father was a mistake. Now, I'm glad that you and Rae come out of it, but that was the only good thing. I've messed up other times, too. But I sure don't need to tell you about 'em. I've done kicked myself enough for both of us!"

"You don't understand Mama, I made a bad mistake."

"You kill anybody?"

He shook his head.

"Break a law?"

"No."

"Anybody hurt?"

"Not really."

"Pregnant?"

Junior screamed, "No!"

Mama misread him, laughed. "Well, I didn't think so." She slapped her knees and sat up straight. "Son," she said, looking deep into his eyes, "you're a man now. You don't need to tell your mama everything and you don't need to worry about what your mama thinks. The man you got to answer to is staring at you in the mirror. My own mama told me that life is made up of choices and the choices that show who you are is the ones that you make when nobody else is around, when nobody else knows. You know something, son? She was right. We all live with our choices. Even Rae."

"Then why you still give Rae money, Mama?"

"Just 'cause your sister's screwing up her life don't mean I don't care for her. Not a day goes by I don't wish I could drag her back here, but I can't. She done made her choices and she's gonna live with 'em. Just like you gotta live with yours and I gotta live with mine. You'll be all right, son, won't you?"

"I guess so," said Junior.

"Well, you guessed right, 'cause by the look on your face, you done kicked yourself enough for both of us. So, stop kicking yourself. You're gonna live through a lot of things in your life, son, and sometimes you don't know the good from the bad, but you just keep on livin'."

Mama smiled, continued. "And speaking of living, son, after this fight, after you come home, there's gonna be some changes. You making all that money and finding me a place to live is nice, but when you stop traveling around, you ain't gonna come back and live with me."

"What?" asked Junior.

"No, you're a man now and you need to find yourself a home. They's building a nice building not far from here called Prairie Shores, everyone's got a kitchen. So, if you really do make all of this money, maybe we can get a couple of rooms there."

"I'm gonna make it, Mama," said Junior, straightening his back, flaring his nostrils. "And if that's where you want to live, that's where we're gonna live."

Mama reached forward and gave him a hug. "That'd be wonderful, son. Only one thing," she said as she stood up and ushered Junior to the door.

"What's that, Mama?"

"Different floors."

One more piece of business, thought Junior, as he spotted the Caddy. He stepped out of the shadow of the el track, crossed the street and knocked on the window.

Cleotis looked up, startled, and rolled down the window. "Damn, boy, you trying to get your head blown off."

Junior could see the gun in his lap, ignored it. "Want to finish my business with you."

"Our business is finished, dummy. Thought we got that straight."

Junior seethed. "We ain't got it straight, Cleotis. You think 'cause a what happened in Kansas City that you can push me around, but that ain't so. I wish it never happened, but it did and I can live with that."

"But can your mama?"

Junior shook his head.

Cleotis smiled.

Junior shook his head even harder. "All the stuff my mama been through, you think that would get her? You don't know my mama and you don't know me."

"What's that supposed to mean?"

"Means I'm gonna pay you. Means you gonna send Rae home. Means you don't do it, I'm gonna quit fightin' so I can spend all my time messing with you."

Cleotis stared at him, nodded his head. "Well there we have it. Junior Hamilton is finally a man. Is that it? You think coming down here and talking to me like that makes you a man? You don't know shit 'bout being a man, Junior. A two-cent bullet takes out a 'man' like you."

"I know this: you don't bring Rae, you don't get the money."

"And s'posing I bring her and she comes back to me, what then?"

Cleotis barely finished the sentence. Junior's right cross knocked him into the passenger seat, blew out the window. Junior walked over to the passenger side, reached in the window, took the gun from Cleotis's lap and pulled the feather out of his cap. He dropped the gun in a nearby Dumpster and jogged to the train.

Saturday, April 6

Noon: phones rang like A-fucking-T and T; rain strafed the windows. Another Dally Richardson column had ragged Junior, stoked the hate money. Odds 9 to 5 favoring Junior; white trash and rich faggots threw money on Tomcat. "A lot of money coming in on Tomcat, Al," said Pete Barnes, as he poured another cup of coffee from a thermos. "We've almost got as much Tomcat money as Junior Hamilton now. If the Hamilton supporters don't start calling, we're gonna get way out of whack."

"Don't worry about it," said Al. "Later on I'll lay some off. The tide will shift soon. We should start getting money on Junior."

Gene straggled in carrying a thermos, large hunk of cheese, and a salami. He dripped from head to toe, courtesy of April in Chicago. "Man, am I getting tired of this. It's still colder than shit and now it won't stop raining. How goes it here?" he asked no one in particular.

No one in particular answered.

Gene set the food and thermos on a table, threw his topcoat and hat on a chair in the corner, repeated the question.

"Going great," said Pete Barnes, tearing off a chunk of cheese. "But we're getting a load on Tomcat."

"That mean anything to you?" asked Al.

"No. Should it?"

"No. I think we'll see a lot more money on Junior, soon. This is just the white bigots throwing out some prayer cash."

Gene sat down in front of a phone, tested his pen on a pad of paper. "That's all it is, prayer cash. Junior's gonna murder him."

"Who did you take the fifty-grand bet from yesterday?" asked Al.

"I told you, Gamey Donato. He said he had a few friends pooled together."

"And I told you that I wanted to know who's betting through me."

Gene sparked defensive: "And you told me that you wanted to see Gamey on settle-up day. You didn't say nothing about quizzing him about his bets. You got a problem with Gamey's bet, call him and cancel it."

Al sighed. "Once it's laid, it's played. Gamey took Tomcat. I hope he's got the money or he's got rich friends, 'cause I don't think he's gonna win this one."

"You turning into a betting man, Al?" asked Gene.

"You turning into the Virgin Mary? I wouldn't put a nickel on a fight in this town. Not when two judges and a referee and a boatload of cash will buy a fight."

"You worried about this one?" asked Pete Barnes.

"Not yet," said Al. "Not yet."

Al picked up a phone, dialed. "It's me," he said into the receiver. "Let me talk to G."

Goldie picked up the other end. "A?"

"Right, what've you got on the fight?"

"This information is for your amusement and information only: eight to five."

"You getting a lot of Tomcat action?"

"Some. This fight ain't playing as well out here. These sun freaks, they don't know a good fight. I might start looking for some more Tomcat action. You got any, you call me. These citrus queens'll start throwing a few dollars on the colored kid and I'll need to balance out."

"Lay low."

"Lay off."

New York, Terre Haute, Kansas City, Oklahoma City, Omaha: Al repeated the process, checked the action, possible layoffs. Results: odds running close, no problems with a layoff.

He walked over to the window, peered out before pulling the curtains shut. The rain fell hard. The streets were covered with mud. Across the street, exhaust from a van caught his attention. He watched as a cripple rolled his wheelchair out of the van, pelted by rain. He held the curtain for a second, forgot about the phones, odds, bets; maybe life wasn't that bad after all.

• • •

The Chicago Stadium, 2:00 P.M., six hours before the fight. The Lip and Don Hansen watched as the workers assembled the ring. "Keep the canvas taut!" yelled the Lip. "I want these guys moving around the ring."

"The girls are all set," said Hansen.

The Lip pulled back his shoulders, stretched his neck, took off his bow tie and unbuttoned the top button of his tuxedo shirt, gently folded the tie and put it in his breast pocket. "That's the least of my worries. You talk to the fighters' managers?"

"All of them. They're set. Abe Rosen wanted to make sure that there was an electrical outlet in Tomcat's locker room. He's going to play some music while he relaxes before the fight."

"Did you tell Abe that there's probably an electrical outlet in every locker room in the city?"

"He also wanted me to remind you that they were going to be selling autographed pictures in the concourse and that we don't participate in that revenue."

"The old saying is true," said the Lip, disgusted.

"Which one?"

"Chicago: the Jews own it, the Micks run it, and the niggers live in it." The Lip thought for a moment, grabbed Hansen by the elbow. "You need to be with Junior from the moment he gets here. Don't let him out of your sight. There's something coming down and I don't want him ducking out."

"Care to let me in on it?"

"If you don't ask, you'll never know."

"Then I'll never know," said Hansen. "Where's Herb Bradley? I'm going to have him get a shot of me and the ring girls before the fight. It might work nice when we publicize our next fight."

The Lip laughed. "Whatever. He's probably in his office, making last-minute calls."

"I'll see you back here in a little while."

Hansen strode off. The Lip watched the ring go up, felt his heart skip a beat when the canvas stretched across the ring, ROBERT J. LIPRANSKI PRODUCTIONS splashed across the canvas for all to see.

One of the workers sat down in a corner of the ring, legs hanging off of the apron, facing the empty stadium. "What are you doing?" yelled the Lip.

"I'm just taking a break," said the man, jumping to his feet.

"No breaks until the ring's set up."

"Sorry," said the man, sarcasm engraved on his face. "Our boss usually gives us fifteen minutes every three hours."

"Well, that ain't the way I do it. You're not working for your boss. You're working for me now."

The man strode across the ring, helped another man finish attaching the apron.

The Lip stared straight ahead, didn't see anything. You're working for me now. You're working for me now. You're working for . . . shit . . .

Rage. Indignation. The Lip even shocked himself as he ran out the door.

Junior woke up, rolled onto his back, and tucked his hands under his head. He'd taken only a two-hour nap, but he felt more rested and refreshed than he had in the past ten years.

No one had been awake when he had returned, and when Aaron woke him up at 7:30 A.M., he realized that he had quickly fallen into a deep, long sleep.

Everyone had been in great spirits at the breakfast table. Frances had served Kid Spinelli first, offered him piping hot waffles, bacon, hash browns, and fresh-squeezed orange juice. Kid Spinelli had responded by leaping to his feet and kissing the old woman square on the lips.

Each fighter had been joyous; the months of hard training, sparring, and sacrifice would culminate with the evening's fights. Wee Willie had called it "the relief"; relief that a fighter had made weight, relief that he had trained as hard as possible, relief that he would finally get to exhibit the skills that the profession rewarded.

"You may be a little tense," Wee Willie had said from the head of the table. "But you've got to acknowledge the relief. It's finally here! It's finally your time! The day of the fight has finally come!"

Junior scratched his thighs, rolled onto his side. Relief. He'd finally told Mama. Nothing, she'd told him when he was young, kept a man awake at night like his secrets. No more confessions in his prayers. No more worries. Cleotis could tell anyone that he wished and Junior wouldn't care, because he knew. He knew that Mama would still love him.

The door cracked open and Junior saw Aaron Green peek inside.

"Come here, Little Chief," he said.

Aaron rushed through the door, screeched, and jumped on top of Junior. He sat up on Junior's chest, a smile splitting his face, and began to throw fake punches. "What you gonna do tonight, Hammer, what you gonna do?"

Junior widened his eyes, pulled up his fists in mock defense, then threw his arms around Aaron and hugged him. His eyes misted as he squeezed him close to his chest. "I'm gonna make my mama proud."

Jack tapped the earpiece, killed the static. All gambling talk; no Sam Giancana. He and Leonard had listened to incoming and outgoing calls all day long and were nearing time to return to the station and interview the pimp.

Leonard fidgeted; *he* wasn't used to sitting in a chair all day long. "Stretch your legs, Leonard," said Jack, ultra loud.

Leonard nodded, took off his headset, and moved toward the back of the room. Jack looked down at the notepad in front of him, went back over the conversation that he'd heard last night that had sent goosebumps up his torso. His notes, the conversation, verbatim:

"Yeah."

"Yeah, it's the Lip."

"Long time."

"Long time. I need fifty thousand on Tomcat. Can you swing it?"

A pause on the receiving end; the voice, muffled: "Is the play legit?"

"I guess you could say it's a lock."

"Does anybody know?"

"Sure, Angelo knows. He set it up."

"I'll figure out a way. Is this public info?"

"Feel free to use the information any way you want."

"Should I tell Al?"

"No, Al can't know. That would alert everybody, and if word gets out, I won't survive it."

"The odds are eight to five in favor of Hamilton. You win, a fifty-thousand-dollar bet on Tomcat nets you sixty-four grand, after juice."

A fix. "The Lip" and Angelo Carpacci set it up. Questions: Who's the Lip? How did he fix the fight? How could the information be used against Sam Giancana?

A ring, quick pickup, conversation: "B-nine."

"This information is for your amusement and information only. Tonight's action, Junior Hamilton is eight to five; Anthony 'Kid' Spinelli is six to five; Spider Gomez is two to one."

"Ten times on Tomcat Gordon, five times on Gomez, five times on whoever's fightin' Spinelli."

"Good luck."

A dial tone. Heavy action on Tomcat Gordon. The bookie was taking it in the shorts and he didn't even know it. Jack took off the headphones as Leonard tapped him on the shoulder. It was time to leave; time to interview the pimp.

Jack smiled as he wheeled out the back door, met the rain. The bookie was going down. His corner was getting awfully tight. Maybe he'd help them nail Sam Giancana.

Al felt like he'd swallowed a quart of crushed glass. "These right?" he asked Pete Barnes.

Pete had sweated through his Hawaiian shirt; pit rings reached his nipples. "Yeah, I'm afraid it is. Jumping the odds really shifted the action. Everybody's taking Tomcat."

"Shifting the odds, my ass," said Al. "Gene, get on the phone. Call New York. I'm calling Goldie. Lay off fifty thousand on Tomcat. I'm gonna do the same thing."

Gene put his hand over the receiver. "Where we at?"

"Fucked, that's where we're at. We've got one hundred ninety-seven thousand dollars on Tomcat and only ninety-two on Hamilton.

The damn phones have gone crazy! Tomcat action jumped in minutes. Shit, this is just what I didn't need."

Al spun the dial; Gene did the same. "Pete, drop the odds to seven to five! Screw it. Fellows," yelled Al, "drop the odds to seven to five. Do you hear me. Now!"

The phone rang and rang and rang and rang and rang and finally someone picked it up. "It's A. Give me G."

"Out."

"What do you mean, out?"

"You hear me? He's out. Who else do you want to talk to?"

"Is J. T. there?"

"Yeah."

"Get him."

A pause that seemed to last all night. A cough. Finally, "Yeah, A. It's J. T. For what can I do you?"

"I need to lay off fifty thousand on Tomcat Gordon. What do you have it at?"

"That ain't the right question."

Al blew. "What the fuck is that supposed to mean. Don't play games with me now. What've you got the fight at?"

"A, I'm telling you, that ain't the right question. We ain't taking any layoff action tonight."

Al's gasp turned his sheetwriters' heads. His fingers went white from gripping the phone and for a moment he lost all thought; all he could hear was the buzz of conversation, nothing made sense. Quiet: "What do you mean, you aren't taking any layoff action?"

"I don't know what's up, A. G told us that he had to run out for a while and not to take any layoff action."

"When is he coming back? Are you taking any when he comes back?"

"On my mother's grave, I do not know anything. I'm figuring he'll be back soon, but I ain't promising anything. Now, I've got to go. We've got bettors to take care of."

The phone went dead in his hand. Goldie had told him to call with any layoff action and now he was out. Nowhere to lay off on the West Coast. He heard Gene next to him, screaming into the receiver.

No layoff action on the East Coast. "That ain't the right question." The right question: *Why can't we lay off?*

Tommy Spector yelled over. "Al, I just took a bet from Poochie. You can start feeling a lot better. He took Tomcat Gordon!"

Al put his head on the table so that he wouldn't pass out.

Big gray Buick in the driveway, no lights, drapes closed. 5:00. Three hours before the fight. What the hell was he doing? He should've been at the stadium, prepping managers, coaching the ring announcer, checking concessions and the gate. What the hell was he doing in Rogers Park? One phone call to Ramon at the bar and his course was set.

"Yes sir, they did ask about Gilda," the bartender had said. "They didn't realize that you had met her at the bar, only asked if you had brought her here. I'm sorry, but I was caught up in the conversation and I volunteered that she had worked here. Yes, they did ask where she was from."

A check with management, and the goons had found out her mailing address. No telling how long they'd been there. No telling what they'd done.

The Lip slipped the car along the curb, half a block short of Gilda's house; could hear the voice pounding inside his head. "Hey, if it was good enough for Big Jim Colosimo, it's good enough for me . . . Tony Torrio got married last night. . . . She's more than a doll. She's a great lay. I had her last night. . . . You're working for me now. . . . You're working for me now!"

Tuxedo jacket in the back seat; he untied his tie and threw it on top. Rage and adrenaline gushed; the shirt felt like a second skin. He scampered around the side of the house, past the garage, slid underneath a window by the kitchen.

The Lip lifted his head slightly, couldn't see anyone, reached around and tested the doorknob. The neighborhood was too damn safe; the doorknob turned easily. He slipped off his shoes, set them by the door and stepped inside, listened. Quiet but not still, a low hum came from the front room. He guessed that it was the television. He peeked around the corner. Confirmation: Vic D'Antonio sat with his feet on the coffee table, watching television.

The Lip surveyed, thought: Vic with his back to him, maybe ten feet from the staircase; a quick strike, noise would bring Angelo and whoever else down the stairs; Angelo would be packing, he had to kill Vic quickly, take his gun. Loaded with danger, but taking out Vic would be a pleasure.

He ran forward, head down, and grabbed Vic around the head. Vic kicked his feet forward, knocked over the coffee table and fell back against the couch. The Lip cradled Vic's head in the crook of his left arm, tried to snap his neck with his right hand.

Vic yelled, dug his shoulder into the back of the couch and spun around. He brought his head up hard and caught the Lip's chin, then leaped over the couch. Momentum drove them into the wall underneath the staircase. Noise was no longer an issue; they screamed like animals. Vic brought a knee up into the Lip's groin; the Lip moved just enough to avoid real damage.

Rummaging upstairs; not much more time. The Lip gathered his rage, drove Vic over the couch, rammed his head through the television set. Glass tore, sparks flew; he got his hands around Vic's neck and choked the life out of him.

"What the hell's going on down there?"

Angelo Carpacci ran down the stairs, shirt half on, a .38 in his hand. He stopped midway down the staircase, froze when he saw the Lip. A pause that seemed to last all night. Angelo shook his head. "Now you've done it, you stupid Polack. Now you've really done it."

The Lip groped the body, somewhere Henry Hamilton laughed: Vic D'Antonio wasn't packing. He dove behind an easy chair, threw a lamp toward Angelo. Angelo ducked the lamp, sprinted down the stairs, and fired at the Lip as the big man lunged across the carpet, pulled himself around a corner and plunged down a set of stairs into the basement.

Angelo slipped on the bottom step. "You are DEAD!" he yelled as he got up and headed for the basement stairs. "I should've killed you a long time ago, you piece of shit. You are dead!"

The Lip tried to slow his breathing, searched the dark for a weapon. He pulled back into a corner, heard Angelo hit the first wood step.

Frantic, he looked for nearly anything. An unfinished basement, nearly empty. Shapes blurred. A rubbing, scratching sound as Angelo searched for a light switch. The Lip fought panic, grabbed at a figure. His hand closed around it, air hissed out: a child's ball, a room full of childhood toys.

The lights came on. Angelo bounded down the step, screamed and raised the gun.

Another sound. Blood painted the wall. Angelo collapsed; the gun skittered harmlessly in front of him.

A wail. The Lip stepped forward, looked up the steps. Gilda, blood on her lips, a torn brassiere and a skirt, her father's suicide Luger still in her hand. He moved close, took the gun from her and lifted her face. "Do you realize what you've just done?" he asked gleefully. "You just saved me seventy thousand dollars!!"

Junior handed the cup of urine to Dr. Lund, jumped back on the table and rolled onto his stomach. He curled his arms up under his head, closed his eyes and relaxed. In a corner of the locker room, Kid Spinelli threw punches, listened to Wee Willie. "This boy's in great shape, Kid, so you're gonna have to take him out early. If it goes past the fifth round, you're gonna be in trouble."

The Kid shot left jabs, tapped his nose, and ran in place. "I'm fine, Willie. I'm fine."

"I know you are, Kid, but taking off that weight took a lot out of you. Finish him quick!"

"Quick," said the Kid. "Quick."

Junior heard the ring announcer announce Kid Spinelli's opponent and suddenly the locker room cleared out. He and Osbie Jones were the only ones left. He drifted away while Osbie spoke. "Nineteen thirty-six, I saw the Clubber fight a club fight. But they called him Clubber on account of that big old club he carried, not 'cause he was a club fighter. Anyways, Clubber was fightin' this tall skinny guy and the tall skinny guy stayed away from him for the first few rounds, and took the lead. But the guy, he started getting cute, you know, dancing and making faces. Well, you just didn't do that to Clubber Jones. So, after the bell sounded to end the fifth round, Clubber's manager moved his stool out so that Clubber could sit down. But Clubber was mad, damn was he mad! He walked back to his corner, looked down at that stool, and while everyone was watching, he slammed a foot down on top of it and just crumpled it. That was a metal stool! That other fighter damn near wet his pants, and when they went out for the sixth round, Clubber just barely tapped him with a right and he went down and stayed down. Didn't want to end up like that stool!"

Tico Hernandez and Spider Gomez entered the locker room, nodded to Osbie, and slapped Junior on the back. "Good luck, Amigo," said Tico. "The Spider and I, we think you are a killer. You gonna spank that gringo, Amigo. That fat Wop, Spinelli, is getting murdered. It's only the second round and he's so tired he can hardly hold his hands up. Wife's lasagna, shit. He's just fat and lazy."

A tall man with a pipe sauntered into the room, one thumb tucked into his suspenders. "Has anyone seen Mr. Lipranski?"

"Ain't seen him," said Osbie Jones.

Junior rolled his head. "No."

"Well, when he finally shows up, please tell him that Commissioner Willoughby is looking for him. Is everything okay?"

"Yes sir," said Osbie. "Mr. Hansen's taken over. He just stepped out to make a phone call."

The commissioner nodded and left the room. Osbie cackled. "Tell you something, Junior. I just can't imagine where Mr. Lipranski is right now. That man's spent the last few days making sure the bolts are tight in every chair in the stadium. Now, the day of the fight and he doesn't show up. I'd just love to know what's holding him up!"

The interrogation room: a small table, two chairs on opposite sides, a tape recorder. Jack sat behind the table, muscles flexed. Leonard Funk ushered Cleotis inside, turned and left the room. Cleotis sat down and his eyes dropped, noticed Al's legs and the chair, cackled: "Ha haaaa!"

"Something funny?"

"Kind of. You're so damn wide I didn't see the chair until I sat down. What happened to you, officer? Fall down those stairs out there?"

Jack forced a smile. "Very funny, shitbird. We're not here to talk about me. We're here to talk about you. You got anything funny to say before I go on?"

Cleotis grinned, flashed his gold-capped teeth. "I'm sorry, officer. It's just that you're so damn big, it's odd seeing them little legs on you."

Jack, poker faced: "You're spending an awful lot of time checking me out."

"What's that s'posed to mean?"

"You tell me. You run hookers for a living, probably don't sample any yourself. Take a look at your fingernails. Haven't you ever cut them? Skip it, Cleotis. You look like a friggin' woman. No big deal to me, but let's settle that and move on."

Cleotis shook. "What you mean by all of that shit? Huh? I ain't no pipe smoker! You don't know shit about me. Sample any, shit. I get 'em all a couple of times a week. Keeps 'em loyal."

"How many times you have Lucy?"

"I told your partner, I don't know no Lucy."

"You know her. You had her bailed out of jail three times and you signed for her at the hospital, too. You might as well make this easy, Cleotis. If she was your girl and you didn't kill her, then I suppose another pimp took her from you. Who's leaning on you, Cleotis? You're scared, we can protect you."

Cleotis leaned back, crossed his legs. "You can stop trying that shit on me right now, gimp. I don't know that girl and I didn't kill her. I told that tall weird-looking cop that I've got an alibi, and it's so air-fucking-tight ain't a fly flying out."

"Refer to him as Detective Funk."

"Funk! That mother fucker's name should be Funk like mine should be White. Man, that's a good one."

"You done?"

"Damn straight I'm done. You can't squeeze shit out of me. I got an alibi tighter than twelve-year-old quiff, so get this over with and get me outta here."

Jack folded his hands, brought them up to his chin. "We'll see. Where were you the night of April second?"

"At Junior Hamilton's fight camp."

"The fighter? Why?"

"Just saying hello."

"To who?"

"Junior Hamilton."

"How do you know him?"

"From the neighborhood. Kinda grew up together. His sister's my girlfriend."

"And Uncle Miltie's really a woman. How long were you there?"

"Hour or so. We talked for a while, then me and his sister made out in the car. You talk to Junior, you tell him that. Tell him his sister says 'hi' and she's looking forward to seeing him after the fight."

"What else did you talk about?"

"Talked about how he's getting screwed. I guess you could say I gave him financial advice. His manager, that Lipronski or Lip-somethingorother, been screwing him outta money. I told Junior what he should be making. Tried to help the dummy."

Jack sat up straight. Lipranski, Lip: Junior's manager. The phone conversation ran through his head: Lip and Angelo Carpacci set up the fight. Giancana in pseudo-hiding. A murder rap ready for his sheet but not hard to beat. The fixed fight hard to resist. He'd be there to watch the money roll in, courtesy of the Lip and Angelo. Jack made up his mind quickly, tried to finish with Cleotis.

"He do that to your face?" asked Jack.

"No, your mama crossed her legs."

Jack lost it, reached across the table and clapped his hands on the sides of Cleotis's head like he was banging cymbals. He got a palm on each of his cheekbones and pressed. Cleotis's eyes bulged, he screamed. Leonard Funk rushed into the room and pulled Jack off of him just as the cheekbones started to cave. Jack spun free, shot out of the room. Leonard watched Cleotis fall to the floor and start to sob, "Face, ears! Broke my face!"

The hallway: Jack hyperventilated. "What were you doing?" cried Leonard. "You may have severely hurt that man."

Between breaths: "Doesn't matter. We'll nail him for the hooker snuff tomorrow. We've got to get going."

"Doesn't matter! If he sings, you could get brought up on

charges! And what do you mean we've got to get going? Where are we going?"

"The fights, Leonard. We're going to the fights."

Al sagged in his seat, put his hands over his eyes. "Oh God. Oh God. No. Poochie's on Tomcat Gordon. Apple. Apple."

"Al, Poochie's never right. You should be glad. If Poochie's on him, he'll never win."

Al looked at Gene, shook his head. "You're wrong this time, Gene. Poochie told me he's got a lock. Junior's manager told him that he was a lock. If Poochie changed his mind, it was for a reason. Oh God, it all fits together. We can't lay off. Goldie's gone. Angelo wanted to bankroll me. It's a fix."

Al screamed, frantic: "Hit 'em all, call for the layoff. Tommy, call K.C.! Pete, call Detroit and Omaha. One of you guys get New York!"

He dialed the number, hollered into the phone. The answer was "No" in Terre Haute, Bookie Shaffer wasn't buying. His men echoed: nobody taking action, a layoff was out.

Al leaped to his feet, grabbed phones, heaved them against the wall. His wail filled the room. "Fuck, fuck, fuck!" He kicked over a folding table, broke a chair against the wall.

Pete Barnes tackled Al, pushed him against the wall. "Al, get hold of yourself! We got work to do. We gotta start laying off! We gotta look around!"

The room was dead silent. Suddenly, the last live phone rang. No one moved to pick it up. "Al," said Gene. "Al, what're you gonna do?"

Al slumped against the wall, sat down. His thoughts jockeyed for position: fuck the small books, lay off a tiny piece at a time. Ring the bettors, cancel all bets. Let the word out, kill the action.

Pete Barnes voiced Al's thoughts. "Al, I see two choices here: either lay off with small books or cancel the bets."

The phone continued to ring: Al flashed on his father—the bloody sanctuary scene etched in his mind forever.

"It's a family curse, Pete."

"What?"

"You want me to answer the phone?" asked Tommy Spector.

Everyone stared at Al. He held his head in his hands, muttered, "Answer the phone, Tommy."

Tommy answered the phone. Pete Barnes moved behind Al. "Al, if it's a fix, we've got to shut down now, start trying to lay off or cancel the bets."

Al rolled his eyes. "There's no layoff, Pete. There's not enough small bookies in the world to take these bets. I screw all of them, I got no business to come back to. Cancel the bets, right. I cancel 'em, it'll send out the word, and the boys don't want that word sent out. No, Pete, they set me up. All these years, and they're taking it all back in one night."

"It's Tony Scarzo, Al," said Tommy Spector. "He said that Momo told him you'd get him Tomcat Gordon at eight to five."

Silence. "How much?"

"Thirty K."

Al didn't blink, stared straight ahead.

"Al, what should I tell him?"

"Al," said Gene.

"Al," said Pete.

"Al," said Gene. "Take the bet, Al."

"He can't take the bet, Gene," said Pete Barnes. "He'd be crazy. This thing is rigged. I started to get that feeling a minute ago and now I know it. No way Tony Scarzo throws thirty grand on a fight unless he knows how it ends. Tell him to fuck off, Al."

"Shut up, Pete," said Gene. He grabbed Al's shoulders, looked him straight in the eyes. "Al, you know what's at stake here. Take the bet, Al."

"What're you doing?" asked Pete.

Gene ignored him. "Take the bet, Al!"

"Who're you with here, Gene?" asked Pete.

"Shut the fuck up, Pete!" yelled Gene. "Al, you know this is about more than a bet. Keep your lines open, Al. You've got to maintain your business. A bookie with no clients ain't any good to no one. Take the bet, Al!"

Pete Barnes jumped out of his chair and grabbed Gene by the back of his shirt. "Why you no good . . . I oughta throw you over the rail."

He moved forward, pulled Gene. Gene fought back, watched his glasses fall off and break on the floor. "Take the bet, Al! Take the bet!" Pete opened the door, kicked the glasses outside, and pushed Gene down the steps. He took a step back, slammed the door as Gene fell to his knees.

"Who'd have guessed it?" said Pete.

"Al?" said Tommy Spector.

Pete turned. "Hang that phone up, Tommy. We're shuttin' down."

A low voice, barely above a whisper. "Take the bet, Tommy."

"What?" yelled Pete.

"You heard me. Take the bet. Keep the phone lines open."

Pete rushed over, threw his hands in front of Al's face, kneeled. "Al! What're you doing? You can't afford this, Al, and you do not want to get into hock with Angelo. Please, Al, I'm begging you!"

"You're a good friend, Pete. I don't take that bet, I'm a dead man. I don't take that bet, word gets to Momo and all over town that I can't handle it. I can't handle it, I lose my people, then I'm no good to them. Angelo's been making his play and Gene's his guy. I knew it."

"What do you mean?" asked Pete.

"Right after I got middled, that banker got murdered. Momo had to go into hiding. Angelo came to me to see if I needed money and he shit when I said no. I get paid to read people, Pete. I read him right away: he thought I made too much money. He hooked up with Gene and what did Gene say? He probably told him he could make more by taking a position. It was coming like winter, nothing I could do to stop it. I just thought I could make it a few more weeks."

"Huh?"

"I figured I'd book until the Fullmer–Robinson fight and then I'd get out. But that ain't gonna happen. Now, call Gamey Donato, see if he made that bet."

Thirty minutes later, only a few stragglers threw down bets. Herman Goetz's brother-in-law dropped $500 on Junior. Al couldn't help but laugh. If the man hadn't been plugging Herman's wife, he might've tipped him off. Al ordered the phone shut down, told his men to leave. Pete stayed, helped him clean up, gathered the phones, and threw them in a box. "I want the figures before you leave," said Al.

Pete set the box down, stood in a corner. He flipped through the sheets, scratched figures on a notepad. "Holy shit," he said.

"Thanks for the tipoff. How much?"

Al's stomach was queasy. His legs felt weak.

"Here's the figures, including juice. Junior wins, you clear a hundred sixty-nine thousand one eighty-eight."

Al slumped in his chair. "Give it to me."

"Tomcat wins, you lose a hundred ninety-eight thousand five hundred sixty."

"Oh my God," said Al. "This can't be happening."

"How much do you need to come up with, Al?"

"Too much."

"Anybody help you?"

"Nobody's got that kind of money but Momo. My whole life, Pete. My whole life."

"What're you gonna do?"

"Hand me a phone."

Pete handed him a phone. "Go on, get out of here."

"You aren't gonna do nothing funny, are you?"

"Like what, run? Kill myself? No, Pete."

"Then what're you gonna do?"

"If I'm going down, I want to see it. I'm calling my uncle. I'm going to the fights."

Pete walked toward the door, stopped. "Al, what the hell did you mean about the family curse?"

Al cradled the receiver, dialed. "Gambling kills us all."

Two dead Dagos in the trunk of Don Hansen's Rambler. One heavy-duty canvas tarp and too much time in the garage. Gilda's stare when he'd thanked her for saving him the money. Her look had said it all: She couldn't get out of Chicago fast enough; he'd never see her again. The Lip's mind raced as he entered the locker room.

"Well, I'll be," said Osbie Jones as he stood up. Junior didn't even open his eyes; the tone of Osbie's voice told him who he'd see.

"Step out for a minute, Osbie. I've got to talk to Junior."

Osbie nodded, slipped out the door. The Lip moved over to Junior, got within inches. "We haven't got much time here, kid. From the sound of that crowd, the fight's almost over, and Willie and the rest of them will be back in here. Look at me, Junior."

Junior lifted his head, craned his neck. "Junior," said the Lip, "there's been a change in plans. This game's run by a bunch of crooks, and tonight the crooks say that you don't win."

An alarm went off. Junior rolled over and sat up. "What do you mean?"

"It's a fix. You lose. But you've got to make it look good."

"I don't get it. Who wants it fixed?"

"Who doesn't? That list is shorter. Believe me, Junior, you don't lose this fight, you'll never fight again, and neither one of us will ever breathe again. You'll get your chance, but you're going down tonight."

Junior stood up. "Why tonight? Why did it have to be tonight? Things was starting to go so well, Mr. Lipranski. Why tonight?"

The Lip raged. "Why tonight? Because, Junior, because. Because I promoted the shit out of this fight! Because everybody and their brother is either at the fight or betting the fight and these men want their piece, the fucking magggots. They've got more money than God, but that's not enough. They want more, and if they know you're going down, they'll make more. I worked my ass off to make this a spectacle, and they barged in at the last second to remind me that I don't control shit! Why tonight, Junior? Because they said it's tonight."

"That can't be! I'm gonna win this fight! Nobody's gonna tell me that I can't win!"

The Lip shot his hands behind Junior's ears, pulled him close. "You just don't get it, do you? You ain't got a choice in this. This ain't no game! These men control everything. There is nowhere that you could go, nowhere that you could hide! C'mon, Junior, play along. You go down tonight, they'll get you your shot, soon. It's Tomcat's turn, first. He's a money magnet right now."

"I can't do that, Mr. Lipranski. I just can't. I've come so far . . . Can't we do something, tell somebody?"

"There's nothing to do and nobody to tell. You shoot your mouth off or blab to anyone, they'll kill you. Junior, there's no decision for you here. You lose this fight. It ain't that bad. You're gonna make a lot of money, and you'll get your shot some other time. One loss ain't the world."

The door of the locker room flew open. Tico Hernandez and Wee Willie came in followed by Spider Gomez and Osbie Jones. Aaron Green skipped in behind them. "He won, Hammer. Spider knocked him out in the eighth round!"

The Lip moved close, whispered in Junior's ear. "That's the round for tonight, Junior. You go down in the eighth round." The Lip started to move away, stopped, and leaned back into Junior's ear. "Oh, and don't worry, I got the bet down. Thirty thousand dollars. Your thirty thousand dollars. All on Tomcat."

The Lip sauntered by the fighters, looked at Wee Willie, shook his head, and kept walking. Osbie Jones slid next to Junior, produced two cotton handwraps, and began to wrap Junior's hands.

"Isn't that great?" asked Aaron as he stepped up to Junior. "The eighth round! I think he could've taken him out earlier, but he just wanted to have some fun with him. The eighth round, Big Chief!"

Junior jumped up from the rubdown table. "I've got to go to the bathroom," he said as Osbie tied the last handwrap and squeezed Junior's hands to make sure that the wraps held his knuckles snugly together. Junior rushed off, moved toward the bathroom, nearly knocked over Kid Spinelli. He saw it in Kid Spinelli's eyes. He'd heard. Kid Spinelli motioned toward his nose; too many jabs had turned it to mush. The result, a fourth-round knockout. "I guess," said Spinelli, eyes gone dead, "it wasn't meant to be our night."

Saturday, April 6

The Fight

The stadium: Jack rolled in, surveyed the scene: a 240,000-square-foot concrete cave; ravenous fight fans filled the seats. Crowd noise reflected the numbers; it had to be a sellout. The ring set up in the middle of the floor: black and white painted ropes, bloodred apron and a canvas with ROBERT J. LIPRANSKI PRODUCTIONS emblazoned in the center. Leonard Funk strode up next to Jack, handed him a paper cup full of coffee and then sat down in the seat in front of him. "Can you see all right, Jack?" asked Leonard.

Jack repositioned his chair, pulled back from the steps to let people through. "Fine. See if you can spot Lipranski. The paper said he shaved his head. He shouldn't be too hard to spot—a big, bald-headed Polack."

They both scanned the crowd, watched as people fidgeted, talked, walked the aisles; twenty minutes before the heavyweight fight—anticipation grew like a late roll at a crap table. "He's probably in the locker room," said Leonard. "The fight should start soon, and I'm sure that he's in there giving last-minute instructions."

"Let's go down there."

They pushed through the crowd, Leonard the lead blocker. They flashed their badges, made their way into the locker room. The entourage questioned them the whole way, a gauntlet to run just to see Lipranski.

Howie the Hat looked at their badges, nodded, returned moments later followed by the Lip.

Jack looked at the Lip: he looked nervous for a guy that stoked a sellout, played a fix.

"What?" asked the Lip, cracking his knuckles. "I'm busier than hell here."

"Easy, mister," said Jack. "We just need to talk to your fighter after the fight."

"Why? What's he done?"

Jack's eyes narrowed. "Nothing, yet."

"What's that supposed to mean?"

Jack pulled forward. "It means nothing to you. You're lucky we don't talk with him now, ruin his concentration. You just find us after the fight. Bring your fighter."

Jack looked toward the back of the room, saw Junior. Junior looked back, puzzled: big arms, big man in a wheelchair.

Jack acknowledged the look, couldn't stop himself. He yelled across the locker room. "Use your head, kid."

Junior slipped on his robe, gloves. Osbie Jones rolled over one of Junior's gloves, pulled the laces tight, rolled them around the glove and then tied them in double knots. He repeated the process on the other glove. Wee Willie walked up behind him, tapped him on the shoulder, and told him to gather the rest of the men and wait at the door.

Wee Willie held out his hands and Junior began to slowly throw punches, bob and weave.

"This is it, Hammer. Your big night."

Junior stopped, rolled his neck, thumbed his nose with his gloves.

"You haven't lost a fight yet and you're not going to lose tonight. But tonight, it's not good enough to just win. Tonight, you got more people watching you than ever seen you before. Tonight, you show the world the Hammer!"

Wee Willie tied Junior's robe, pulled him close. "This is your show, Hammer, but it ain't just about you. It's about your mama. It's about those men standing in the doorway, your sparring partners, cut man, friends! Most of all, it's about sacrifice. All them sacrifices you made these past years. You could've been drinking, chasing women, eating all the food you want, but you ain't done it. Why? For nights like this. This night belongs to you!"

Wee Willie grabbed him by the gloves, wheeled, raced for the door—tried to ignore the vacant stare on Junior's face.

Jack and Leonard moved back through the stadium. Leonard grabbed an aisle seat, Jack moved in next to him. Jack continued to search the crowd, laughed when he saw two men walk in, take off their top-coats, and sit down in the second row. "Well I'll be damned."

"What?"

"Take a look at the two guys sitting down in the second row. Look familiar?"

"They just sat down. I can't quite make them out."

"I don't know who the old geezer in the sweater is, but the guy in the suit and tie that's taking his hat off is Al Kelly."

"The bookie you've been watching?"

"One and the same. No pun intended here, but I'll bet the farm that he finally figured out what's going on and decided to witness it himself."

Leonard took a sip of his beer, crossed his legs, and draped an arm over the back of the chair. He turned and looked back at Al. "From what you've told me, if he's figured out what's going on, then he's not a happy man. Why would he want to see it himself? Don't you think that would be torture?"

"Our bookie's become a bettor tonight, Leonard. He's here to root for his fighter."

Al took a gulp of his draft, scoured the crowd for the Lip. The fix was in and the Lip was part of it. Al wanted to eyeball him at least once.

The beer tweaked his nerves; he knew he was cursed when even the scalpers raped him for the pair of tickets. Why hadn't he seen it coming? He knew the answer; he'd lulled himself to sleep with dreams of moving to Florida. Now, it would never happen. One hundred seventy-two grand plus. His savings, Florida, everything wiped out in one fell swoop. He'd have to go to Angelo, ask for the money. He'd get it, along with the juice that would make him a prisoner for the rest of his life. He could see his future, booking for Angelo, giving him his hold, scraping just to live. He swallowed the rest of his beer, foam and all, flagged down a vendor. "Two more."

Pat pulled out some coins. "I've got these, Nephew." He paid for the beers, handed one to Al. "They're vicious snakes, Al. I'm not going to tell you what you should've done or what you could've done, but you definitely should've told me about your plan earlier. The first thing that I would've done is told you to get rid of Gene. The man's got bad ambition!"

"I just figured that if I let Gene go, Angelo would figure out that something was up. I stopped listening to Gene after the NCAA semifinal game. Screw him. He wants to be the man, let him. He's gonna find out that it isn't all that it's cracked up to be."

"What're you going to do for a bankroll?" asked Pat.

"I can't cover it, if that's what you mean. I've got a little over half of it. That NCAA game really tapped me out."

"We'll talk later. I might be able to help you."

Al shook his head, vehemently, said, "No, Pat, no. I got myself into this mess, I'm gonna get myself out of it. I just can't think about it now. I'm doing my best just not throwing up right here."

The man in front of him looked over his shoulder, scooted forward in his seat. Al smiled. "Don't worry, buddy. I launch, I'll do it in my own lap."

The Lip surveyed the stadium, fought his nerves. He nodded to Don Hansen, who waved his hand. Suddenly, Elvis Presley's voice filled the room. On cue, someone cranked "Blue Suede Shoes" so loud that the Lip's ears hurt. Men in TOMCAT GORDON T-shirts spilled into the aisle, Tomcat followed, gloves on the man in front of him, all of them trotting in unison. They got to the ring, climbed inside. Tomcat stepped to the center of the ring, threw punches and danced, Elvis wailed, the crowd screamed when they saw Tomcat's blue-painted boxing shoes.

Tomcat skipped back to his corner, and one of his handlers removed his robe. He worked the ropes, leaned way out into the crowd, blew kisses. Finally, he returned to his corner and ran in place as the song ended and the crowd yelled their support.

A drumbeat cut through the crowd noise. The cheap seats, mostly colored and Hispanic, went wild. The drumbeat: African;

Junior jogged out behind his entourage, glistening under the stadium lights. He climbed into the ring to boos from the lower seats, cheers from the uppers; the mixture came across like a wild animal's roar.

Junior jogged in place and threw jabs, kept his eyes on the ground. He was emotionless, drained by the Lip's decree. Wee Willie had scorched him with his pep talk.

The ring announcer: tall and slender with a voice like a cannon. "In this corner, weighing in at two hundred and eighteen pounds, with a record of twenty-six wins, eighteen by knockout, and only three losses; a ladies' man, a man's man, ranked number three by the National Boxing Association. Ladies and gentlemen, Tom! Cat! Gordon!"

The crowd went ballistic; a few women's screams punctuated the cry. The announcer waited for the applause to die, filled his chest with air, and bellowed. "And in this corner; weighing in at two hundred and twenty six pounds! He's undefeated with thirty-seven wins, thirty-five coming by knockout! He's the Hammer! Ladies and gentlemen, please welcome Junior, the Hammer, Hamilton!!!"

The crowd barked equal parts cheers and venom. Anticipation cut the applause short. The referee called them to the center of the ring, started to give them instructions. Junior looked up briefly, caught a Tomcat wink, felt sick to his stomach. "And above all else," continued the referee, "I'm in charge of this fight. If I tell you to break apart, break apart. Is that understood, gentlemen? I run this fight!" Both men nodded. "Then let's come out fighting!" yelled the referee as they touched gloves, turned and headed back to their corners.

Junior touched his gloves to Wee Willie's hands, looked down at Aaron Green. Aaron's eyes popped. "This is your night, Hammer!"

Osbie Jones smeared petroleum jelly over Junior's face, Wee Willie barked: "Now get on your bicycle these first few rounds. He's got a little bit of flab left. You stick and move and keep moving, he'll tire out. And remember, use your combinations. He drops an elbow to block your body blows. That leaves his head wide open!"

The bell rang and Junior moved slowly to the center of the ring and held out his gloves. Tomcat ignored the gesture and shot a right hand at Junior's head. Junior chewed his mouthpiece, snarled. That was no way to start the fight. He popped Tomcat's brow with a left jab and followed it with another. Tomcat moved forward, stunned.

"Stick and move!" yelled Wee Willie.

"Stick and move!" yelled Aaron.

Junior shot another left, followed with another and moved to his left. Suddenly, he stopped and threw a right-hand lead. Tomcat had been following him and was surprised by the quick shift. The right hand caught him flush on the nose and staggered him into the ropes.

The Lip bit his tongue. What the fuck was Junior doing? His heart beat overtime. He snuck a peek at Lincoln Johnson, read the stoic gaze as pissed.

His mind raced. Could the kid screw him? Not a chance. He'd never blow the money, risk the damage. Junior needed the fight as much as any of them. He might be dumb, but not that dumb.

What did the cops want with Junior? If they had wind of the fix, they sure wouldn't wait until after the fight to talk to him. They hadn't let on shit. Something going down and it wasn't good. Not enough prayers to beg that they wouldn't check the trunk of the car.

The Lip blew around the ring, heard the radio announcer scream into the microphone as Junior landed another right. Way too early in the fight, the crowd smelled blood and screamed.

Tomcat rolled off the ropes and scooted away. The bell sounded as Junior started to stalk him and each fighter returned to his corner. "Good round, Hammer!" yelled Wee Willie. Osbie Jones jumped into the ring, reached into Junior's mouth and pulled out his mouthpiece. Then he pulled a squeeze bottle out from underneath his arm and squeezed a stream of water into Junior's mouth. Junior swallowed the water, took another mouthful and spit it into the bucket that Osbie Jones offered. Aaron Green pulled himself up onto the corner of the apron and glowed at Junior.

"Just keep doing what you're doing, Hammer," said Wee Willie. "But move more. You need to wear him out. Every time he throws that left hook, counter with a right."

Junior nodded, tapped his gloves together. Tomcat was a joke. Any other night, he knew he could take him out at will. But not tonight, he thought. Kid Spinelli had been right, it just wasn't their night. The thought saddened him; everything straight with Mama, the fear in his gut gone, he'd finally pay for *her* and now this. A bad way to end it all. No way to make Mama proud.

The bell sounded and he moved out for round two.

"He isn't looking too shabby right now," remarked Pat.

"It's early," said Al. "Got to give the audience their show."

"He keeps giving a show like the last round, Tomcat won't be able to hold up his end."

The crowd leaped to its feet, and the man next to Pat knocked his elbow and drenched him with beer. Al and Pat jumped to attention. Tomcat Gordon had rocked Junior with a haymaker, had him in a corner.

"See, Pat. Spoke too soon," said Al.

Junior covered up while Tomcat slugged at his arms. The punches had no effect on him, but they were sure to wear out Tomcat. Junior absorbed a few more, popped Tomcat with a jab when he dropped his arms for a moment.

The crowd booed lustily as Junior slipped out of the corner and danced around the ring. Tomcat, tired from the barrage of punches, slowly moved after him, tried to cut off the ring, watched helplessly as Junior easily skipped out of his way.

"This kid should murder him," said Al. "This is a crying shame!"

"You're wrong there, Mister," said a man in front of them. "Tomcat always starts slow. I've seen him fight a bunch. Don't worry, Mister. He'll turn it around soon."

Al smirked. "Let's hope so."

The Lip passed Lincoln Johnson between rounds, rested a hand on his shoulder. Johnson looked at his hand, lifted his eyes. "Yes?"

"Everything's fine, Mr. Johnson."

"It sure is, Mr. Lipranski," said Johnson. "I believe that Junior is looking pretty good tonight. I like him." He beamed, looked around, made sure that the people surrounding him knew of his allegiance. "Reg and I were just talking about how good he looks."

"Great," said Reg Lewis. "He keeps fighting like this, there's no telling how far he'll go."

"My point exactly, Reg," said Johnson, a grin crossing his face. "I do believe that he'll be fighting for a championship soon."

The Lip smiled, stared at him. "Let's hope so."

The Lip moved back around the ring. Nerves made him search the crowd. No Momo. No cops with him in their eyesight. The car in the parking lot with two corpses and a life sentence in the trunk, if he was lucky. The bell sounded for the third round, he dashed back to his chair, caught a glimpse of the man as he rounded the corner. He turned away quickly, unable to meet Al's eyes.

Leonard leaned back in his chair, beckoned Jack close. "Lipranski looks nervous. Maybe the outcome is no foregone conclusion."

"You never know," said Jack. "But, from the sound of those conversations, they're doing their best. You know, you don't always have to have a fighter to fix a fight."

"What do you mean?" asked Leonard.

"Well, if you pay off one of the judges, you can sway a decision. But that takes balls. Your guy gets knocked out or hurt bad enough that they call it a technical knockout, you're screwed. The easiest way to fix a fight is to get a fighter *and* the referee. You want the fighter for obvious reasons, but you also want the ref so that if the other fighter gets a lucky punch, he can break it up, or whatever. You see what I mean."

"Well, we're going to have a hard time proving anything."

"It's not for us to prove anyway. Leave that to the boxing commission. We've got more important stuff to do."

"Like disprove that pimp's alibi," said Leonard.

"More."

"What more?"

Jack chuckled. "I'm playing a hunch, Leonard. Al Kelly had to be here to watch his fate played out. I'm betting that Momo's doing the same thing." Jack saw Leonard's startled expression. "That's right.

He's the most wanted man in town right now, but I'm betting that Sam Giancana's right here, watching the fight."

Junior sat on his stool, watched the Lip glare at him from a seat behind a neutral corner. Junior knew that he was dominating the fight and he didn't care. It was his message to the Lip and all of his cronies: I'm the better fighter; I'm the better man.

"Third round, Junior, and you're ahead, but you're not following the game plan." Wee Willie grabbed his chin and pulled his face toward him. "Look at me. You are not following our plan! What's wrong with you? Start moving more! And follow up on your combinations. Tomcat's leaving his guard down every time you attack his body! Pound on his ribs with your hook and finish him off upstairs. Come on now!"

The bell rang and Junior moved slowly toward the center of the ring. He had to have the money! He needed the money for Mama. He wanted to win the fight so bad, but he couldn't, not since Mr. Lipranski had bet his money on Tomcat. Six more rounds, and he'd lay down. He didn't want to, but he didn't have a choice. He'd lay down or he'd end up broke.

Junior moved forward, fast, tried to ignore his instincts. Pop him with the jab, keep him off-balance. Dropping his right elbow every time he takes a left to the ribs, combo up top. No! Dammit, move, keep moving, keep the punches weak, don't hurt the man.

Tomcat lunged at Junior, threw a hook from the floor. He missed badly and as he fell by, Junior hit him with a right hand. Momentum took him into the ropes. Junior followed, ready to strike. Tomcat turned, pulled his elbows tight, covered up for the onslaught, but it didn't come. Junior retreated momentarily and the bell rang.

"What the hell happened in there, Junior?" screamed Wee Willie. "You work him into the corner and don't follow up! You gone crazy? Now start listening to me. He's done. He's tired, and when a fighter's tired he starts making mistakes. He thinks you're gonna rush him. Don't rush him. Let him come to you. Then, when he does, come with a straight right hand. He'll never expect it."

Junior gulped at the water that Osbie Jones offered, barely heard Wee Willie. Five more rounds. Worse torture than he could've imagined. The only place he'd ever felt perfect and now they were taking that from him, too.

Aaron Green interrupted his thoughts. "Come on, Hammer. You can do it! All of that training, all of that running, all of that was so you could beat him. Come on, Hammer!"

Junior stared down at Aaron, felt his smile. He returned it when Osbie Jones pushed him in the center of the back and grabbed the stool when he stood back up.

"If this is a fix, it's the strangest one I've ever seen," said Pat. "Not like when Crandy Williams took a dive against Sean McCoy. He walked out for the first round, put his hands in front of his face, and took a punch right in the stomach. Then, he dove, literally, face first into the canvas and stayed there for ten minutes. It was sublimely ridiculous. I, thank God, had McCoy."

"It ain't looking that good anymore," said Al, gesturing toward the ring. Tomcat had worked Junior into a corner and was pummeling his arms.

"He's not hitting him at all," said Pat.

"That's not what concerns me, Pat. What concerns me is that Junior could easily slip out of that and isn't. First he doesn't follow up when Tomcat's hurt, now he's just standing there, letting the guy hit him."

Suddenly, the balcony came to life. "Apple, apple," they began to yell. "Fix!"

"Move!" yelled Pat.

"Move!" yelled Al.

The fighters fell into a clinch, Tomcat so tired that he could barely lift his arms. Junior broke the clinch and started to circle, snapped jabs into Tomcat's face, kept him honest with combinations. Tomcat rushed him, threw an overhand right that missed completely and nearly toppled from the momentum. Tomcat turned around in horror, expecting a punch, but Junior had stepped away, moved to the other side of the ring. Tomcat shuffled over, tried to hold his hands high, nearly had to jump as Junior began to circle again. Tomcat ran forward, stumbled and fell into Junior. He came up off of his knees quickly and tackled Junior, propelling them into a corner. "Quit running, nigger," hissed Tomcat as the referee broke them up and the bell rang.

Junior walked slowly to his corner, dreading the tongue-lashing that he was about to receive. Wee Willie didn't disappoint him. "What's going on in there? I mean it! What's going on in there? You look terrible. Are you sick or something?" Wee Willie stopped, gasped. "Oh my God. What did Lipranski tell you that night that you met him downtown? What's going on in there, Junior?"

Junior looked at the ground, motioned Osbie Jones to give him water. "Junior, I'm talking to you! What did Lipranski say?"

Junior ignored him. Aaron Green looked up at Junior, pleaded: "What's he talking about, Hammer? What's wrong with you? You can murder this guy! Please, Hammer, beat him. You've just got to win, Hammer, you've got to!"

Wee Willie pushed Aaron and Osbie Jones away from the ring. "Hammer, I don't know what you've got going with Lipranski, but it can't be good. Don't listen to him, Hammer. You sleep with them, you wake up with them. Don't do it, Hammer!"

"Not much time left," said Jack. "I want you to get on a phone, get me Andy Scott and whoever he's got available down here. Tell him that we're worried about a riot. The Mexicans and the Negroes in the balcony are going to go batshit if this is a fix."

"Do you believe that?" asked Leonard as he stood up and moved out of the row.

"No," said Jack. "But if we can get a few more bodies down here, with all of the security that we've got, if Giancana's here, we'll spot him."

"All right," said Leonard. "But what makes you think the fight's almost over? Don't you think it will go the distance?"

"A fixed fight never goes the distance; even the boys have limits. You ask a guy to take a dive, you don't ask him to take the punishment for fifteen rounds."

Junior leaned into the corner, felt the rope burn his shoulders. He let Tomcat get close, held back an uppercut. Tomcat fired sloppy hooks toward his ribs, he caught them with his elbows. Gotta hold back; I win, Mama loses. Let him keep throwing at the ribs, cover the face.

That smell in the hallway, gas. Always gas. Rats as big as cats, clothes that never fit.

Quit running, nigger? The hell with you. Gonna win this fight, you gonna remember it.

One for the kidneys: piss blood tonight, Tomcat! Couple of jabs, no petroleum jelly on his face, the leather'll catch the skin, break blood vessels. Gonna win, you gonna remember it.

Junior slipped out of the corner, rushed away from Tomcat. Tomcat followed, slow.

Junior held his distance, kept Tomcat at bay, fought the urge.

Wee Willie screamed, Aaron Green pleaded. Osbie Jones pushed the spit bucket into the corner, refused to rinse Junior's mouthpiece.

Junior looked into the crowd; smoke hovered everywhere, curled around the huge lights that dropped from the ceiling. Losing, now. Three more rounds and it's over. Money for Mama. Move her away. Go away, too. Forget about all this. Willie said it, ain't flawed like him. Don't need no championship. Don't need all that. Just need money and peace.

He felt the stool come out from underneath him. He danced forward.

Losing now. No sense in getting hit. Move around for three rounds and then take the dive.

Junior backpedaled, waited for Tomcat to rush. Tomcat came, weaved in front of him, and threw a lazy left hook. Junior caught it with his right elbow and snapped Tomcat's head back with his own left.

So easy. Could take this man out anytime. Take out his body, leave his head to die. Dance around him, humiliate him. Could do it, but not tonight.

Junior moved to his left, instinct took over. Tomcat followed, but

Junior peppered him with jabs, kept him away. The crowd seethed, they wanted a slugfest. One voice stood out: "Come on, Junior. You can do it!"

They got me, he thought. Even Lipranski's voice can come out of the dark and find me. First it was her and that stupid mistake, now it's Lipranski. Maybe they can't be escaped. Maybe someone's always on you.

Tomcat followed Junior into a corner, watched as Junior seemed to stop, misread it as the fix. Junior was out of it, didn't see it coming, didn't know what happened until he felt the canvas hammer his face. He'd left himself open and walked right into Tomcat's left hook.

The Lip leaped out of his chair, screamed at the top of his lungs. "It's over! Tomcat knocked him out! It's over!"

"Careful," whispered Don Hansen, pointing toward the Commissioner, who sat, a few rows back, with Lou Brown. Lou saw the Lip and waved.

"I don't care," said the Lip. "They'll never pin this one. It looked too good. Junior deserves a bonus."

He barely heard himself over the crowd, couldn't stop from rushing the ring. He stopped at the apron, moved through the photographers. Flashbulbs exploded: The Lip was blinded, rubbed 'em right, couldn't believe his eyes.

All that and it comes down to this. They wanted me to throw the fight and with me worrying about it, he actually caught me with a real punch. Shoot. Just lay here for a few more seconds and it's all over. We got the money and I didn't do anything wrong. I won't need this no more. I can just go on being . . .

Junior's heart stopped. He grabbed the bottom rope and pulled himself up, scrambled to his feet right before the referee could finish the count, turned to face Tomcat. Turned . . . away from Aaron Green, who stood, screaming in his corner, eyes pleading, little fists pumping. Pumping so hard that he nearly lost it off his shoulder. The black silk, with the gold trim: Junior's robe.

● ● ●

The referee yelled, "Nine," opened his mouth to finish the count and stopped as Junior struggled to his feet. Junior held his gloves to his face. The ref stepped forward and touched them. Junior and Al knew it at the same moment, he was legit: the ref wasn't part of the fix.

Junior worked Tomcat around the ring, stung him with jabs, kept him at bay. Tomcat tried to cut off the ring: Junior slipped away easily.

Al stood with the rest of the crowd. "Kill him, Hammer, kill him!" yelled Al. The man in front of him turned, glared. "Who're you for, Mister?"

"Wrong guy," said Al.

"You're for the wrong guy?"

"No. I'm the wrong guy for you to fuck with tonight, so shut your mouth, turn around and watch the fight."

The man turned around and Pat elbowed Al in the side, grinned.

Al resumed his cheers, screamed for Junior. "Take him out, Junior! Take him out!"

The crowd around him gawked at him, cursed. Al ignored them, forgot the rules, allowed himself to hope.

Two more rounds! Don't lose your head. Stay back on the man. You showed 'em you can fight. Tomcat knows the better man. Stay back and collect the money.

Junior danced, stayed away from Tomcat. Tomcat seethed, launched haymakers from every angle: Junior ducked, dodged, moved.

The crowd stood: the fight close, Tomcat looked tired, Junior looked fresh.

Junior slipped a right cross, came up behind Tomcat. He moved to his left and Tomcat did a three sixty, tried to find him. Tomcat toppled over but leaped to his feet quickly, spit rage.

Man should never lose his temper in the ring. Worst thing a fighter can do is get all mad.

Junior moved clockwise, Tomcat struggled to keep up. Suddenly, Junior stopped, moved the other way—Tomcat slipped by like a child playing a poor game of tag.

It's not your night because they said it's not your night. Tomcat's a money magnet. A money magnet.

Junior continued to move, heard the crowd for the first time. They were on their feet, yelling, as he slipped another punch.

The bell rang early. The Lip moved away from the judges' table, ran to Tomcat's corner.

Junior moved into his corner. Wee Willie met him. "I don't get it, Hammer. I'm praying you're hurt. You're moving like a champion but not throwing any punches. You hurt?"

Junior ignored him, watched Tomcat on his stool. Tomcat's arms hung at his sides. He gulped water but didn't spit it out. His trainer washed his mouthpiece and when he reinserted it, Tomcat let it hang out so that he could suck air.

No wind left and he's mad. Use your head, kid. Use my head. Use my head.

Junior looked up at Wee Willie. "You wanna see me move? Watch this."

Aaron Green clapped his hands in anticipation; Al stood with the rest of the crowd, screamed for action; Jack wheeled as close to the doors as he could while still being able to see the ring; the Lip pushed Abe Rosen out of his way, grabbed Tomcat's trainer and screamed: "Cut 'em! Cut the leather on his gloves! Tomcat, if you can't hit him, then slice the son of a bitch up!" Tomcat nodded, stared back at Junior as he stood in his corner and threw punches.

Tomcat's trainer took out a pocket knife, made small incisions on each glove and exposed the edges. Any punches that brushed Junior's face would cut him like a butcher's knife nicking a tomato.

The bell sounded and Tomcat rushed forward. Junior stepped aside and Tomcat threw an off-balance right. Junior slipped it, but it glanced off his forehead and sliced him to the bone.

Junior whipped his head as he felt his skin split. The sight of the blood on the canvas surprised him and he caught a left hand square in the face, felt his nose tear open. Another right ripped open an eyebrow and suddenly it was clear to him: they'd doctored Tomcat's gloves in order to have the fight stopped. He hadn't convinced them that he'd throw it, so they wanted to make sure. He raised himself up on his toes and began to move.

The Lip pounded on the canvas in Tomcat's corner. "Slice him, Tomcat! Slice that son of a bitch!"

Junior raced around the ring. The crowd screamed at a fevered pitch. A fight broke out in the upper balcony but no one watched. Al jumped on top of his chair to see over the men in front of him and the rest of the crowd on the floor followed suit. Jack craned his neck around a column and Leonard waved him off when he told him to get to the telephone.

A chant broke out in the balcony. "Hammer, Hammer!!"

Junior slipped another punch, ran circles around Tomcat. Tomcat's mouthpiece hung out; he sucked air through his mouth.

Blood ran down Junior's cheeks and gurgled as it spurted out of his nose. His eyes burned from the blood leaking from his brow, and his ribs ached where Tomcat had landed a lucky hook.

Junior dropped his right hand, feigned an injury. He kept his left hand high and moved around the ring. Tomcat lunged, missed, lunged again, and missed.

Junior shot a quick jab at Tomcat's face, pulled it short. Annoy him. Nothing else needed. Worst thing a fighter can do is get all mad.

Tomcat bulled after Junior, missed a punch and threw his arm around him, tried to muscle him into the corner. Junior feinted to his left, watched Tomcat overcompensate. Junior moved to his right, came behind Tomcat and watched him fall again, trying to find Junior.

Tomcat jumped up, tackled Junior, threw him toward the ropes.

Junior squared up, let Tomcat throw punches. He slipped them easily. Junior dropped both hands, dodged the punches, watched the fury grow in Tomcat's eyes.

The crowd shrieked.

Tomcat screamed, his mouthpiece shot across the ring. Junior barely heard the bell over the crowd noise. He turned slowly, *waited for it.*

The crowd gasped in unison as Tomcat threw the punch. It caught Junior behind the ear. He fell through the ropes and rolled off the apron, came to rest at Lincoln Johnson's feet.

The referee shot through the ropes, stood over Junior and quickly climbed back into the ring. He threw his hands in the air, waved them like a shipwreck survivor waving for a plane.

"What the hell?" screamed Pat.

"It was after the bell," yelled Al. "It was after the bell! Wasn't it?"

The Lip ran toward the judges' table, nearly knocked over the commissioner. The judges were huddled. The commissioner held the Lip back by his shoulders.

Wee Willie rushed around the ring, pushed through the crowd hovering over Junior.

Junior lay on the concrete, one glove raised, shielding his eyes from the flashes.

The ring announcer moved back to the center of the ring, grabbed the microphone when it descended from the ceiling. "Ladies aaaaaaand gentlemen."

Al clenched his fists, felt his heart try to beat its way out of his chest.

"We have a winner!"

The Lip held his breath, tried to see past the photographers, hear over the radio announcer.

"In the seventh round . . . the winner . . . by disqualification . . . Junior, The Hammer, Hamilton!"

Bedlam. Beer cups flew, arguments turned to fistfights. Al stood on his chair, hands raised high, tears of joy gushed down his cheeks. "He did it!" he yelled as the highbrows moved away from him. "He did it!"

The Lip glared as the commissioner congratulated him on an interesting fight, promised to investigate. Lincoln Johnson smiled for the crowd, yelled, "Great fight!" turned and whispered to the Lip that he was a dead man and had better start running.

Junior felt Wee Willie and Howie the Hat lift him, drape his arms over their shoulders. He bit his tongue to stop the grin: he finally knew why Jack Johnson smiled. Relief.

• • •

Jack wheeled double-time. He hit the exit just ahead of Leonard
Funk, herded the uniforms and off duties, told them to watch for
Giancana. A fix gone bad; someone with hell to pay. He sent four
uniforms to Tomcat's dressing room; he and Leonard would question
Junior, watch his back.

A quick twenty minutes, no sightings reported. Cheap-seaters
filed out, exchanged bills in plain sight. Ringsiders milled about,
screamed about the decision.

Exit banter: "It was at the bell, not after it. . . . The colored kid
could've gone on—they should've given him a few minutes and
started back up. . . . Deeesqualifcation is no decision, fuck your
dinero! . . . Hammer hurt his shoulder early, drug it like a dog with a
bad leg. . . . Next time, he'll kill him."

Jack searched the crowd, fingered the .38 in his jacket.

Junior sat in the shower, let the hot water run all over him. The
reporters had already left and everyone else had dressed and left him
to clean up and dress. They were taking him to dinner. "Somewhere
nice and quiet, where I can hear the whole story," Wee Willie had
said. He finally summoned the energy and stood up, wrapped a towel
around himself and moved toward his locker.

The door flew open just as Junior sat down. "Nice fight!" said the
Lip. His shirt was drenched from perspiration and he'd torn the bow
tie from his neck. "That was some fighting!"

Junior shrugged his shoulders, raised an icepack to the back of
his head.

"You dumb son of a bitch!" screamed the Lip. "You dumb, dumb
son of a bitch. Do you know what you just did?"

"Sure do. I tried to throw a fight. Anyone could see I was injured.
I wasn't coming out for the next round. Eighth round, ain't that the
one you wanted?"

The Lip blew. "You don't have any idea of what you just did.
Don't feed me that crap about not coming out. You could've stayed
down when he knocked you down. You could've let him take you,
but no, you had to run rings around him. You had to show everyone

how fucking talented you are. You dumb son of a bitch, you just threw away all of our money and might have gotten us killed."

Junior slipped an arm into a shirtsleeve, calm. "You know what I just did, Mr. Lipranski? I just won over the crowd. I just became the money magnet. Nobody can prove I was trying to throw that fight. And nobody can prove that I wasn't. But every man that was at that fight tonight knows that I'm the better fighter."

The Lip shook his head. "Got it all figured out, have you? Well, there are a lot of people who're gonna want a word with you. Explain it to them."

"Easy enough. I'll tell 'em you told me I had to stay until the eighth round or I woulda stayed down when he knocked me down. Tell 'em I didn't hit him for the last two rounds, knew I was behind on the points. Tell 'em I'm looking for a new manager, see if they know anybody. Should make a lot of money on the rematch."

"You dumb son of a bitch," said the Lip as he unbuttoned his tuxedo jacket.

"You know, Mr. Lipranski," said Junior as he set down the icepack and stood up. "Some people mistake quiet for dumb."

The Lip shouted, rushed toward Junior. Someone blindsided him, hit him from the side. He didn't even catch a glimpse of him as Kid Spinelli fired a right hand directly into his chin. The Lip toppled over a bench, banged into a row of lockers and slid to the ground, unconscious.

"My best punch all night," said Kid Spinelli. "Now get your clothes on and let's get out of here. There's nothing left for us here."

Al damn near ran the whole two and a half miles down Madison. Pat waited for a cab at the stadium, Al caught one as he hit the Loop. He directed the driver north, fought for breath, savored every one. Not even a five-minute ride, but he counted all $169,188—adding it to the totals since the basketball game made it clear: he was right back where he'd been. Almost like there was no game, no fight, no bets at all. He shook his head and laughed.

The cab shot north up Rush Street, stopped in front of Roxies. Al paid the driver and walked inside.

Dark and smoky, Janet stood at the end of the bar, coaxed a sponge into buying her a drink. The bartender cut the booze by two, doubled the price.

Al strode up alongside them, nudged the drunk. "Free drinks tonight."

The drunk swiveled, "Where?"

Al handed him a fin. "Anywhere but here."

The drunk looked at Al, turned back to Janet. She shrugged her shoulders. He got up from the stool, didn't wait for Al to change his mind.

"Thank you for scaring off a paying customer. The owner will appreciate it."

"I'm the owner."

"Well, then, this employee doesn't appreciate it." She smiled, lit a cigarette. "What brings you out of hiding?"

"Good news and bad news."

"Great, give me the bad news first, I can rinse with the good news."

"You've only got two days left. You're fired."

Janet's eyes popped. "What the . . ."

"The good news is that'll still give you one day to pack. We're heading to Florida."

Janet jumped into his arms, kissed him straight.

Al held on tight.

The kids spotted him first; they flocked around Junior, asked for autographs. He signed while Kid Spinelli tried to pull kids his way.

Jack and Leonard moved close, waited for the kids to disperse. Jack scanned the crowd, refused to give up.

Another twenty minutes, Jack couldn't take it anymore, sent Leonard to bring Junior over. Leonard came back, Junior in tow. Wee Willie, Aaron and the rest huddled, talked. "What now?"

"Interesting fight, Mr. Hamilton," said Jack, reaching for Junior's hand. Junior shook it, held his gaze.

"Thanks. I'll get him my own way next time."

"I'll bet you will," said Jack. "Listen, we'll make this quick. A friend of yours, Cleotis Gibson, said that you could substantiate his whereabouts a few nights ago."

"I know him, but Cleotis ain't no friend of mine. What did he say?"

"Said that he visited you at your fight camp earlier this week, Tuesday, April 2."

"True enough."

"How long did he stay?"

"Five, ten minutes."

Leonard interrupted. "That's not what he said. He said that he talked with you for a few minutes and then spent nearly an hour in the car with . . . er, umm. Well, he said that he was in the parking lot for another hour."

Junior shook his head. "He was with my sister, but they left right away. Believe me, only thing you remember more than Cleotis showing up is Cleotis leaving. What'd he do?"

Leonard started to explain. Jack listened for a minute, watched the crowd. Andy Frain security guards started to leave. Two men had climbed the fire escape, handed a brown-bagged bottle back and forth. A line formed outside the Stadium Grill. Not enough cabs and a long walk east on Madison Street.

Jack spun his chair toward the street; three men worked against the crowd, made their way toward an Olds. Jack pulled the .38 from his jacket, yelled, "Momo!"

One of the three lowered his head, the other two looked up, startled. "Momo!" yelled Jack, again.

He started to move toward the street, saw another car whip to the curb. A man got out, lurched through the crowd.

Jack saw him, recognized trouble, looked back at the Olds and shook. He screamed, turned back toward the man.

"You son of a bitch!" yelled the man.

Jack saw it; instinct said no time to shout. He drew the .38 from his lap, fired as the man raised his gun. The recoil blew his chair back. It hit a crack and spilled Jack onto the concrete.

The man's gun went off as he fell, Jack felt the air explode.

Leonard Funk screamed.

Jack turned, saw Junior lying in a pool of blood, clutching the right side of his chest.

"Ambulance!" yelled Jack.

Wee Willie, Aaron Green rushed over. Howie the Hat and Jack Albano ran into the street, yelling for an ambulance.

Jack rolled over, saw the Olds take off, missed the license plate. He turned his attention back to the man, just in time to see Poochie die in the street.

"They took him to Provident," said Leonard. "It's the only colored hospital. Only six other hospitals take coloreds, and five of them have quotas. The dead man has a better chance of getting in one of them than Junior."

"How did he look?"

"Terrible. But I don't know how much of that was the fight. The ambulance driver thought it missed his heart, might've caught a lung."

"Let's head over there," said Jack. "Pull the van around."

"You know," said Leonard. "He seemed pretty happy when I told him the pimp would probably go away for a long time."

"I hope he lives to enjoy that."

"Me, too." Leonard started to walk away, turned. "Jack," he said. "How did you get your gun out so fast?"

Jack looked him in the eye, flashed on the Olds pulling away, weighed it as a good thing. "Just lucky."

"Did you really see Giancana?"

Jack looked up as the Chicago Stadium sign went dark. "Always."

BEHIND THE NEWS
By Dally Richardson

Tuesday, April 9

The stench is finally wearing off, Chicago. Aided by the antiseptics permeating the hospital room of the noble Negro, Junior Hamilton, the foul odor of Tomcat Gordon's ring antics is finally wearing off.

As anyone who saw the fight would guess, the Hammer is pulling through. Lucky for Hamilton and fight fans everywhere, the man who attempted to shoot the Hammer had Tomcat's aim. The shot was nothing more than a flesh wound. Hamilton was stitched up and released, and he told this reporter that he expects to be ready to fight again, soon.

But change is imminent for the dazzling dancer. He has hired noted Negro lawyer Reg Lewis to help set him free from a shady contract that he was forced to sign by soon-to-be-former manager Don Hansen. Hansen is said to have an "ooze" problem—consult the second and third letters of the alphabet for more info.

Hamilton has also received an unexpected endorsement: the brain and brawn of Bronzeville! Yes, folks, Lincoln Johnson has offered to help promote Hamilton's next fight. Johnson confirmed that the Hammer has offered to fight an exhibition match during this year's Bud Billiken parade, and that his offer has been accepted.

What is to become of the other participants in Saturday's dubious debacle?

Illinois State Boxing Commissioner James Willoughby said that a full investigation is under way and that Tomcat Gordon, his manager, and his trainer will all be suspended. Gordon is guilty of the lowly late hit, and all are culpable for the devious doctoring of his gloves. Referee Ernie Batz is also subject to suspension for missing the dangerous mitts.

Finally, promoter Robert J. Lipranski is set to receive a lifetime ban from the State Boxing Commission. Commissioner Willoughby failed to elaborate on Lipranski's indiscretions. Lipranski has not been seen since the fight. This reporter simply hopes that he headed downwind.

Tuesday, April 9

Settle-up Day

Al stepped into the bathroom. Sandy and one of the bouncers stood in the doorway and made sure that none of the other patrons of the Trocadero followed. The door swung shut and closed their view of the dance floor: a stripper shedding her g-string to a Chico Hamilton jazz tune.

He walked toward the urinals, turned and faced the stall. He saw the shoes from under the door, unzipped, started to drain.

"What the hell?" yelled Gene as he pulled the door open.

Al continued to leak, Gene stepped back, tugged at his pants.

"Momo sent some of the boys over to have a talk with Gamey Donato," said Al. "He never placed those bets. You paid him to lie the first time, but Momo's boys are a little harder to convince. You know something, you were right about the way they work people over. It works pretty good."

"It was Angelo. He had Gamey lay the money on Michigan State for him. He didn't want Momo to know that he was playing—something about drug money."

"What about the fight? Who played the fifty grand?"

Gene slid back into the corner, trembled. "Lip."

"Explain."

"Angelo and a couple of colored guys fixed the fight with the Lip. Lip owed both of 'em money and they told him that it was his only way out. He called me to play the fifty grand."

"Well, then you've got more problems than I knew about."

"What do you mean?"

"What I mean is that you've been hiding at your brother's and this hell hole the past few days when you should've had your ear to the ground. Angelo and Vic D'Antonio are missing, and nobody's seen the Lip since the kid got shot. Angelo never told Momo nothing about the colored guys, and he's plenty pissed. I turned over my action to him and somebody owes him that fifty grand plus juice."

"Oh my God, Al. What's going on? All I did was take the bet. You won! You should be happy! I mean, maybe you don't want me working for you anymore, but that's all there should be between you and me."

Al bit his lower lip and threw his head back, zipped up. "You're still not there yet, Gene. See, you wanted to be the man. You wanted to take a position and be responsible and you know what? You got your chance. Momo sees you as being responsible for that fifty grand, and you know something else? He's letting a lot of people that lost money on that fix know that you were in on it."

"But I wasn't! All I did was take the money!"

Al bobbed his head. "That's enough. A smart bookie doesn't take a position. You did. Now, you know that I'm not a betting man, but I'd be willing to bet that you're never gonna see Angelo or Vic or maybe even the Lip ever again. Momo's never gotten along with the coloreds here real well, and I don't think he's starting now. Word has it that Lincoln Johnson was expecting quite a payout, so he dropped a bundle on Tomcat. Momo, Lincoln Johnson, a lot of bettors. Shit, Gene, the odds ain't favoring you."

Al nodded at Sandy and he opened the door. Crowd noise and a Chuck Berry tune filled the restroom. "Not bad business for a Tuesday," said Al. He started to walk out.

"Al!" cried Gene. "You've got to straighten this out for me. They'll kill me, Al! Please!"

Al turned around, poker faced: "You made a bet, Gene, and you lost."

Gene wailed. "Is that it? Twenty-eight years and that's all you've got to say?"

"No," said Al. He glanced down, laughed. "Pull up your zipper."

A three-day bender. The Lip woke with a start as the farmer turned his tractor off the road and pulled up next to Don Hansen's Rambler. The farmer motioned at the window and the Lip rolled it down.

"You've been here for quite a spell," said the farmer as the Lip sat up, rubbed his eyes and turned the rearview mirror so that he could look at himself. His eyes were yellow with deep gashes of red and his face was lined from lying against the car door.

"How long have I been here, old man?"

The farmer had left the tractor in neutral, and the Lip felt nauseous as he watched the man bounce up and down. "Pert near thirteen hours. You was here when I started my chores at four A.M. and you're still here."

"Where's here?"

"Here's Indiana and here's also my cornfield, so I'd appreciate it if you'd get your car out of my cornfield."

The Lip straightened up, fished the keys out of the ashtray. "Anything you say."

The farmer nodded, started to pull away. "Hey old man," yelled the Lip. "What day is it?"

The farmer laughed. "Mister, you must've had a wild one. It's Tuesday. And you know something else, Mister? It's 1957!" The farmer cackled, turned the tractor's front wheels back onto the road and drove back toward his farmhouse.

The Lip took inventory: eighty-six dollars, gas tank on empty, tux jacket on the floorboard—ruined by the dirt and blood that he'd wiped from his hands. Saturday night, a nightmare: most of the night at hospital, mugging for the cameras while two bodies rotted in his trunk, then a two-hour drive into Indiana and a veer off the road. Irony: he'd buried the bodies in a cornfield. The coup de grace: he'd stripped them nude, thrown an aluminum comb into the grave. The discovery would send two messages: the cops would link them to the Marcus murder, Momo would blame it on the coons. The signal: go over the body, the fix, whatever, with a fine tooth comb.

A three-day bender. Sunday and Monday hiding out in a whorehouse in Indianapolis—the madam had asked him to leave after he'd slapped around his third girl. Tuesday, early, in the cornfield, swigging from a bottle of bourbon.

Mistakes: losing control, confidence in Junior, letting the debt hang with Angelo.

Solutions: never lose control, offer confidence, or get in debt.

The situation: the money was tied up; Judge Willoughby had informed him at the hospital that a full investigation was being launched. No money, nowhere to turn, plenty of enemies. Don't worry about the shines, Momo would be looking for them. Don't worry about Momo, Angelo had kept their debt to himself. The kid had paid for the fix, the shooter had paid for the kid. The bet, the $50,000— that was a problem. He'd have to visit Gene, find out what he'd spilled, make sure he didn't spill any more, maybe spill Gene.

Next time: the fight game wasn't enough. Small-time hoods screwed up a peach of a deal. Set sights higher, go after the rackets, control everything, take it all. The Lip rammed the gas pedal to the floor, shot back out onto the road, fishtailed as he made a quick turn for the highway. His town, his time. He threw the ruined tux jacket out the window and headed back toward Chicago.